Running Water

A. E. W. Mason

Contents

RUNNING WATER

BY

A. E. W. Mason

CHAPTER I
SHOWS MRS. THESIGER IN HER HOME

The Geneva express jerked itself out of the Gare de Lyons. For a few minutes the lights of outer Paris twinkled past its windows and then with a spring it reached the open night. The jolts and lurches merged into one regular purposeful throb, the shrieks of the wheels, the clatter of the coaches, into one continuous hum. And already in the upper berth of her compartment Mrs. Thesiger was asleep. The noise of a train had no unrest for her. Indeed, a sleeping compartment in a Continental express was the most permanent home which Mrs. Thesiger had possessed for a good many more years than she would have cared to acknowledge. She spent her life in hotels with her daughter for an unconsidered companion. From a winter in Vienna or in Rome she passed to a spring at Venice or at Constantinople, thence to a June in Paris, a July and August at the bathing places, a September at Aix, an autumn in Paris again. But always she came back to the sleeping-car. It was the one familiar room which was always ready for her; and though the prospect from its windows changed, it was the one room she knew which had always the same look, the same cramped space, the same furniture--the one room where, the moment she stepped into it, she was at home.

Yet on this particular journey she woke while it was yet dark. A noise slight in comparison to the clatter of the train, but distinct in character and quite near, told her at once what had disturbed her. Some one was moving stealthily in the compartment--her daughter. That was all. But Mrs. Thesiger lay quite still, and, as would happen to her at times, a sudden terror gripped her by the heart. She heard the girl beneath her, dressing very quietly, subduing the rustle of her garments, even the sound of her breathing.

"How much does she know?" Mrs. Thesiger asked of herself; and her heart sank and she dared not answer.

The rustling ceased. A sharp click was heard, and the next moment through a broad pane of glass a faint twilight crept into the carriage. The blind had been raised from one of the windows. It was two o'clock on a morning of July and the dawn was breaking. Very swiftly the daylight broadened, and against the window there came into view the profile of a girl's head and face. Seen as Mrs. Thesiger saw it, with the light still dim behind it, it was black like an ancient daguerreotype. It was also as motionless and as grave.

"How much does she know?"

The question would thrust itself into the mother's thoughts. She watched her daughter intently from the dark corner where her head lay, thinking that with the broadening of the day she might read the answer in that still face. But she read nothing even when every feature was revealed in the clear dead light, for the face which she saw was the face of one who lived much apart within itself, building amongst her own dreams as a child builds upon the sand and pays no heed to those who pass. And to none of her dreams had Mrs. Thesiger the key. Deliberately her daughter had withdrawn herself amongst them, and they had given her this return for her company. They had kept her fresh and gentle in a circle where freshness was soon lost and gentleness put aside.

Sylvia Thesiger was at this time seventeen, although her mother dressed her to look younger, and even then overdressed her like a toy. It was of a piece with the nature of the girl that, in this matter as in the rest, she made no protest. She foresaw the scene, the useless scene, which would follow upon her protest, exclamations against her ingratitude, abuse for her impertinence, and very likely a facile shower of tears at the end; and her dignity forbade her to enter upon it. She just let her mother dress her as she chose, and she withdrew just a little more into the secret chamber of her dreams. She sat now looking steadily out of the window, with her eyes uplifted and aloof, in a fashion which had become natural to her, and her mother was seized with a pang of envy at the girl's beauty. For beauty Sylvia Thesiger had, uncommon in its quality rather than in its degree. From the temples to the round point of her chin the contour of her face described a perfect oval. Her forehead was broad and low and her hair, which in color was a dark chestnut, parted in the middle, whence it rippled in two thick daring waves to the ears, a fashion which noticeably became her, and it was gathered behind into a plait which lay rather low upon the nape of her neck. Her eyes were big, of a dark gray hue and very quiet in their scrutiny; her mouth, small and provoking. It provoked, when still, with the promise of a very winning smile, and the smile itself was not so frequent but that it provoked a desire to summon it to her lips again. It had a way of hesitating, as though Sylvia were not sure whether she would smile or not; and when she had made up her mind, it dimpled her cheeks and transfigured her whole face, and revealed in her tenderness and a sense of humor. Her complexion was pale, but clear, her figure was slender and active, but without angularities, and she was of the middle height. Yet the quality which the eye first remarked in her was not so much her beauty, as a certain purity, a look almost of the Madonna, a certainty, one might say, that even in the circle in which she moved, she had kept herself unspotted from the world.

Thus she looked as she sat by the carriage window. But as the train drew near to Amberieu, the air brightened and the sunlight ministered to her beauty like a careful handmaid, touching her pale cheeks to a rosy warmth, giving a luster to her hair, and humaning her to a smile. Sylvia sat forward a little, as though to meet the sunlight, then she turned toward the carriage and saw her mother's eyes intently watching her.

"You are awake?" she said in surprise.

"Yes, child. You woke me."

"I am very sorry. I was as quiet as I could be. I could not sleep."

"Why?" Mrs. Thesiger repeated the question with insistence. "Why couldn't you sleep?"

"We are traveling to Chamonix," replied Sylvia. "I have been thinking of it all night," and though she smiled in all sincerity, Mrs. Thesiger doubted. She lay silent for a little while. Then she said, with a detachment perhaps slightly too marked:

"We left Trouville in a hurry yesterday, didn't we?"

"Yes," replied Sylvia, "I suppose we did," and she spoke as though this was the first time that she had given the matter a thought.

"Trouville was altogether too hot," said Mrs. Thesiger; and again silence followed. But Mrs. Thesiger was not content. "How much does she know?" she speculated again, and was driven on to find an answer. She raised herself upon her elbow, and while rearranging her pillow said carelessly:

"Sylvia, our last morning at Trouville you were reading a book which seemed to interest you very much."

"Yes."

Sylvia volunteered no information about that book.

"You brought it down to the sands. So I suppose you never noticed a strange-looking couple who passed along the deal boards just in front of us." Mrs. Thesiger laughed and her head fell back upon her pillow. But during that movement her eyes had never left her daughter's face. "A middle-aged man with stiff gray hair, a stiff, prim face, and a figure like a ramrod. Oh, there never was anything so stiff." A no-ticeable bitterness began to sound in her voice and increased as she went on. "There was an old woman with him as precise and old-fashioned as himself. But you didn't see them? I never saw anything so ludicrous as that couple, austere and provincial as their clothes, walking along the deal boards between the rows of smart people." Mrs. Thesiger laughed as she recalled the picture. "They must have come from the Provinces. I could imagine them living in a chateau on a hill overlooking some tiny village in--where shall we say?" She hesitated for a moment, and then with an air of audacity she shot the word from her lips--"in Provence."

The name, however, had evidently no significance for Sylvia, and Mrs. Thesiger was relieved of her fears.

"But you didn't see them," she repeated, with a laugh.

"Yes, I did," said Sylvia, and brought her mother up on her elbow again. "It struck me that the old lady must be some great lady of a past day. The man bowed to you and--"

She stopped abruptly, but her mother completed the sentence with a vindic-tiveness she made little effort to conceal.

"And the great lady did not, but stared in the way great ladies have. Yes, I had met the man--once--in Paris," and she lay back again upon her pillow, watching her daughter. But Sylvia showed no curiosity and no pain. It was not the first time when people passed her mother that she had seen the man bow and the woman ignore. Rather she had come to expect it. She took her book from her berth and opened it.

Mrs. Thesiger was satisfied. Sylvia clearly did not suspect that it was just the appearance of that stiff, old-fashioned couple which had driven her out of Trouville a good month before her time--her, Mrs. Thesiger of the many friends. She fell to wondering what in the world had brought M. de Camours and his mother to that watering place amongst the brilliant and the painted women. She laughed again at the odd picture they had made, and her thoughts went back over twenty years to the time when she had been the wife of M. de Camours in the chateau overlooking the village in Provence, and M. de Camours' mother had watched her with an unceasing jealousy. Much had happened since those days. Madame de Camours' watchings had not been in vain, a decree had been obtained from the Pope annulling the marriage. Much had happened. But even after twenty years the memory of that formal life in the Provencal chateau was vivid enough; and Mrs. Thesiger yawned. Then she laughed. Monsieur de Camours and his mother had always been able to make people yawn.

"So you are glad that we are going to Chamonix, Sylvia--so glad that you couldn't sleep?"

"Yes."

It sounded rather unaccountable to Mrs. Thesiger, but then Sylvia was to her a rather unaccountable child. She turned her face to the wall and fell asleep.

Sylvia's explanation, however, happened to be true. Chamonix meant the great range of Mont Blanc, and Sylvia Thesiger had the passion for mountains in her blood. The first appearance of their distant snows stirred her as no emotion ever had, so that she came to date her life by these appearances rather than by the calendar of months and days. The morning when from the hotel windows at Glion she had first seen the twin peaks of the Dent du Midi towering in silver high above a blue corner of the Lake of Geneva, formed one memorable date. Once, too, in the winter-time, as the Rome express stopped at three o'clock in the morning at the frontier on the Italian side of the Mont Cenis tunnel, she had carefully lifted the blind on the right-hand side of the sleeping compartment and had seen a great wall of mountains tower up in a clear frosty moonlight from great buttresses of black rock to delicate pinnacles of ice soaring infinite miles away into a cloudless sky of blue. She had come near to tears that night as she looked from the window; such a tumult of vague longings rushed suddenly in upon her and uplifted her. She was made aware of dim uncomprehended thoughts stirring in the depths of her being, and her soul was drawn upward to those glittering spires, as to enchanted magnets. Ever afterward Sylvia looked forward, through weeks, to those few moments in her mother's annual itinerary, and prayed with all her heart that the night might be clear of mist and rain.

She sat now at the window with no thought of Trouville or their hurried flight. With each throb of the carriage-wheels the train flashed nearer to Chamonix. She opened the book which lay upon her lap--the book in which she had been so interested when Monsieur de Camours and his mother passed her by. It was a volume of the "Alpine Journal," more than twenty years old, and she could not open it but some exploit of the pioneers took her eyes, some history of a first ascent of an unclimbed peak. Such a history she read now. She was engrossed in it, and yet at times a little frown of annoyance wrinkled her forehead. She gave an explanation of her annoyance; for once she exclaimed half aloud, "Oh, if only he wouldn't be so *funny*!" The author was indeed being very funny, and to her thinking never so funny as when the narrative should have been most engrossing. She was reading the account of the first ascent of an aiguille in the Chamonix district, held by guides to be impossible and conquered at last by a party of amateurs. In spite of its humor Sylvia Thesiger was thrilled by it. She envied the three men who had taken part in that ascent, envied them their courage, their comradeship, their bivouacs in the open air beside glowing fires, on some high shelf of rock above the snows. But most of all her imagination was touched by the leader of that expedition, the man who sometimes alone, sometimes in company, had made sixteen separate attacks upon that peak. He stared from the pages of the volume--Gabriel Strood. Something of his great reach of limb, of his activity, of his endurance, she was able to realize. Moreover he had a particular blemish which gave to him a particular interest in her eyes, for it would have deterred most men altogether from his pursuit and it greatly hampered him. And yet in spite of it, he had apparently for some seasons stood prominent in the Alpine fraternity. Gabriel Strood was afflicted with a weakness in the muscles of one thigh. Sylvia, according to her custom, began to picture him, began to talk with him.

She wondered whether he was glad to have reached that summit, or whether he was not on the whole rather sorry--sorry for having lost out of his life a great and never-flagging interest. She looked through the subsequent papers in the volume, but could find no further mention of his name. She perplexed her fancies that morning. She speculated whether having made this climb he had stopped and climbed no more; or whether he might not get out of this very train on to the platform at Chamonix. But as the train slowed down near to Annemasse, she remembered that the exploit of which she had read had taken place more than twenty years ago.

CHAPTER II
INTRODUCES ONE OF STROOD'S SUCCESSORS

But though Gabriel Strood occupied no seat in that train, one of his successors was traveling by it to Chamonix after an absence of four years. Of those four years Captain Chayne had passed the last two among the coal-stacks of Aden, with the yellow land of Arabia at his back, longing each day for this particular morning, and keeping his body lithe and strong against its coming. He left the train at Annemasse, and crossing the rails to the buffet, sat down at the table next to that which Mrs. Thesiger and her daughter already occupied.

He glanced at them, placed them in their category, and looked away, utterly uninterested. They belonged to the great class of the continental wanderers, people of whom little is known and everything suspected--people with no kinsfolk, who flit from hotel to hotel and gather about them for a season the knowing middle-aged men and the ignorant young ones, and perhaps here and there an unwary woman deceived by the more than fashionable cut of their clothes. The mother he put down as nearer forty than thirty, and engaged in a struggle against odds to look nearer twenty than thirty. The daughter's face Chayne could not see, for it was bent persistently over a book. But he thought of a big doll in a Christmas toy-shop. From her delicate bronze shoes to her large hat of mauve tulle everything that she wore was unsuitable. The frock with its elaborations of lace and ribbons might have passed on the deal boards of Trouville. Here at Annemasse her superfineness condemned her.

Chayne would have thought no more of her, but as he passed her table on his way out of the buffet his eyes happened to fall on the book which so engrossed her. There was a diagram upon the page with which he was familiar. She was reading an old volume of the "Alpine Journal." Chayne was puzzled--there was so marked a contradiction between her outward appearance and her intense absorption in such a subject as Alpine adventure. He turned at the door and looked back. Sylvia Thesiger had raised her head and was looking straight at him. Thus their eyes met, and did more than meet.

Chayne, surprised as he had been by the book which she was reading, was almost startled by the gentle and rather wistful beauty of the face which she now showed to him. He had been prepared at the best for a fresh edition of the mother's worn and feverish prettiness. What he saw was distinct in quality. It seemed to him that an actual sympathy and friendliness looked out from her dark and quiet eyes, as though by instinct she understood with what an eager exultation he set out upon his holiday. Sylvia, indeed, living as she did within herself, was inclined to hero-worship naturally; and Chayne was of the type to which, to some extent through contrast with the run of her acquaintance, she gave a high place in her thoughts. A spare, tall man, clear-eyed and clean of feature, with a sufficient depth of shoulder and wonderfully light of foot, he had claimed her eyes the moment that he entered the buffet. Covertly she had watched him, and covertly she had sympathized with the keen enjoyment which his brown face betrayed. She had no doubts in her mind as to the intention of his holiday; and as their eyes met now involuntarily, a smile began to hesitate upon her lips. Then she became aware of the buffet, and her ignorance of the man at whom she looked, and, with a sudden mortification, of her own over-elaborate appearance. Her face flushed, and she lowered it again somewhat quickly to the pages of her book. But it was as though for a second they had spoken.

Chayne, however, forgot Sylvia Thesiger. As the train moved on to Le Fayet he was thinking only of the plans which he had made, of the new expeditions which were to be undertaken, of his friend John Lattery and his guide Michel Revailloud who would be waiting for him upon the platform of Chamonix. He had seen neither of them for four years. The electric train carried the travelers up from Le Fayet. The snow-ridges and peaks came into view; the dirt-strewn Glacier des Bossons shot out a tongue of blue ice almost to the edge of the railway track, and a few minutes afterward the train stopped at the platform of Chamonix.

Chayne jumped down from his carriage and at once suffered the first of his disappointments. Michel Revailloud was on the platform to meet him, but it was a Michel Revailloud whom he hardly knew, a Michel Revailloud grown very old. Revailloud was only fifty-two years of age, but during Chayne's absence the hardships of his life had taken their toll of his vigor remorselessly. Instead of the upright, active figure which Chayne so well remembered, he saw in front of him a little man with bowed shoulders, red-rimmed eyes, and a withered face seamed with tiny wrinkles.

At this moment, however, Michel's pleasure at once more seeing his old patron gave to him at all events some look of his former alertness, and as the two men shook hands he cried:

"Monsieur, but I am glad to see you! You have been too long away from Chamonix. But you have not changed. No, you have not changed."

In his voice there was without doubt a note of wistfulness. "I would I could say as much for myself." That regret was as audible to Chayne as though it had been uttered. But he closed his ears to it. He began to talk eagerly of his plans. There were familiar peaks to be climbed again and some new expeditions to be attempted.

"I thought we might try a new route up the Aiguille sans Nom," he suggested, and Michel assented but slowly, without the old heartiness and without that light in his face which the suggestion of something new used always to kindle. But again Chayne shut his ears.

"I was very lucky to find you here," he went on cheerily. "I wrote so late that I hardly hoped for it."

Michel replied with some embarrassment:

"I do not climb with every one, monsieur. I hoped perhaps that one of my old patrons would want me. So I waited."

Chayne looked round the platform for his friend.

"And Monsieur Lattery?" he asked.

The guide's face lit up.

"Monsieur Lattery? Is he coming too? It will be the old days once more."

"Coming? He is here now. He wrote to me from Zermatt that he would be here."

Revailloud shook his head.

"He is not in Chamonix, monsieur."

Chayne experienced his second disappointment that morning, and it quite chilled him. He had come prepared to walk the heights like a god in the perfection of enjoyment for just six weeks. And here was his guide grown old; and his friend, the comrade of so many climbs, so many bivouacs above the snow-line, had failed to keep his tryst.

"Perhaps there will be a letter from him at Couttet's," said Chayne, and the two men walked through the streets to the hotel. There was no letter, but on the other hand there was a telegram. Chayne tore it open.

"Yes it's from Lattery," he said, as he glanced first at the signature. Then he read the telegram and his face grew very grave. Lattery telegraphed from Courmayeur, the Italian village just across the chain of Mont Blanc:

"Starting now by Col du Geant and Col des Nantillons."

The Col du Geant is the most frequented pass across the chain, and no doubt the easiest. Once past its great ice-fall, the glacier leads without difficulty to the Montanvert hotel and Chamonix. But the Col des Nantillons is another affair. Having passed the ice-fall, and when within two hours of the Montanvert, Lattery had turned to the left and had made for the great wall of precipitous rock which forms the western side of the valley through which the Glacier du Geant flows down, the wall from which spring the peaks of the Dent du Requin, the Aiguille du Plan, the Aiguille de Blaitiere, the Grepon and the Charmoz. Here and there the ridge sinks between the peaks, and one such depression between the Aiguille de Blaitiere and the Aiguille du Grepon is called the Col des Nantillons. To cross that pass, to descend on the other side of the great rock-wall into that bay of ice facing Chamonix, which is the Glacier des Nantillons, had been Lattery's idea.

Chayne turned to the porter.

"When did this come?"

"Three days ago."

The gravity on Chayne's face changed into a deep distress. Lattery's party would have slept out one night certainly. They would have made a long march from Courmayeur and camped on the rocks at the foot of the pass. It was likely enough that they should have been caught upon that rock-wall by night upon the second day. The rock-wall had never been ascended, and the few who had descended it bore ample testimony to its difficulties. But a third night, no! Lattery should have been in Chamonix yesterday, without a doubt. He would not indeed have food for three nights and days.

Chayne translated the telegram into French and read it out to Michel Revailloud.

"The Col des Nantillons," said Michel, with a shake of the head, and Chayne saw the fear which he felt himself looking out from his guide's eyes.

"It is possible," said Michel, "that Monsieur Lattery did not start after all."

"He would have telegraphed again."

"Yes," Michel agreed. "The weather has been fine too. There have been no fogs. Monsieur Lattery could not have lost his way."

"Hardly in a fog on the Glacier du Geant," replied Chayne.

Michel Revailloud caught at some other possibility.

"Of course, some small accident--a sprained ankle--may have detained him at the hut on the Col du Geant. Such things have happened. It will be as well to telegraph to Courmayeur."

"Why, that's true," said Chayne, and as they walked to the post-office he argued more to convince himself than Michel Revailloud. "It's very likely--some quite small accident--a sprained ankle." But the moment after he had sent the telegram, and when he and Michel stood again outside the post-office, the fear which was in him claimed utterance.

"The Col des Nantillons is a bad place, Michel, that's the truth. Had Lattery been detained in the hut he would have found means to send us word. In weather like this, that hut would be crowded every night; every day there would be some one coming from Courmayeur to Chamonix. No! I am afraid of the steep slabs of that rock-wall."

And Michael Revailloud said slowly:

"I, too, monsieur. It is a bad place, the Col des Nantillons; it is not a quick way or a good way to anywhere, and it is very dangerous. And yet I am not sure. Monsieur Lattery was very safe on rocks. Ice, that is another thing. But he would be on rock."

It was evident that Michel was in doubt, but it seemed that Chayne could not force himself to share it.

"You had better get quietly together what guides you can, Michel," he said. "By the time a rescue party is made up the answer will have come from Courmayeur."

Chayne walked slowly back to the hotel. All those eager anticipations which had so shortened his journey this morning, which during the last two years had so often raised before his eyes through the shimmering heat of the Red Sea cool visions of ice-peaks and sharp spires of rock, had crumbled and left him desolate. Anticipations of disaster had taken their place. He waited in the garden of the hotel at a spot whence he could command the door and the little street leading down to it. But for an hour no messenger came from the post-office. Then, remembering that a long sad work might be before him, he went into the hotel and breakfasted. It was twelve o'clock and the room was full. He was shown a place amongst the other newcomers at one of the long tables, and he did not notice that Sylvia Thesiger sat beside him. He heard her timid request for the salt, and passed it to her; but he did not speak, he did not turn; and when he pushed back his chair and left the room, he had no idea who had sat beside him, nor did he see the shadow of disappointment on her face. It was not until later in the afternoon when at last the blue envelope was brought to him. He tore it open and read the answer of the hotel proprietor at Courmayeur:

"Lattery left four days ago with one guide for Col du Geant."

He was standing by the door of the hotel, and looking up he saw Michel Revailloud and a small band of guides, all of whom carried ice-axes and some *Ruecksacks* on their backs, and ropes, come tramping down the street toward him.

Michel Revailloud came close to his side and spoke with excitement.

"He has been seen, monsieur. It must have been Monsieur Lattery with his one guide. There were two of them," and Chayne interrupted him quickly.

"Yes, there were two," he said, glancing at his telegram. "Where were they seen?"

"High up, monsieur, on the rocks of the Blaitiere. Here, Jules"; and in obedience to Michel's summons, a young brown-bearded guide stepped out from the rest. He lifted his hat and told his story:

"It was on the Mer de Glace, monsieur, the day before yesterday. I was bringing a party back from the Jardin, and just by the Moulin I saw two men very high up on the cliffs of the Blaitiere. I was astonished, for I had never seen any one upon those cliffs before. But I was quite sure. None of my party could see them, it is true, but

I saw them clearly. They were perhaps two hundred feet below the ridge between the Blaitiere and the Grepon and to the left of the Col."

"What time was this?"

"Four o'clock in the afternoon."

"Yes," said Chayne. The story was borne out by the telegram. Leaving Courmayeur early, Lattery and his guide would have slept the night on the rocks at the foot of the Blaitiere, they would have climbed all the next day and at four o'clock had reached within two hundred feet of the ridge, within two hundred feet of safety. Somewhere within those last two hundred feet the fatal slip had been made; or perhaps a stone had fallen.

"For how long did you watch them?" asked Chayne.

"For a few minutes only. My party was anxious to get back to Chamonix. But they seemed in no difficulty, monsieur. They were going well."

Chayne shook his head at the hopeful words and handed his telegram to Michel Revailloud.

"The day before yesterday they were on the rocks of the Blaitiere," he said. "I think we had better go up to the Mer de Glace and look for them at the foot of the cliffs."

"Monsieur, I have eight guides here and two will follow in the evening when they come home. We will send three of them, as a precaution, up the Mer de Glace. But I do not think they will find Monsieur Lattery there."

"What do you mean?"

"I mean that I believe Monsieur Lattery has made the first passage of the Col des Nantillons from the east," he said, with a peculiar solemnity. "I think we must look for them on the western side of the pass, in the crevasses of the Glacier des Nantillons."

"Surely not," cried Chayne. True, the Glacier des Nantillons in places was steep. True, there were the seracs--those great slabs and pinnacles of ice set up on end and tottering, high above, where the glacier curved over a brow of rock and broke--one of them might have fallen. But Lattery and he had so often ascended and descended that glacier on the way to the Charmoz and the Grepon and the Plan. He could not believe his friend had come to harm that way.

Michel, however, clung to his opinion.

"The worst part of the climb was over," he argued. "The very worst pitch, monsieur, is at the very beginning when you leave the glacier, and then it is very bad again half way up when you descend into a gully; but Monsieur Lattery was very safe on rock, and having got so high, I think he would have climbed the last rocks with his guide."

Michel spoke with so much certainty that even in the face of his telegram, in the face of the story which Jules had told, hope sprang up within Chayne's heart.

"Then he may be still up there on some ledge. He would surely not have slipped on the Glacier des Nantillons."

That hope, however, was not shared by Michel Revailloud.

"There is very little snow this year," he said. "The glaciers are uncovered as I have never seen them in all my life. Everywhere it is ice, ice, ice. Monsieur Lattery had only one guide with him and he was not so sure on ice. I am afraid, monsieur, that he slipped out of his steps on the Glacier des Nantillons."

"And dragged his guide with him?" exclaimed Chayne. His heart rather than his judgment protested against the argument. It seemed to him disloyal to believe it. A man should not slip from his steps on the Glacier des Nantillons. He turned toward the door.

"Very well," he said. "Send three guides up the Mer de Glace. We will go up to the Glacier des Nantillons."

He went up to his room, fetched his ice-ax and a new club-rope with the twist of red in its strands, and came down again. The rumor of an accident had spread. A throng of tourists stood about the door and surrounded the group of guides, plying them with questions. One or two asked Chayne as he came out on what peak the accident had happened. He did not reply. He turned to Michel Revailloud and forgetful for the moment that he was in Chamonix, he uttered the word so familiar in the High Alps, so welcome in its sound.

"***Vorwaerts**, Michel," he said, and the word was the Open Sesame to a chamber which he would gladly have kept locked. There was work to do now; there would be time afterward to remember--too long a time. But in spite of himself his recollections rushed tumultuously upon him. Up to these last four years, on some day in each July his friend and he had been wont to foregather at some village in the Alps, Lattery coming from a Government Office in Whitehall, Chayne now from some garrison town in England, now from Malta or from Alexandria, and sometimes from a still farther dependency. Usually they had climbed together for six weeks, although there were red-letter years when the six weeks were extended to eight, six weeks during which they lived for the most part on the high level of the glaciers, sleeping in huts, or mountain inns, or beneath the stars, and coming down only for a few hours now and then into the valley towns. *Vorwaerts*! The months of their comradeship seemed to him epitomized in the word. The joy and inspiration of many a hard climb came back, made bitter with regret for things very pleasant and now done with forever. Nights on some high ledge, sheltered with rocks and set in the pale glimmer of snow-fields, with a fire of brushwood lighting up the faces of well-loved comrades; half hours passed in rock chimneys wedged overhead by a boulder, or in snow-gullies beneath a bulge of ice, when one man struggled above, out of sight, and the rest of the party crouched below with what security it might waiting for the cheery cry, "*Es geht. Vorwaerts*!"; the last scramble to the summit of a virgin peak; the swift glissade down the final snow-slopes in the dusk of the evening with the lights of the village twinkling below; his memories tramped by him fast and always in the heart of them his friend's face shone before his eyes. Chayne stood for a moment dazed and bewildered. There rose up in his mind that first helpless question of distress, "Why?" and while he stood, his face puzzled and greatly troubled, there fell upon his ears from close at hand a simple message of sympathy uttered in a whisper gentle but distinct:

"I am very sorry."

Chayne looked up. It was the overdressed girl of the Annemasse buffet, the girl who had seemed to understand then, who seemed to understand now. He raised his hat to her with a sense of gratitude. Then he followed the guides and went up among the trees toward the Glacier des Nantillons.

CHAPTER III
THE FINDING OF JOHN LATTERY

The rescue party marched upward between the trees with the measured pace of experience. Strength which would be needed above the snow-line was not to be wasted on the lower slopes. But on the other hand no halts were made; steadily the file of men turned to the right and to the left and the zigzags of the forest path multiplied behind them. The zigzags increased in length, the trees became sparse; the rescue party came out upon the great plateau at the foot of the peaks called the Plan des Aiguilles, and stopped at the mountain inn built upon its brow, just over Chamonix. The evening had come, below them the mists were creeping along the hillsides and blotting the valley out.

"We will stop here," said Michel Revailloud, as he stepped on to the little platform of earth in front of the door. "If we start again at midnight, we shall be on the glacier at daybreak. We cannot search the Glacier des Nantillons in the dark."

Chayne agreed reluctantly. He would have liked to push on if only to lull thought by the monotony of their march. Moreover during these last two hours, some faint rushlight of hope had been kindled in his mind which made all delay irksome. He himself would not believe that his friend John Lattery, with all his skill, his experience, had slipped from his ice-steps like any tyro; Michel, on the other hand, would not believe that he had fallen from the upper rocks of the Blaitiere on the far side of the Col. From these two disbeliefs his hope had sprung. It was possible that either Lattery or his guide lay disabled, but alive and tended, as well as might be, by his companion on some insecure ledge of that rock-cliff. A falling stone, a slip checked by the rope might have left either hurt but still living. It was true that for two nights and a day the two men must have already hung upon their ledge, that a third night was to follow. Still such endurance had been known in the annals of the Alps, and Lattery was a hard strong man.

A girl came from the chalet and told him that his dinner was ready. Chayne forced himself to eat and stepped out again on to the platform. A door opened and closed behind him. Michel Revailloud came from the guides' quarters at the end of the chalet and stood beside him in the darkness, saying nothing since sympathy taught him to be silent, and when he moved moving with great gentleness.

"I am glad, Michel, that we waited here since we had to wait," said Chayne.

"This chalet is new to you, monsieur. It has been built while you were away."

"Yes. And therefore it has no associations, and no memories. Its bare whitewashed walls have no stories to tell me of cheery nights on the eve of a new climb when he and I sat together for a while and talked eagerly of the prospects of to-morrow."

The words ceased. Chayne leaned his elbows on the wooden rail. The mists in the valley below had been swept away; overhead the stars shone out of an ebony sky very bright as on some clear winter night of frost, and of all that gigantic amphitheater of mountains which circled behind them from right to left there was hardly a hint. Perhaps here some extra cube of darkness showed where a pinnacle soared, or there a vague whiteness glimmered where a high glacier hung against the cliff, but for the rest the darkness hid the mountains. A cold wind blew out of the East and Chayne shivered.

"You are cold, monsieur?" said Michel. "It is your first night."

"No, I am not cold," Chayne replied, in a low and quiet voice. "But I am thinking it will be deadly cold up there in the darkness on the rocks of the Blaitiere."

Michel answered him in the same quiet voice. On that broad open plateau both men spoke indeed as though they were in a sick chamber.

"While you were away, monsieur, three men without food sat through a night on a steep ice-sheltered ice-slope behind us, high up on the Aiguille du Plan, as high up as the rocks of the Blaitiere. And not one of them came to any harm."

"I know. I read of it," said Chayne, but he gathered little comfort from the argument.

Michel fumbled in his pocket and drew out a pipe. "You do not smoke any more?" he asked. "It is a good thing to smoke."

"I had forgotten," said Chayne.

He filled his pipe and then took a fuse from his match-box.

"No, don't waste it," cried Michel quickly before he could strike it. "I remember your fuses, monsieur."

Michel struck a sulphur match and held it as it spluttered, and frizzled, in the hollow of his great hands. The flame burnt up. He held it first to Chayne's pipe-bowl and then to his own; and for a moment his face was lit with the red glow. Its age thus revealed, and framed in the darkness, shocked Chayne, even at this moment, more than it had done on the platform at Chamonix. Not merely were its deep lines shown up, but all the old humor and alertness had gone. The face had grown mask-like and spiritless. Then the match went out.

Chayne leaned upon the rail and looked downward. A long way below him, in the clear darkness of the valley the lights of Chamonix shone bright and very small. Chayne had never seen them before so straight beneath him. As he looked he began to notice them; as he noticed them, more and more they took a definite shape. He rose upright, and pointing downward with one hand he said in a whisper, a whisper of awe--

"Do you see, Michel? Do you see?"

The great main thoroughfare ran in a straight line eastward through the town, and, across it, intersecting it at the little square where the guides gather of an evening, lay the other broad straight road from the church across the river. Along those two roads the lights burned most brightly, and thus there had emerged before Chayne's eyes a great golden cross. It grew clearer and clearer as he looked; he looked away and then back again, and now it leapt to view, he could not hide it from his sight, a great cross of light lying upon the dark bosom of the valley.

"Do you see, Michel?"

"Yes." The answer came back very steadily. "But so it was last night and last year. Those three men on the Plan had it before their eyes all night. It is no sign of disaster." For a moment he was silent, and then he added timidly: "If you look for a sign, monsieur, there is a better one."

Chayne turned toward Michel in the darkness rather quickly.

"As we set out from the hotel," Michel continued, "there was a young girl upon the steps with a very sweet and gentle face. She spoke to you, monsieur. No doubt she told you that her prayers would be with you to-night."

"No, Michel," Chayne replied, and though the darkness hid his face, Michel knew that he smiled. "She did not promise me her prayers. She simply said: 'I am sorry.'"

Michel Revailloud was silent for a little while, and when he spoke again, he spoke very wistfully. One might almost have said that there was a note of envy in his voice.

"Well, that is still something, monsieur. You are very lonely to-night, is it not so? You came back here after many years, eager with hopes and plans and not thinking at all of disappointments. And the disappointments have come, and the hopes are all fallen. Is not that so, too? Well, it is something, monsieur--I, who am lonely too, and an old man besides, so that I cannot mend my loneliness, I tell you-

-it is something that there is a young girl down there with a sweet and gentle face who is sorry for you, who perhaps is looking up from among those lights to where we stand in the darkness at this moment."

But it seemed that Chayne did not hear, or, if he heard, that he paid no heed. And Michel, knocking the tobacco from his pipe, said:

"You will do well to sleep. We may have a long day before us"; and he walked away to the guides' quarters.

But Chayne could not sleep; hope and doubt fought too strongly within him, wrestling for the life of his friend. At twelve o'clock Michel knocked upon his door. Chayne got up from his bed at once, drew on his boots, and breakfasted. At half past the rescue party set out, following a rough path through a wilderness of boulders by the light of a lantern. It was still dark when they came to the edge of the glacier, and they sat down and waited. In a little while the sky broke in the East, a twilight dimly revealed the hills, Michel blew out the lantern, the blurred figures of the guides took shape and outline, and silently the morning dawned upon the world.

The guides moved on to the glacier and spread over it, ascending as they searched.

"You see, monsieur, there is very little snow this year," said Michel, chipping steps so that he and Chayne might round the corner of a wide crevasse.

"Yes, but it does not follow that he slipped," said Chayne, hotly, for he was beginning to resent that explanation as an imputation against his friend.

Slowly the party moved upward over the great slope of ice into the recess, looking for steps abruptly ending above a crevasse or for signs of an avalanche. They came level with the lower end of a long rib of rock which crops out from the ice and lengthwise bisects the glacier. Here the search ended for a while. The rib of rocks is the natural path, and the guides climbed it quickly. They came to the upper glacier and spread out once more, roped in couples. They were now well within the great amphitheater. On their left the cliffs of the Charmoz overlapped them, on the right the rocks of the Blaitiere. For an hour they advanced, cutting steps since the glacier was steep, and then from the center of the glacier a cry rang out. Chayne at the end of the line upon the right looked across. A little way in front of the two men who had shouted something dark lay upon the ice. Chayne, who was with Michel Revailloud, called to him and began hurriedly to scratch steps diagonally toward the object.

"Take care, monsieur," cried Michel.

Chayne paid no heed. Coming up from behind on the left-hand side, he passed his guide and took the lead. He could tell now what the dark object was, for every now and then a breath of wind caught it and whirled it about the ice. It was a hat. He raised his ax to slice a step and a gust of wind, stronger than the others, lifted the hat, sent it rolling and skipping down the glacier, lifted it again and gently dropped it at his feet. He stooped down and picked it up. It was a soft broad-brimmed hat of dark gray felt. In the crown there was the name of an English maker. There was something more too. There were two initials--J.L.

Chayne turned to Michel Revailloud.

"You were right, Michel," he said, solemnly. "My friend has made the first passage of the Col des Nantillons from the East."

The party moved forward again, watching with redoubled vigilance for some spot in the glacier, some spot above a crevasse, to which ice-steps descended and from which they did not lead down. And three hundred yards beyond a second cry rang out. A guide was standing on the lower edge of a great crevasse with a hand upheld above his head. The searchers converged quickly upon him. Chayne hurried forward, plying the pick of his ax as never in his life had he plied it. Had the guide come upon the actual place where the accident took place, he asked himself? But before he reached the spot, his pace slackened, and he stood still. He had no longer any doubt. His friend and his friend's guide were not lying upon any ledge of the rocks of the Aiguille de Blaitiere; they were not waiting for any succor.

On the glacier, a broad track, littered with blocks of ice, stretched upward in a straight line from the upper lip of the crevasse to the great ice-fall on the sky-line where the huge slabs and pinnacles of ice, twisted into monstrous shapes, like a sea suddenly frozen when a tempest was at its height, stood marshaled in serried rows. They stood waiting upon the sun. One of them, melted at the base, had crashed down the slope, bursting into huge fragments as it fell, and cleaving a groove even in that hard glacier.

Chayne went forward and stopped at the guide's side on the lower edge of the crevasse. Beyond the chasm the ice rose in a blue straight wall for some three feet, and the upper edge was all crushed and battered; and then the track of the falling serac ended. It had poured into the crevasse.

The guide pointed to the left of the track.

"Do you see, monsieur? Those steps which come downward across the glacier and stop exactly where the track meets them? They do not go on, on the other side of the track, monsieur."

Chayne saw clearly enough. The two men had been descending the glacier in the afternoon, the avalanche had fallen and swept them down. He dropped upon his knees and peered into the crevasse. The walls of the chasm descended smooth and precipitous, changing in gradual shades and color from pale transparent green to the darkest blue, until all color was lost in darkness. He bent his head and shouted into the depths:

"Lattery! Lattery!"

And only his voice came back to him, cavernous and hollow. He shouted again, and then he heard Michel Revailloud saying solemnly behind him:

"Yes, they are here."

Suddenly Chayne turned round, moved by a fierce throb of anger.

"It's not true, you see," he cried. "He didn't slip out of his steps and drag his guide down with him. You were wrong, Michel."

Michel was standing with his hat in his hand.

"Yes, monsieur, I was quite wrong," he said, gently. He turned to a big and strong man:

"Francois, will you put on the rope and go down?"

They knotted the rope securely about Francois' waist and he took his ice-ax in his hand, sat down on the edge of the crevasse with his legs dangling, turned over upon his face and said:

"When I pull the rope, haul in gently."

They lowered him carefully down for sixty feet, and at that depth the rope slackened. Francois had reached the bottom of the crevasse. For a few moments they watched the rope move this way and that, and then there came a definite pull.

"He has found them," said Michel.

Some of the guides lined out with the rope in their hands. Chayne took his position in the front, at the head of the line and nearest to the crevasse. The pull upon the rope was repeated, and slowly the men began to haul it in. It did not occur to Chayne that the weight upon the rope was heavy. One question filled his mind, to the exclusion of all else. Had Francois found his friend? What news would he bring of them when he came again up to the light? Francois' voice was heard now, faintly, calling from the depths. But what he said could not be heard. The line of men hauled in the rope more and more quickly and then suddenly stopped and drew it in very gently. For they could now hear what Francois said. It was but one word, persistently repeated:

"Gently! Gently!"

And so gently they drew him up toward the mouth of the crevasse. Chayne was standing too far back to see down beyond the edge, but he could hear Francois' ax clattering against the ice-walls, and the grating of his boots. Michel, who was kneeling at the edge of the chasm, held up his hand, and the men upon the rope ceased to haul. In a minute or two he lowered it.

"Gently," he said, "gently," gazing downward with a queer absorption. Chayne began to hear Francois' labored breathing and then suddenly at the edge of the crevasse he saw appear the hair of a man's head.

"Up with him," cried a guide; there was a quick strong pull upon the rope and out of the chasm, above the white level of the glacier, there appeared a face--not Francois' face--but the face of a dead man. Suddenly it rose into the colorless light, pallid and wax-like, with open, sightless eyes and a dropped jaw, and one horrid splash of color on the left forehead, where blood had frozen. It was the face of Chayne's friend, John Lattery; and in a way most grotesque and horrible it bobbed and nodded at him, as though the neck was broken and the man yet lived. When Francois just below cried, "Gently! Gently," it seemed that the dead man's mouth was speaking.

Chayne uttered a cry; then a deathly sickness overcame him. He dropped the rope, staggered a little way off like a drunken man and sat down upon the ice with his head between his hands.

Some while later a man came to him and said:

"We are ready, monsieur."

Chayne returned to the crevasse. Lattery's guide had been raised from the crevasse. Both bodies had been wrapped in sacks and cords had been fixed about their legs. The rescue party dragged the bodies down the glacier to the path, and placing them upon doors taken from a chalet, carried them down to Chamonix. On the way down Francois talked for a while to Michel Revailloud, who in his turn fell back to where at the end of the procession Chayne walked alone.

"Monsieur," he said, and Chayne looked at him with dull eyes like a man dazed.

"There is something which Francois noticed, which he wished me to tell you. Francois is a good lad. He wishes you to know that your friend died at once--there was no sign of a movement. He lay in the bottom of the crevasse in some snow which was quite smooth. The guide--he had kicked a little with his feet in the snow--but your friend had died at once."

"Thank you," said Chayne, without the least emotion in his voice. But he walked with uneven steps. At times he staggered like one overdone and very tired. But once or twice he said, as though he were dimly aware that he had his friend's reputation to defend:

"You see he didn't slip on the ice, Michel. You were quite wrong. It was the avalanche. It was no fault of his."

"I was wrong," said Michel, and he took Chayne by the arm lest he should fall; and these two men came long after the others into Chamonix.

CHAPTER IV
MR. JARVICE

The news of Lattery's death was telegraphed to England on the same evening. It appeared the next morning under a conspicuous head-line in the daily newspapers, and Mr. Sidney Jarvice read the item in the Pullman car as he traveled from Brighton to his office in London. He removed his big cigar from his fat red lips, and became absorbed in thought. The train rushed past Hassocks and Three Bridges and East Croydon. Mr. Jarvice never once looked at his newspaper again. The big cigar of which the costliness was proclaimed by the gold band about its middle had long since gone out, and for him the train came quite unexpectedly to a stop at the ticket platform on Battersea Bridge.

Mr. Jarvice was a florid person in his looks and in his dress. It was in accordance with his floridness that he always retained the gold band about his cigar while he smoked it. He was a man of middle age, with thick, black hair, a red, broad face, little bright, black eyes, a black mustache and rather prominent teeth. He was short and stout, and drew attention to his figure by wearing light-colored trousers adorned with a striking check. From Victoria Station he drove at once to his office in Jermyn Street. A young and wizened-looking clerk was already at work in the outer room.

"I will see no one this morning, Maunders," said Mr. Jarvice as he pressed through.

"Very well, sir. There are a good number of letters," replied the clerk.

"They must wait," said Mr. Jarvice, and entering his private room he shut the door. He did not touch the letters upon his table, but he went straight to his bureau, and unlocking a drawer, took from it a copy of the Code Napoleon. He studied the document carefully, locked it up again and looked at his watch. It was getting on toward one o'clock. He rang the bell for his clerk.

"Maunders," he said, "I once asked you to make some inquiries about a young man called Walter Hine."

"Yes, sir."

"Do you remember what his habits were? Where he lunched, for instance?"

Maunders reflected for a moment.

"It's a little while ago, sir, since I made the inquiries. As far as I remember, he did not lunch regularly anywhere. But he went to the American Bar of the Criterion restaurant most days for a morning drink about one."

"Oh, he did? You made his acquaintance, of course?"

"Yes, sir."

"Well, you might find him this morning, give him some lunch, and bring him round to see me at three. See that he is sober."

At three o'clock accordingly Mr. Walter Hine was shown into the inner room of Mr. Jarvice. Jarvice bent his bright eyes upon his visitor. He saw a young man with very fair hair, a narrow forehead, watery blue eyes and a weak, dissipated face. Walter Hine was dressed in a cheap suit of tweed much the worse for wear, and he entered the room with the sullen timidity of the very shy. Moreover, he was a little unsteady as he walked, as though he had not yet recovered from last night's intoxication.

Mr. Jarvice noted these points with his quick glance, but whether they pleased him or not there was no hint upon his face.

"Will you sit down?" he said, suavely, pointing to a chair. "Maunders, you can go."

Walter Hine turned quickly, as though he would have preferred Maunders to stay, but he let him go. Mr. Jarvice shut the door carefully, and, walking across the room, stood over his visitor with his hands in his pockets, and renewed his scrutiny. Walter Hine grew uncomfortable, and blurted out with a cockney twang--

"Maunders told me that if I came to see you it might be to my advantage."

"I think it will," replied Mr. Jarvice. "Have you seen this morning's paper?"

"On'y the 'Sportsman'."

"Then you have probably not noticed that your cousin, John Lattery, has been killed in the Alps." He handed his newspaper to Hine, who glanced at it indifferently.

"Well, how does that affect me?" he asked.

"It leaves you the only heir to your uncle, Mr. Joseph Hine, wine-grower at Macon, who, I believe, is a millionaire. Joseph Hine is domiciled in France, and must by French law leave a certain portion of his property to his relations, in other words, to you. I have taken some trouble to go into the matter, Mr. Hine, and I find that your share must at the very least amount to two hundred thousand pounds."

"I know all about that," Hine interrupted. "But as the old brute won't acknowledge me and may live another twenty years, it's not much use to me now."

"Well," said Mr. Jarvice, smiling suavely, "my young friend, that is where I come in."

Walter Hine looked up in surprise. Suspicion followed quickly upon the surprise.

"Oh, on purely business terms, of course," said Jarvice. He took a seat and resumed gaily. "Now I am by profession--what would you guess? I am a money-lender. Luckily for many people I have money, and I lend it--I lend it upon very easy terms. I make no secret of my calling, Mr. Hine. On the contrary, I glory in it. It gives me an opportunity of doing a great deal of good in a quiet way. If I were to show you my books you would realize that many famous estates are only kept going through my assistance; and thus many a farm laborer owes his daily bread to me and never knows his debt. Why should I conceal it?"

Mr. Jarvice turned toward his visitor with his hands outspread. Then his voice dropped.

"There is only one thing I hide, and that, Mr. Hine, is the easiness of the terms on which I advance my loans. I must hide that. I should have all my profession against me were it known. But you shall know it, Mr. Hine." He leaned forward and patted his young friend upon the knee with an air of great benevolence. "Come, to business! Your circumstances are not, I think, in a very flourishing condition."

"I should think not," said Walter Hine, sullenly. "I have a hundred and fifty a year, paid weekly. Three quid a week don't give a fellow much chance of a flutter."

"Three pounds a week. Ridiculous!" cried Mr. Jarvice, lifting up his hands. "I am shocked, really shocked. But we will alter all that. Oh yes, we will soon alter that."

He sprang up briskly, and unlocking once more the drawer in which he kept his copy of the Code Napoleon, he took out this time a slip of paper. He seated himself again, drawing up his chair to the table.

"Will you tell me, Mr. Hine, whether these particulars are correct? We must be business-like, you know. Oh yes," he said, gaily wagging his head and cocking his bright little eyes at his visitor. And he began to read aloud, or rather paraphrase, the paper which he held:

"Your father inherited the same fortune as your uncle, Joseph Hine, but lost almost the entire amount in speculation. In middle life he married your mother, who was--forgive me if I wound the delicacy of your feelings, Mr. Hine--not quite his equal in social position. The happy couple then took up their residence in Arcade Street, Croydon, where you were born on March 6, twenty-three years ago."

"Yes," said Walter Hine.

"In Croydon you passed your boyhood. You were sent to the public school there. But the rigorous discipline of school life did not suit your independent character." Thus did Mr. Jarvice gracefully paraphrase the single word "expelled" which was written on his slip of paper. "Ah, Mr. Hine," he cried, smiling indulgently at the sullen, bemused weakling who sat before him, stale with his last night's drink. "You and Shelley! Rebels, sir, rebels both! Well, well! After you left school, at the age of sixteen, you pursued your studies in a desultory fashion at home. Your father died the following year. Your mother two years later. You have since lived in Russell Street, Bloomsbury, on the income which remained from your father's patrimony. Three pounds a week--to be sure, here it is--paid weekly by trustees appointed by your mother. And you have adopted none of the liberal professions. There we have it, I think."

"You seem to have taken a lot of trouble to find out my history," said Walter Hine, suspiciously.

"Business, sir, business," said Mr. Jarvice. It was on the tip of his tongue to add, "The early bird, you know," but he was discreet enough to hold the words back. "Now let me look to the future, which opens out in a brighter prospect. It is altogether absurd, Mr. Hine, that a young gentleman who will eventually inherit a quarter of a million should have to scrape through meanwhile on three pounds a week. I put it on a higher ground. It is bad for the State, Mr. Hine, and you and I, like good citizens of this great empire, must consider the State. When this great fortune comes into your hands you should already have learned how to dispose of it."

"Oh, I could dispose of it all right," interrupted Mr. Hine with a chuckle. "Don't you worry your head about that."

Mr. Jarvice laughed heartily at the joke. Walter Hine could not but think that he had made a very witty remark. He began to thaw into something like confidence. He sat more easily on his chair.

"You will have your little joke, Mr. Hine. You could dispose of it! Very good indeed! I must really tell that to my dear wife. But business, business!" He checked his laughter with a determined effort, and lowered his voice to a confidential pitch. "I propose to allow you two thousand pounds a year, paid quarterly in advance. Five hundred pounds each quarter. Forty pounds a week, Mr. Hine, which with your three will make a nice comfortable living wage! Ha! Ha!"

"Two thousand a year!" gasped Mr. Hine, leaning back in his chair. "It ain't possible. Two thou--here, what am I to do for it?"

"Nothing, except to spend it like a gentleman," said Mr. Jarvice, beaming upon his visitor. It did not seem to occur to either man that Mr. Jarvice had set to his loan the one condition which Mr. Walter Hine never could fulfil. Walter Hine was troubled with doubts of quite another kind.

"But you come in somewhere," he said, bluntly. "On'y I'm hanged if I see where."

"Of course I come in, my young friend," replied Jarvice, frankly. "I or my executors. For we may have to wait a long time. I propose that you execute in my favor a post-obit on your uncle's life, giving me--well, we may have to wait a long time. Twenty years you suggested. Your uncle is seventy-three, but a hale man, living in a healthy climate. We will say four thousand pounds for every two thousand which I lend you. Those are easy terms, Mr. Hine. I don't make you take cigars and sherry! No! I think such practices almost reflect discredit on my calling. Two thousand a year! Five hundred a quarter! Forty pounds a week! Forty-three with your little income! Well, what do you say?"

Mr. Hine sat dazzled with the prospect of wealth, immediate wealth, actually within his reach now. But he had lived amongst people who never did anything for nothing, who spoke only a friendship when they proposed to borrow money, and at the back of his mind suspicion and incredulity were still at work. Somehow Jarvice would be getting the better of him. In his dull way he began to reason matters out.

"But suppose I died before my uncle, then you would get nothing," he objected.

"Ah, to be sure! I had not forgotten that point," said Mr. Jarvice. "It is a contingency, of course, not very probable, but still we do right to consider it." He leaned back in his chair, and once again he fixed his eyes upon his visitor in a long and silent scrutiny. When he spoke again, it was in a quieter voice than he had used. One might almost have said that the real business of the interview was only just beginning.

"There is a way which will save me from loss. You can insure your life as against your uncle's, for a round sum--say for a hundred thousand pounds. You will make over the policy to me. I shall pay the premiums, and so if anything were to happen to you I should be recouped."

He never once removed his eyes from Hine's face. He sat with his elbows on the arms of his chair and his hands folded beneath his chin, quite still, but with a queer look of alertness upon his whole person.

"Yes, I see," said Mr. Hine, as he turned the proposal over in his mind.

"Do you agree?" asked Jarvice.

"Yes," said Walter Hine.

"Very well," said Jarvice, all his old briskness returning. "The sooner the arrangement is pushed through, the better for you, eh? You will begin to touch the dibs." He laughed and Walter Hine chuckled. "As to the insurance, you will have to get the company's doctor's certificate, and I should think it would be wise to go steady for a day or two, what? You have been going the pace a bit, haven't you? You had better see your solicitor to-day. As soon as the post-obit and the insurance policy are in this office, Mr. Hine, your first quarter's income is paid into your bank. I will have an agreement drawn, binding me on my side to pay you two thousand a year until your uncle's death."

Mr. Jarvice rose as if the interview was ended. He moved some papers on his table, and added carelessly--"You have a good solicitor, I suppose?"

"I haven't a solicitor at all," said Walter Hine, as he, too, rose.

"Oh, haven't you?" said Mr. Jarvice, with all the appearance of surprise. "Well, shall I give you an introduction to one?" He sat down, wrote a note, placed it in an envelope, which he left unfastened, and addressed it. Then he handed the envelope to his client.

"Messrs. Jones and Stiles, Lincoln's Inn Fields," he said. "But ask for Mr. Driver. Tell him the whole proposal frankly, and ask his advice."

"Driver?" said Hine, fingering the envelope. "Hadn't I ought to see one of the partners?"

Mr. Jarvice smiled.

"You have a business head, Mr. Hine, that's very clear. I'll let you into a secret. Mr. Driver is rather like yourself--something of a rebel, Mr. Hine. He came into disagreement with that very arbitrary body the Incorporated Law Society, so,--well his name does not figure in the firm. But he *is* Jones and Stiles. Tell him everything! If he advises you against my proposal, I shall even say take his advice. Good-morning." Mr. Jarvice went to the door and opened it.

"Well, this is the spider's web, you know," he said, with the good-humored laugh of one who could afford to despise the slanders of the ill-affected. "Not such a very uncomfortable place, eh?" and he bowed Mr. Fly out of his office.

He stood at the door and waited until the outer office closed. Then he went to his telephone and rang up a particular number.

"Are you Jones and Stiles?" he asked. "Thank you! Will you ask Mr. Driver to come to the telephone"; and with Mr. Driver he talked genially for the space of five minutes.

Then, and not till then, with a smile of satisfaction, Mr. Jarvice turned to the unopened letters which had come to him by the morning post.

CHAPTER V
MICHEL REVAILLOUD EXPOUNDS
HIS PHILOSOPHY

That summer was long remembered in Chamonix. July passed with a procession of cloudless days; valley and peak basked in sunlight. August came, and on a hot starlit night in the first week of that month Chayne sat opposite to Michel Revailloud in the balcony of a cafe which overhangs the Arve. Below him the river tumbling swiftly amidst the boulders flashed in the darkness like white fire. He sat facing the street. Chamonix was crowded and gay with lights. In the little square just out of sight upon the right, some traveling musicians were singing, and up and down the street the visitors thronged noisily. Women in light-colored evening frocks, with lace shawls thrown about their shoulders and their hair; men in attendance upon them, clerks from Paris and Geneva upon their holidays; and every now and then a climber with his guide, come late from the mountains, would cross the bridge quickly and stride toward his hotel. Chayne watched the procession in silence quite aloof from its light-heartedness and gaiety. Michel Revailloud drained his glass of beer, and, as he replaced it on the table, said wistfully:

"So this is the last night, monsieur. It is always sad, the last night."

"It is not exactly as we planned it," replied Chayne, and his eyes moved from the throng before him in the direction of the churchyard, where a few days before his friend had been laid amongst the other Englishmen who had fallen in the Alps. "I do not think that I shall ever come back to Chamonix," he said, in a quiet and heart-broken voice.

Michel gravely nodded his head.

"There are no friendships," said he, "like those made amongst the snows. But this, monsieur, I say: Your friend is not greatly to be pitied. He was young, had known no suffering, no ill-health, and he died at once. He did not even kick the snow for a little while."

"No doubt that's true," said Chayne, submitting to the commonplace, rather than drawing from it any comfort. He called to the waiter. "Since it is the last night, Michel," he said, with a smile, "we will drink another bottle of beer."

He leaned back in his chair and once more grew silent, watching the thronged street and the twinkling lights. In the little square one of the musicians with a very clear sweet voice was singing a plaintive song, and above the hum of the crowd, the melody, haunting in its wistfulness, floated to Chayne's ears, and troubled him with many memories.

Michel leaned forward upon the table and answered not merely with sympathy but with the air of one speaking out of full knowledge, and speaking moreover in a voice of warning.

"True, monsieur. The happiest memories can be very bitter--if one has no one to share them. All is in that, monsieur. If," and he repeated his phrase--"If one has no one to share them." Then the technical side of Chayne's proposal took hold of him.

"The Col Dolent? You will have to start early from the Chalet de Lognan, monsieur. You will sleep there, of course, to-morrow. You will have to start at midnight--perhaps even before. There is very little snow this year. The great bergschrund will be very difficult. In any season it is always difficult to cross that bergschrund on to the steep ice-slope beyond. It is so badly bridged with snow. This season it will be as bad as can be. The ice-slope up to the Col will also take a long time. So start very early."

As Michel spoke, as he anticipated the difficulties and set his thoughts to overcome them, his eyes lit up, his whole face grew younger.

Chayne smiled.

"I wish you were coming with me Michel," he said, and at once the animation died out of Michel's face. He became once more a sad, dispirited man.

"Alas, monsieur," he said, "I have crossed my last Col. I have ascended my last mountain."

"You, Michel?" cried Chayne.

"Yes, monsieur, I," replied Michel, quietly. "I have grown old. My eyes hurt me on the mountains, and my feet burn. I am no longer fit for anything except to lead mules up to the Montanvert and conduct parties on the Mer de Glace."

Chayne stared at Michel Revailloud. He thought of what the guide's life had been, of its interest, its energy, its achievement. More than one of those aiguilles towering upon his left hand, into the sky, had been first conquered by Michel Revailloud. And how he had enjoyed it all! What resource he had shown, what cheerfulness. Remorse gradually seized upon Chayne as he looked across the little iron table at his guide.

"Yes, it is a little sad," continued Revailloud. "But I think that toward the end, life is always a little sad, if"--and the note of warning once more was audible--"if one has no well-loved companion to share one's memories."

The very resignation of Michel's voice brought Chayne to a yet deeper compunction. The wistful melody still throbbed high and sank, and soared again above the murmurs of the passers-by and floated away upon the clear hot starlit night. Chayne wondered with what words it spoke to his old guide. He looked at the tired sad face on which a smile of friendliness now played, and his heart ached. He felt some shame that his own troubles had so engrossed him. After all, Lattery was not greatly to be pitied. That was true. He himself too was young. There would come other summers, other friends. The real irreparable trouble sat there before him on the other side of the iron table, the trouble of an old age to be lived out in loneliness.

"You never married, Michel?" he said.

"No. There was a time, long ago, when I would have liked to," the guide answered, simply. "But I think now it was as well that I did not get my way. She was very extravagant. She would have needed much money, and guides are poor people, monsieur--not like your professional cricketers," he said, with a laugh. And then he turned toward the massive wall of mountains. Here and there a slim rock spire, the Dru or the Charmoz, pointed a finger to the stars, here and there an ice-field glimmered like a white mist held in a fold of the hills. But to Michel Revailloud, the whole vast range was spread out as on a raised map, buttress and peak, and dome of snow from the Aiguille d'Argentiere in the east to the summit of Mont Blanc in the west. In his thoughts he turned from mountain to mountain and found each one, majestic and beautiful, dear as a living friend, and hallowed with recollections. He remembered days when they had called, and not in vain, for courage and endurance, days of blinding snow-storms and bitter winds which had caught him half-way up some ice-glazed precipice of rock or on some long steep ice-slope crusted dangerously with thin snow into which the ax must cut deep hour after hour, however frozen the fingers, or tired the limbs. He recalled the thrill of joy with which, after many vain attempts, he, the first of men, had stepped on to the small topmost pinnacle of this or that new peak. He recalled the days of travel, the long glacier walks on the high level from Chamonix to Zermatt, and from Zermatt again to the Oberland; the still clear mornings and the pink flush upon some high white cone which told that somewhere the sun had risen; and the unknown ridges where expected difficulties suddenly vanished at the climber's approach, and others where an easy scramble suddenly turned into the most difficult of climbs. Michel raised his glass in the air. "Here is good-by to you--the long good-by," he said, and his voice broke. And abruptly he turned to Chayne with his eyes full of tears and began to speak in a quick passionate whisper, while the veins stood out upon his forehead and his face quivered.

"Monsieur, I told you your friend was not greatly to be pitied. I tell you now something more. The guide we brought down with him from the Glacier des Nantillons a fortnight back--all this fortnight I have been envying him--yes, yes, even though he kicked the snow with his feet for a little before he died. It is better to do so than to lead mules up to the Montanvert."

"I am sorry," said Chayne.

The words sounded, as he spoke them, lame enough and trivial in the face of Michel's passionate lament. But they had an astonishing effect upon the guide. The flow of words stopped at once, he looked at his young patron almost whimsically and a little smile played about his mouth.

"'I am sorry,'" he repeated. "Those were the words the young lady spoke to you on the steps of the hotel. You have spoken with her, monsieur, and thanked her for them?"

"No," said Chayne, and there was much indifference in his voice.

Women had, as yet, not played a great part in Chayne's life. Easy to please, but difficult to stir, he had in the main just talked with them by the way and gone on forgetfully: and when any one had turned and walked a little of his road beside him, she had brought to him no thought that here might be a companion for all the way. His indifference roused Michel to repeat, and this time unmistakably, the warning he had twice uttered.

He leaned across the table, fixing his eyes very earnestly on his patron's face. "Take care, monsieur," he said. "You are lonely to-night--very lonely. Then take good care that your old age is not one lonely night like this repeated and repeated through many years! Take good care that when you in your turn come to the end, and say good-by too"--he waved his hand toward the mountains--"you have some one to share your memories. See, monsieur!" and very wistfully he began to plead, "I go home to-night, I go out of Chamonix, I cross a field or two, I come to Les Praz-Conduits and my cottage. I push open the door. It is all dark within. I light my own lamp and I sit there a little by myself. Take an old man's wisdom, monsieur! When it is all over and you go home, take care that there is a lighted lamp in the room and the room not empty. Have some one to share your memories when life is nothing but memories." He rose as he ended, and held out his hand. As Chayne took it, the guide spoke again, and his voice shook:

"Monsieur, you have been a good patron to me," he said, with a quiet and most dignified simplicity, "and I make you what return I can. I have spoken to you out of my heart, for you will not return to Chamonix and after to-night we shall not meet again."

"Thank you," said Chayne, and he added: "We have had many good days to-gether, Michel."

"We have, monsieur."

"I climbed my first mountain with you."

"The Aiguille du Midi. I remember it well."

Both were silent after that, and for the same reason. Neither could trust his voice. Michel Revailloud picked up his hat, turned abruptly away and walked out of the cafe into the throng of people. Chayne resumed his seat and sat there, silent and thoughtful, until the street began to empty and the musicians in the square ceased from their songs.

Meanwhile Michel Revailloud walked slowly down the street, stopping to speak with any one he knew however slightly, that he might defer his entrance into the dark and empty cottage at Les Praz-Conduits. He drew near to the hotel where Chayne was staying and saw under the lamp above the door a guide whom he knew talking with a young girl. The young girl raised her head. It was she who had said, "I am sorry." As Michel came within the circle of light she recognized him. She spoke quickly to the guide and he turned at once and called "Michel," and when Revailloud approached, he presented him to Sylvia Thesiger. "He has made many first ascents in the range of Mont Blanc, mademoiselle."

Sylvia held out her hand with a smile of admiration.

"I know," she said. "I have read of them."

"Really?" cried Michel. "You have read of them--you, mademoiselle?"

There was as much pleasure as wonder in his tone. After all, flattery from the lips of a woman young and beautiful was not to be despised, he thought, the more especially when the flattery was so very well deserved. Life had perhaps one or two compensations to offer him in his old age.

"Yes, indeed. I am very glad to meet you, Michel. I have known your name a long while and envied you for living in the days when these mountains were un-known."

Revailloud forgot the mules to the Montanvert and the tourists on the Mer de Glace. He warmed into cheerfulness. This young girl looked at him with so frank an envy.

"Yes, those were great days, mademoiselle," he said, with a thrill of pride in his voice. "But if we love the mountains, the first ascent or the hundredth--there is just the same joy when you feel the rough rock beneath your fingers or the snow crisp under your feet. Perhaps mademoiselle herself will some time--"

At once Sylvia interrupted him with an eager happiness--

"Yes, to-morrow," she said.

"Oho! It is your first mountain, mademoiselle?"

"Yes."

"And Jean here is your guide. Jean and his brother, I suppose?" Michel laid his hand affectionately on the guide's shoulder. "You could not do better, mademoiselle."

He looked at her thoughtfully for a little while. She was fresh--fresh as the smell of the earth in spring after a fall of rain. Her eyes, the alertness of her face, the eager tones of her voice, were irresistible to him, an old tired man. How much more irresistible then to a younger man. Her buoyancy would lift such an one clear above his melancholy, though it were deep as the sea. He himself, Michel Revailloud, felt twice the fellow he had been when he sat in the balcony above the Arve.

"And what mountain is it to be, mademoiselle?" he asked.

The girl took a step from the door of the hotel and looked upward. To the south, but quite close, the long thin ridge of the Aiguille des Charmoz towered jagged and black against the starlit sky. On one pinnacle of that ridge a slab of stone was poised like the top of a round table on the slant. It was at that particular pinnacle that Sylvia looked.

"L'Aiguille des Charmoz," said Michel, doubtfully, and Sylvia swung round to him and argued against his doubt.

"But I have trained myself," she said. "I have been up the Brevent and Flegere. I am strong, stronger than I look."

Michel Revailloud smiled.

"Mademoiselle, I do not doubt you. A young lady who has enthusiasm is very hard to tire. It is not because of the difficulty of that rock-climb that I thought to suggest--the Aiguille d'Argentiere."

Sylvia turned with some hesitation to the younger guide.

"You too spoke of that mountain," she said.

Michel pressed his advantage.

"And wisely, mademoiselle. If you will let me advise you, you will sleep to-morrow night at the Pavillon de Lognan and the next day climb the Aiguille d'Argentiere."

Sylvia looked regretfully up to the ridge of the Charmoz which during this last fortnight had greatly attracted her. She turned her eyes from the mountain to Revailloud and let them rest quietly upon his face.

"And why do you advise the Aiguille d'Argentiere?" she asked.

Michel saw her eyes softly shining upon him in the darkness, and all the more persisted. Was not his dear patron who must needs be helped to open his eyes, since he would not open them himself, going to sleep to-morrow in the Pavillon de Lognan? The roads to the Col Dolent and the Aiguille d'Argentiere both start from that small mountain inn. But this was hardly the reason which Michel could give to the young girl who questioned him. He bethought him of another argument, a subtle one which he fancied would strongly appeal to her. Moreover, there was truth in it.

"I will tell you why, mademoiselle. It is to be your first mountain. It will be a day in your life which you will never forget. Therefore you want it to be as complete as possible--is it not so? It is a good rock-climb, the Aiguille des Charmoz--yes. But the Argentiere is more complete. There is a glacier, a rock traverse, a couloir up a rock-cliff, and at the top of that a steep ice-slope. And that is not all. You want your last step on to the summit to reveal a new world to you. On the Charmoz, it is true, there is a cleft at the very top up which you scramble between two straight walls and you pop your head out above the mountain. Yes, but you see little that is new; for before you enter the cleft you see both sides of the mountain. With the Argentiere it is different. You mount at the last, for quite a time behind the mountain with your face to the ice-slope; and then suddenly you step out upon the top and the chain of Mont Blanc will strike suddenly upon your eyes and heart. See, mademoiselle, I love these mountains with a very great pride and I would dearly like you to have that wonderful white revelation of a new strange world upon your first ascent."

Before he had ended, he knew that he had won. He heard the girl draw sharply in her breath. She was making for herself a picture of the last step from the ice-slope to summit ridge.

"Very well," she said. "It shall be the Aiguille d'Argentiere."

Michel went upon his way out of Chamonix and across the fields. They would be sure to speak, those two, to-morrow at the Pavillon de Lognan. If only there were no other party there in that small inn! Michel's hopes took a leap and reached beyond the Pavillon de Lognan. To ascend one's first mountain--yes, that was enviable and good. But one should have a companion with whom one can live over again the raptures of that day, in the after time. Well--perhaps--perhaps!

Michel pushed open the door of his cottage, and lit his lamp, without after all bethinking him that the room was dark and empty. His ice-axes stood in a corner, the polished steel of their adz-heads gleaming in the light; his **Ruecksack** and some coils of rope hung upon pegs; his book with the signatures and the comments of his patrons lay at his elbow on the table, a complete record of his life. But he was not thinking that they had served him for the last time. He sat down in his chair and so remained for a little while. But a smile was upon his face, and once or twice he chuckled aloud as he thought of his high diplomacy. He did not remember at all that to-morrow he would lead mules up to the Montanvert and conduct parties on the Mer de Glace.

CHAPTER VI
THE PAVILLON DE LOGNAN

The Pavillon de Lognan is built high upon the southern slope of the valley of Chamonix, under the great buttresses of the Aiguille Verte. It faces the north and from the railed parapet before its door the path winds down through pastures bright with Alpine flowers to the pine woods, and the village of Les Tines in the bed of the valley. But at its eastern end a precipice drops to the great ice-fall of the Glacier d'Argentiere, and night and day from far below the roar of the glacier streams enters in at the windows and fills the rooms with the music of a river in spate.

At five o'clock on the next afternoon, Chayne was leaning upon the rail looking straight down to the ice-fall. The din of the torrent was in his ears, and it was not until a foot sounded lightly close behind him that he knew he was no longer alone. He turned round and saw to his surprise the over-dainty doll of the Annemasse buffet, the child of the casinos and the bathing beaches, Sylvia Thesiger. His surprise was very noticeable and Sylvia's face flushed. She made him a little bow and went into the chalet.

Chayne noticed a couple of fresh guides by the door of the guides' quarters. He remembered the book which he had seen her reading with so deep an interest in the buffet. And in a minute or two she came out again on to the earth platform and he saw that she was not overdressed to-day. She was simply and warmly dressed in a way which suggested business. On the other hand she had not made herself ungainly. He guessed her mountain and named it to her.

"Yes," she replied. "Please say that it will be fine to-morrow!"

"I have never seen an evening of better promise," returned Chayne, with a smile at her eagerness. The brown cliffs of the Aiguille du Chardonnet just across the glacier glowed red in the sunlight; and only a wisp of white cloud trailed like a lady's scarf here and there in the blue of the sky. The woman of the chalet came out and spoke to him.

"She wants to know when we will dine," he explained to Sylvia. "There are only you and I. We should dine early, for you will have to start early"; and he repeated the invariable cry of that year: "There is so very little snow. It may take you some time to get off the glacier on to your mountain. There is always a crevasse to cross."

"I know," said Sylvia, with a smile. "The bergschrund."

"I beg your pardon," said Chayne, and in his turn he smiled too. "Of course you know these terms. I saw you reading a copy of the 'Alpine Journal.'"

They dined together an hour later with the light of the sunset reddening the whitewashed walls of the little simple room and bathing in glory the hills without. Sylvia Thesiger could hardly eat for wonder. Her face was always to the window, her lips were always parted in a smile, her gray eyes bright with happiness.

"I have never known anything like this," she said. "It is all so strange, so very beautiful."

Her freshness and simplicity laid their charm on him, even as they had done on Michel Revailloud the night before. She was as eager as a child to get the meal done with and to go out again into the open air, before the after-glow had faded from the peaks. There was something almost pathetic in her desire to make the very most of such rare moments. Her eagerness so clearly told him that such holidays came but seldom in her life. He urged her, however, to eat, and when she had done they went out together and sat upon the bench, watching in silence the light upon the peaks change from purple to rose, the rocks grow cold, and the blue of the sky deepen as the night came.

"You too are making an ascent?" she asked.

"No," he answered. "I am crossing a pass into Italy. I am going away from Chamonix altogether."

Sylvia turned to him; her eyes were gentle with sympathy.

"Yes, I understand that," she said. "I am sorry."

"You said that once before to me, on the steps of the hotel," said Chayne. "It was kind of you. Though I said nothing, I was grateful"; and he was moved to open his heart to her, and to speak of his dead friend. The darkness gathered about them; he spoke in the curt sentences which men use who shrink from any emotional display; he interrupted himself to light his pipe. But none the less she understood the reality of his distress. He told her with a freedom of which he was not himself at the moment quite aware, of a clean, strong friendship which owed nothing to sentiment, which was never fed by protestations, which endured through long intervals, and was established by the memory of great dangers cheerily encountered and overcome. It had begun amongst the mountains, and surely, she thought, it had retained to the end something of their inspiration.

"We first met in the Tyrol, eight years ago. I had crossed a mountain with a guide--the Glockturm--and came down in the evening to the Radurschal Thal where I had heard there was an inn. The evening had turned to rain; but from a shoulder of the mountain I had been able to look right down the valley and had seen one long low building about four miles from the foot of the glacier. I walked through the pastures toward it, and found sitting outside the door in the rain the man who was to be my friend. The door was locked, and there was no one about the house, nor was there any other house within miles. My guide, however, went on. Lattery and I sat out there in the rain for a couple of hours, and then an old woman with a big umbrella held above her head came down from the upper pastures, driving some cows in front of her. She told us that no one had stayed at her inn for fourteen years. But she opened her door, lit us a great fire, and cooked us eggs and made us coffee. I remember that night as clearly as if it were yesterday. We sat in front of the fire with the bedding and the mattresses airing behind us until late into the night. The rain got worse too. There was a hole in the thatch overhead, and through it I saw the lightning slash the sky, as I lay in bed. Very few people ever came up or down that valley; and the next morning, after the storm, the chamois were close about the inn, on the grass. We went on together. That was the beginning."

He spoke simply, with a deep quietude of voice. The tobacco glowed and grew dull in the bowl of his pipe regularly; the darkness hid his face. But the tenderness, almost the amusement with which he dwelt on the little insignificant details of that first meeting showed her how very near to him it was at this moment.

"We went from the Tyrol down to Verona and baked ourselves in the sun there for a day, under the colonnades, and then came back through the St. Gotthard to Goeschenen. Do you know the Goeschenen Thal? There is a semicircle of mountains, the Winterbergen, which closes it in at the head. We climbed there together for a week, just he and I and no guides. I remember a rock-ridge there. It was barred by a pinnacle which stood up from it--'a gendarme,' as they call it. We had to leave the arete and work out along the face of the pinnacle at right angles to the mountain. There was a little ledge. You could look down between your feet quite straight to the glacier, two thousand feet below. We came to a place where the wall of the pinnacle seemed possible. Almost ten feet above us, there was a flaw in the rock which elsewhere was quite perpendicular. I was the lightest. So my friend planted himself as firmly as he could on the ledge with his hands flat against the rock face. There wasn't any handhold, you see, and I climbed out on to his back and stood upon his shoulders. I saw that the rock sloped back from the flaw or cleft in quite a practicable way. Only there was a big boulder resting on the slope within reach, and which we could hardly avoid touching. It did not look very secure. So I put out my hand and just touched it--quite, quite gently. But it was so exactly balanced that the least little vibration overset it, and I saw it begin to move, very slowly, as if it meant no harm whatever. But it was moving, nevertheless, toward me. My chest was on a level with the top of the cleft, so that I had a good view of the boulder. I couldn't do anything at all. It was much too heavy and big for my arms to stop and I couldn't move, of course, since I was standing on Jack Lattery's shoulders. There did not seem very much chance, with nothing below us except two thousand feet of vacancy. But there was just at my side a little bit of a crack in the edge of the cleft, and there was just a chance that the rock might shoot out down that cleft past me. I remember standing and watching the thing sliding down, not in a rush at all, but very smoothly, almost in a friendly sort of way, and I wondered how long it would be before it reached me. Luckily some irregularity in the slope of rock just twisted it into the crack, and it suddenly shot out into the air at my side with a whizz. It was so close to me that it cut the cloth of my sleeve. I had been so fascinated by the gentle movement of the boulder that I had forgotten altogether to tell Lattery what was happening; and when it whizzed out over his head, he was so startled that he nearly lost his balance on the little shelf and we were within an ace of following our rock down to the glacier. Those were our early days." And he laughed with a low deep ring of amusement in his voice.

"We were late that day on the mountain," he resumed, "and it was dark when we got down to a long snow-slope at its foot. It was new ground to us. We were very tired. We saw it glimmering away below us. It might end in a crevasse and a glacier for all we knew, and we debated whether we should be prudent or chance it. We chanced the crevasse. We sat down and glissaded in the dark with only the vaguest idea where we should end. Altogether we had very good times, he and I. Well, they have come to an end on the Glacier des Nantillons."

Chayne became silent; Sylvia Thesiger sat at his side and did not interrupt. In front of them the pastures slid away into darkness. Only a few small clear lights shining in the chalets told them there were other people awake in the world. Except for the reverberation of the torrent deep in the gorge at their right, no sound at all broke the deep silence. Chayne knocked the ashes from his pipe.

"I beg your pardon," he said. "I have been talking to you about one whom you never knew. You were so quiet that I seemed to be merely remembering to myself."

"I was so quiet," Sylvia explained, "because I wished you to go on. I was very glad to hear you. It was all new and strange and very pleasant to me--this story of your friendship. As strange and pleasant as this cool, quiet night here, a long way from the hotels and the noise, on the edge of the snow. For I have heard little of such friendships and I have seen still less."

Chayne's thoughts were suddenly turned from his dead friend to this, the living companion at his side. There was something rather sad and pitiful in the tone of her voice, no less than in the words she used. She spoke with so much humility. He was aware with a kind of shock, that here was a woman, not a child. He turned his eyes to her, as he had turned his thoughts. He could see dimly the profile of her face. It was still as the night itself. She was looking straight in front of her into the darkness. He pondered upon her life and how she bore with it, and how she had kept herself unspoiled by its associations. Of the saving grace of her dreams he knew nothing. But the picture of her mother was vivid to his eyes, the outlawed mother, shunned instinctively by the women, noisy and shrill, and making her companions of the would-be fashionable loiterers and the half-pay officers run to seed. That she bore it ill her last words had shown him. They had thrown a stray ray of light upon a dark place which seemed a place of not much happiness.

"I am very glad that you are here to-night," he said. "It has been kind of you to listen. I rather dreaded this evening."

Though what he said was true, it was half from pity that he said it. He wished her to feel her value. And in reply she gave him yet another glimpse into the dark place.

"Your friend," she said, "must have been much loved in Chamonix."

"Why?"

"So many guides came of their own accord to search for him."

Again Chayne's face was turned quickly toward her. Here indeed was a sign of the people amongst whom she lived, and of their unillumined thoughts. There must be the personal reason always, the personal reason or money. Outside of these, there were no motives. He answered her gently:

"No; I think that was not the reason. How shall I put it to you?" He leaned forward with his elbows upon his knees, and spoke slowly, choosing his words. "I think these guides obeyed a law, a law not of any man's making, and the one law last broken--the law that what you know, that you must do, if by doing it you can save a life. I should think nine medals out of ten given by the Humane Society are given because of the compulsion of that law. If you can swim, sail a boat, or climb a mountain, and the moment comes when a life can only be saved if you use your knowledge--well, you have got to use it. That's the law. Very often, I have no doubt, it's quite reluctantly obeyed, in most cases I think it's obeyed by instinct, without consideration of the consequences. But it *is* obeyed, and the guides obeyed it when so many of them came with me on to the Glacier des Nantillons."

He heard the girl at his side draw in a sharp breath. She shivered.

"You are cold?"

"No," she answered. "But that, too, is all strange to me. I should have known of that law without the need to be told of it. But I shall not forget it."

Again humility was very audible in the quiet tone of her voice. She understood that she had been instructed. She felt she should not have needed it. She faced her ignorance frankly.

"What one knows, that one must do," she repeated, fixing the words in her mind, "if by doing it one can save a life. No, I shall not forget that."

She rose from the seat.

"I must go in."

"Yes," cried Chayne, starting up. "You have stayed up too long as it is. You will be tired to-morrow."

"Not till to-morrow evening," she said, with a laugh. She looked upward to the starlit sky. "It will be fine, I hope. Oh, it *must* be fine. To-morrow is my one day. I do so want it to be perfect," she exclaimed.

"I don't think you need fear."

She held out her hand to him.

"This is good-by, I suppose," she said, and she did not hide the regret the words brought to her.

Chayne took her hand and kept it for a second or two. He ought to start an hour and a half before her. That he knew very well. But he answered:

"No. We go the same road for a little while. When do you start?"

"At half past one."

"I too. It will be daybreak before we say good-by. I wonder whether you will sleep at all to-night. I never do the first night."

He spoke lightly, and she answered him in the same key.

"I shall hardly know whether I sleep or wake, with the noise of that stream rising through my window. For so far back as I can remember I always dream of running water."

The words laid hold upon Chayne's imagination and fixed her in his memories. He knew nothing of her really, except just this one curious fact. She dreamed of running water. Somehow it was fitting that she should. There was a kind of resemblance; running water was, in a way, an image of her. She seemed in her nature to be as clear and fresh; yet she was as elusive; and when she laughed, her laugh had a music as light and free.

She went into the chalet. Through the window Chayne saw her strike a match and hold it to the candle. She stood for a moment looking out at him gravely, with the light shining upward upon her young face. Then a smile hesitated upon her lips and slowly took possession of her cheeks and eyes. She turned and went into her room.

CHAPTER VII
THE AIGUILLE D'ARGENTIERE

Chayne smoked another pipe alone and then walking to the end of the little terrace looked down on to the glistening field of ice below. Along that side of the chalet no light was burning. Was she listening? Was she asleep? The pity which had been kindled within him grew as he thought upon her. To-morrow she would be going back to a life she clearly hated. On the whole he came to the conclusion that the world might have been better organized. He lit his candle and went to bed, and it seemed that not five minutes had passed before one of his guides knocked upon his door. When he came into the living-room Sylvia Thesiger was already break-fasting.

"Did you sleep?" he asked.

"I was too excited," she answered. "But I am not tired"; and certainly there was no trace of fatigue in her appearance.

They started at half past one and went up behind the hut.

The stars shimmered overhead in a dark and cloudless sky. The night was still; as yet there was no sign of dawn. The great rock cliffs of the Chardonnet across the glacier and the towering ice-slopes of the Aiguille Verte beneath which they passed were all hidden in darkness. They might have been walking on some desolate plain of stones flat from horizon to horizon. They walked in single file, Jean leading with a lighted lantern in his hand, so that Sylvia, who followed next, might pick her way amongst the boulders. Thus they marched for two hours along the left bank of the glacier and then descended on to ice. They went forward partly on moraine, partly on ice at the foot of the crags of the Aiguille Verte. And gradually the darkness thinned. Dim masses of black rock began to loom high overhead, and to all seeming very far away. The sky paled, the dim masses of rock drew near about the climbers, and over the steep walls, the light flowed into the white basin of the glacier as though from every quarter of the sky.

Sylvia stopped and Chayne came up with her.

"Well?" he asked; and as he saw her face his thoughts were suddenly swept back to the morning when the beauty of the ice-world was for the first time vouch-safed to him. He seemed to recapture the fine emotion of that moment.

Sylvia stood gazing with parted lips up that wide and level glacier to its rock-embattled head. The majestic silence of the place astounded her. There was no whisper of wind, no rustling of trees, no sound of any bird. As yet too there was no crack of ice, no roar of falling stones. And as the silence surprised her ears, so the simplicity of color smote upon her eyes. There were no gradations. White ice filled the basin and reached high into the recesses of the mountains, hanging in rugged glaciers upon their flanks, and streaking the gullies with smooth narrow ribands. And about the ice, and above it, circling it in, black walls of rock towered high, as-tonishingly steep and broken at the top into pinnacles of an exquisite beauty.

"I shall be very glad to have seen this," said Sylvia, as she stored the picture in her mind, "more glad than I am even now. It will be a good memory to fall back upon when things are troublesome."

"Must things be troublesome?" he asked.

"Don't let me spoil my one day," she said, with a smile.

She moved on, and Chayne, falling back, spoke for a little with his guides. A little further on Jean stopped.

"That is our mountain, mademoiselle," he said, pointing eastward across the glacier.

Sylvia turned in that direction.

Straight in front of her a bay of ice ran back, sloping ever upward, and around the bay there rose a steep wall of cliffs which in the center sharpened precipitously to an apex. The apex was not a point but a rounded level ridge of snow which curved over on the top of the cliffs like a billow of foam. A tiny black tower of rock stood alone on the northern end of the snow-ridge.

"That, mademoiselle, is the Aiguille d'Argentiere. We cross the glacier here."

Jean put the rope about her waist, fixing it with the fisherman's bend, and tied one end about his own, using the overhand knot, while his brother tied on behind. They then turned at right angles to their former march and crossed the glacier, keeping the twenty feet of rope which separated each person extended. Once Jean looked back and uttered an exclamation of surprise. For he saw Chayne and his guides following across the glacier behind, and Chayne's road to the Col Dolent at the head of the glacier lay straight ahead upon their former line of advance. However he said nothing.

They crossed the bergschrund with less difficulty than they had anticipated, and ascending a ridge of debris, by the side of the lateral glacier which descended from the cliffs of the Aiguille d'Argentiere, they advanced into the bay under the southern wall of the Aiguille du Chardonnet. On the top of this moraine Jean halted, and the party breakfasted, and while they breakfasted Chayne told Sylvia something of that mountain's history. "It is not the most difficult of peaks," said he, "but it has associations, which some of the new rock-climbs have not. The pioneers came here." Right behind them there was a gap, the pass between their mountain and the Aiguille du Chardonnet. "From that pass Moore and Whymper first tried to reach the top by following the crest of the cliffs, but they found it impracticable. Whymper tried again, but this time up the face of the cliffs further on to the south and just to the left of the summit. He failed, came back again and conquered. We follow his road."

And while they looked up the dead white of that rounded summit ridge changed to a warm rosy color and all about that basin the topmost peaks took fire.

"It is the sun," said he.

Sylvia looked across the valley. The great ice-triangle of the Aiguille Verte flashed and sparkled. The slopes of the Les Droites and Mont Dolent were hung with jewels; even the black precipices of the Tour Noir grew warm and friendly. But at the head of the glacier a sheer unbroken wall of rock swept round in the segment of a circle, and this remained still dead black and the glacier at its foot dead white. At one point in the knife-like edge of this wall there was a depression, and from the depression a riband of ice ran, as it seemed from where they sat, perpendicularly down to the Glacier d'Argentiere.

"That is the Col Dolent," said Chayne. "Very little sunlight ever creeps down there."

Sylvia shivered as she looked. She had never seen anything so somber, so sinister, as that precipitous curtain of rock and its riband of ice. It looked like a white band painted on a black wall.

"It looks very dangerous," she said, slowly.

"It needs care," said Chayne.

"Especially this year when there is so little snow," added Sylvia.

"Yes. Twelve hundred feet of ice at an angle of fifty degrees."

"And the bergschrund's just beneath."

"Yes, you must not slip on the Col Dolent," said he, quietly.

Sylvia was silent a little while. Then she said with a slight hesitation:

"And you cross that pass to-day?"

There was still more hesitation in Chayne's voice as he answered:

"Well, no! You see, this is your first mountain. And you have only two guides."

Sylvia looked at him seriously.

"How many should I have taken for the Aiguille d'Argentiere? Twelve?"

Chayne smiled feebly.

"Well, no," and his confusion increased. "Two, as a rule, are enough--unless--"

"Unless the amateur is very clumsy," she added. "Thank you, Captain Chayne."

"I didn't mean that," he cried. He had no idea whether she was angry or not. She was just looking quietly and steadily into his face and waiting for his explanation.

"Well, the truth is," he blurted out, "I wanted to go up the Aiguille d'Argentiere with you," and he saw a smile dimple her cheeks.

"I am honored," she said, and the tone of her voice showed besides that she was very glad.

"Oh, but it wasn't only for the sake of your company," he said, and stopped. "I don't seem to be very polite, do I?" he said, lamentably.

"Not very," she replied.

"What I mean is this," he explained. "Ever since we started this morning, I have been recapturing my own sensations on my first ascent. Watching you, your enjoyment, your eagerness to live fully every moment of this day, I almost feel as if I too had come fresh to the mountains, as if the Argentiere were my first peak."

He saw the blood mount into her cheeks.

"Was that the reason why you questioned me as to what I thought and felt?"

she asked.

"Yes."

"I thought you were testing me," she said, slowly. "I thought you were trying whether I was--worthy"; and once again humility had framed her words and modulated their utterance. She recognized without rancor, but in distress, that people had the right to look on her as without the pale.

The guides packed up the ***Ruecksacks***, and they started once more up the moraine. In a little while they descended on to the lateral glacier which descending from the recesses of the Aiguille d'Argentiere in front of them flowed into the great basin behind. They roped together now in one party and ascended the glacier diagonally, rounding a great buttress which descends from the rock ledge and bisects the ice, and drawing close to the steep cliffs. In a little while they crossed the bergschrund from the glacier on to the wall of mountain, and traversing by easy rocks at the foot of the cliffs came at last to a big steep gully filled with hard ice which led up to the ridge just below the final peak.

"This is our way" said Jean. "We ascend by the rocks at the side."

They breakfasted again and began to ascend the rocks to the left of the great gully, Sylvia following second behind her leading guide. The rocks were not difficult, but they were very steep and at times loose. Moreover, Jean climbed fast and Sylvia had much ado to keep pace with him. But she would not call on him to slacken his pace, and she was most anxious not to come up on the rope but to climb with her own hands and feet. This they ascended for the better part of an hour and Jean halted on a convenient ledge. Sylvia had time to look down. She had climbed with her face to the wall of rock, her eyes searching quickly for her holds, fixing her feet securely, gripping firmly with her hands, avoiding the loose boulders. Moreover, the rope had worried her. When she had left it at its length between herself and the guide in front of her, it would hang about her feet, threatening to trip her, or catch as though in active malice in any crack which happened to be handy. If she shortened it and held it in her hands, there would come a sudden tug from above as the leader raised himself from one ledge to another which almost overset her.

Now, however, flushed with her exertion and glad to draw her breath at her ease, she looked down and was astonished. So far below her already seemed the glacier she had left, so steep the rocks up which she had climbed.

"You are not tired?" said Chayne.

Sylvia laughed. Tired, when a dream was growing real, when she was actually on the mountain face! She turned her face again to the rock-wall and in a little more than an hour after leaving the foot of the gully she stepped out on to a patch of snow on the shoulder of the mountain. She stood in sunlight, and all the country to the east was suddenly unrolled before her eyes. A moment before and her face was to the rock, now at her feet the steep snow-slopes dropped to the Glacier of Saleinaz. The crags of the Aiguille Dorees, and some green uplands gave color to the glittering world of ice, and far away towered the white peaks of the Grand Combin and the Weisshorn in a blue cloudless sky, and to the left over the summit of the Grande Fourche she saw the huge embattlements of the Oberland. She stood absorbed while the rest of the party ascended to her side. She hardly knew indeed that they were there until Chayne standing by her asked:

"You are not disappointed?"

She made no reply. She had no words wherewith to express the emotion which troubled her to the depths.

They rested for a while on this level patch of snow. To their right the ridge ran sharply up to the summit. But not by that ridge was the summit to be reached. They turned over on to the eastern face of the mountain and traversed in a straight line across the great snow-slope which sweeps down in one white unbroken curtain toward the Glacier of Saleinaz. Their order had been changed. First Jean advanced. Chayne followed and after him came Sylvia.

The leading guide kicked a step or two in the snow. Then he used the adz of his ax. A few steps still, and he halted.

"Ice," he said, and from that spot to the mountain top he used the pick.

The slope was at a steep angle, the ice very hard, and each step had to be cut with care, especially on the traverse where the whole party moved across the mountain upon the same level, and there was no friendly hand above to give a pull upon the rope. The slope ran steeply down beneath them, then curved over a brow and steepened yet more.

"Are the steps near enough together?" Chayne asked.

"Yes," she replied, though she had to stretch in her stride.

And upon that Jean dug his pick in the slope at his side and turned round.

"Lean well way from the slope, mademoiselle, not toward it. There is less chance then of slipping from the steps," he said anxiously, and there came a look of surprise upon his face. For he saw that already of her own thought she was standing straight in her steps, thrusting herself out from the slope by pressing the pick of her ax against it at the level of her waist. And more than once thereafter Jean turned about and watched her with a growing perplexity. Chayne looked to see whether her face showed any sign of fear. On the contrary she was looking down that great sweep of ice with an actual exultation. And it was not ignorance which allowed her to exult. The evident anxiety of Chayne's words, and the silence which since had fallen upon one and all were alone enough to assure her that here was serious work. But she had been reading deeply of the Alps, and in all the histories of mountain exploits which she had read, of climbs up vertical cracks in sheer walls of rocks, balancings upon ridges sharp as a knife edge, crawlings over smooth slabs with nowhere to rest the feet or hands, it was the ice-slope which had most kindled her imagination. The steep, smooth, long ice-slope, white upon the surface, grayish-green or even black where the ax had cut the step, the place where no slip must be made. She had lain awake at nights listening to the roar of the streets beneath her window and picturing it, now sleeping in the sunlight, now enwreathed in mists which opened and showed still higher heights and still lower depths, now whipped angrily with winds which tore off the surface icicles and snow, and sent them swirling like smoke about the shoulders of the peak. She had dreamed herself on to it, half shrinking, half eager, and now she was actually upon one and she felt no fear. She could not but exult.

The sunlight was hot upon this face of the mountain; yet her feet grew cold, as she stood patiently in her steps, advancing slowly as the man before her moved. Once as she stood, she moved her foot and scratched the sole of her boot on the ice to level a roughness in the step, and at once she saw Chayne and the guide in front drive the picks of their axes hard into the slope at their side and stand tense as if expecting a jerk upon the rope. Afterward they both looked round at her, and seeing she was safe turned back again to their work, the guide cutting the steps, Chayne polishing them behind him.

In a little while the guide turned his face to the slope and cut upward instead of across. The slope was so steep that instead of cutting zigzags across its face, he chopped pigeon holes straight up. They moved from one to the other as on a ladder, and their knees touched the ice as they stood upright in the steps. For a couple of hours the axes never ceased, and then the leader made two or three extra steps at the side of the staircase. On to one of them he moved out, Chayne went up and joined him.

"Come, mademoiselle," he said, and he drew in the rope as Sylvia advanced. She climbed up level with them on the ladder and waited, not knowing why they stood aside.

"Go on, mademoiselle," said the guide. She took another step or two upon snow and uttered a cry. She had looked suddenly over the top of the mountain on to the Aiguille Verte and the great pile of Mont Blanc, even as Revailloud had told her that she would. The guide had stood aside that she might be the first to step out upon the summit of the mountain. She stood upon the narrow ridge of snow, at her feet the rock-cliffs plastered with bulging masses of ice fell sheer to the glacier.

Her first glance was downward to the Col Dolent. Even at this hour when the basin of the valley was filled with sunshine that one corner at the head of the Glacier d'Argentiere was still dead white, dead black. She shivered once more as she looked at it--so grim and so menacing the rock-wall seemed, so hard and steep the riband of ice. Then Chayne joined her on the ridge. They sat down and ate their meal and lay for an hour sunning themselves in the clear air.

"You could have had no better day," said Chayne.

Only a few white scarfs of cloud flitted here and there across the sky and their shadows chased each other across the glittering slopes of ice and snow. The triangle of the Aiguille Verte was over against her, the beautiful ridges of Les Courtes and Les Droites to her right and beyond them the massive domes and buttresses of the great white mountain. Sylvia lay upon the eastern slope of the Argentiere looking over the brow, not wanting to speak, and certainly not listening to any word that was uttered. Her soul was at peace. The long-continued tension of mind and muscle, the excitement of that last ice-slope, both were over and had brought their reward. She looked out upon a still and peaceful world, wonderfully bright, wonderfully beautiful, and wonderfully colored. Here a spire would pierce the sunlight with slabs of red rock interspersed amongst its gray; there ice-cliffs sparkled as though strewn with jewels, bulged out in great green knobs, showed now a grim gray, now a transparent blue. At times a distant rumble like thunder far away told that the ice-fields were hurling their avalanches down. Once or twice she heard a great roar near at hand, and Chayne pointing across the valleys would show her what seemed to be a handful of small stones whizzing down the rocks and ice-gullies of the Aiguille Verte. But on the whole this new world was silent, communing with the heavens. She was in the hushed company of the mountains. Days there would be when these sunlit ridges would be mere blurs of driving storm, when the wind would shriek about the gullies, and dark mists swirl around the peaks. But on this morning there was no anger on the heights.

"Yes--you could have had no better day for your first mountain, mademoiselle," said Jean, as he stood beside her. "But this is not your first mountain."

She turned to him.

"Yes, it is."

Her guide bowed to her.

"Then, mademoiselle, you have great gifts. For you stood upon that ice-slope and moved along and up it, as only people of experience stand and move. I noticed you. On the rocks, too, you had the instinct for the hand-grip and the foothold and with which foot to take the step. And that instinct, mademoiselle, comes as a rule only with practice." He paused and looked at her perplexity.

"Moreover, mademoiselle, you remind me of some one," he added. "I cannot remember who it is, or why you remind me of him. But you remind me of some one very much." He picked up the **Ruecksack** which he had taken from his shoulders.

It was half past eleven. Sylvia took a last look over the wide prospect of jagged ridge, ice pinnacles and rock spires. She looked down once more upon the slim snow peak of Mont Dolent and the grim wall of rocks at the Col.

"I shall never forget this," she said, with shining eyes. "Never."

The fascination of the mountains was upon her. Something new had come into her life that morning which would never fail her to the very end, which would color all her days, however dull, which would give her memories in which to find solace, longings wherewith to plan the future. This she felt and some of this her friend understood.

"Yes," he said. "You understand the difference it makes to one's whole life. Each year passes so quickly looking back and looking forward."

"Yes, I understand," she said.

"You will come back?"

But this time she did not answer at once. She stood looking thoughtfully out over the bridge of the Argentiere. It seemed to Chayne that she was coming slowly to some great decision which would somehow affect all her life. Then she said--and it seemed to him that she had made her decision:

"I do not know. Perhaps I never shall come back."

They turned away and went carefully down the slope. Again her leading guide, who on the return journey went last, was perplexed by that instinct for the mountain side which had surprised him. The technique came to her so naturally. She turned her back to the slope, and thus descended, she knew just the right level at which to drive in the pick of her ax that she might lower herself to the next hole in their ice-ladder. Finally as they came down the rocks by the great couloir to the glacier, he cried out:

"Ah! Now, mademoiselle, I know who it is you remind me of. I have been watching you. I know now."

She looked up.

"Who is it?"

"An English gentleman I once climbed with for a whole season many years ago. A great climber, mademoiselle! Captain Chayne will know his name. Gabriel Strood."

"Gabriel Strood!" she cried, and then she laughed. "I too know his name. You are flattering me, Jean."

But Jean would not admit it.

"I am not, mademoiselle," he insisted. "I do not say you have his skill--how should you? But there are certain movements, certain neat ways of putting the hands and feet. Yes, mademoiselle, you remind me of him."

Sylvia thought no more of his words at the moment. They reached the lateral glacier, descended it and crossed the Glacier d'Argentiere. They found their stone-encumbered pathway of the morning and at three o'clock stood once more upon the platform in front of the Pavillon de Lognan. Then she rested for a while, saying very little.

"You are tired?" he said.

"No," she replied. "But this day has made a great difference to me."

Her guides approached her and she said no more upon the point. But Chayne had no doubt that she was referring to that decision which she had taken on the summit of the peak. She stood up to go.

"You stay here to-night?" she said.

"Yes."

"You cross the Col Dolent to-morrow?"

"Yes."

She looked at him quickly and then away.

"You will be careful? In the shadow there?"

"Yes."

She was silent for a moment or two, looking up the glacier toward the Aiguille d'Argentiere.

"I thank you very much for coming with me," and again the humility in her voice, as of one outside the door, touched and hurt him. "I am very grateful," and here a smile lightened her grave face, "and I am rather proud!"

"You came up to Lognan at a good time for me," he answered, as they shook hands. "I shall cross the Col Dolent with a better heart to-morrow."

They shook hands, and he asked:

"Shall I see no more of you?"

"That is as you will," she replied, simply.

"I should like to. In Paris, perhaps, or wherever you are likely to be. I am on leave now for some months."

She thought for a second or two. Then she said:

"If you will give me your address, I will write to you. I think I shall be in England."

"I live in Sussex, on the South Downs."

She took his card, and as she turned away she pointed to the Aiguille d'Argentiere.

"I shall dream of that to-night."

"Surely not," he replied, laughing down to her over the wooden balustrade. "You will dream of running water."

She glanced up at him in surprise that he should have remembered this strange quality of hers. Then she turned away and went down to the pine woods and the village of Les Tines.

CHAPTER VIII
SYLVIA PARTS FROM HER MOTHER

Meanwhile Mrs. Thesiger laughed her shrill laugh and chatted noisily in the garden of the hotel. She picnicked on the day of Sylvia's ascent amongst the sham ruins on the road to Sallanches with a few detached idlers of various nationalities.

"Quite, quite charming," she cried, and she rippled with enthusiasm over the artificial lake and the artificial rocks amongst which she seemed so appropriate a figure; and she shrugged her pretty shoulders over the eccentricities of her daughter, who was undoubtedly burning her complexion to the color of brick-dust among those stupid mountains. She came back a trifle flushed in the cool of the afternoon, and in the evening slipped discreetly into the little Cercle at the back of the Casino, where she played baccarat in a company which flattery could hardly have termed doubtful. She was indeed not displeased to be rid of her unsatisfactory daughter for a night and a couple of days.

"Sylvia won't fit in."

Thus for a long time she had been accustomed piteously to complain; and with ever more reason. Less and less did Sylvia fit in with Mrs. Thesiger's scheme of life. It was not that the girl resisted or complained. Mrs. Thesiger would have understood objections and complaints. She would not have minded them; she could have coped with them. There would have been little scenes, with accusations of ingratitude, of undutifulness, and Mrs. Thesiger was not averse to the excitement of little scenes. But Sylvia never complained; she maintained a reserve, a mystery which her mother found very uncomfortable. "She has no sympathy," said Mrs. Thesiger. Moreover, she would grow up, and she would grow up in beauty and in freshness. Mrs. Thesiger did her best. She kept her dressed in a style which suited a younger girl, or rather, which would have suited a younger girl had it been less decorative and extreme. Again Sylvia did not complain. She followed her usual practice and shut her mind to the things which displeased her so completely, that they ceased to trouble her. But Mrs. Thesiger never knew that secret; and often, when in the midst of her chatter she threw a glance at the elaborate figure of her daughter, sitting apart with her lace skirts too short, her heels too high, her hat too big and too fancifully trimmed, she would see her madonna-like face turned toward her, and her dark eyes thoughtfully dwelling upon her. At such times there would come an uncomfortable sensation that she was being weighed and found wanting; or a question would leap in her mind and bring with it fear, and the same question which she had asked herself in the train on the way to Chamonix.

"You ask me about my daughter?" she once exclaimed pettishly to Monsieur Pettigrat. "Upon my word, I really know nothing of her except one ridiculous thing. She always dreams of running water. Now, I ask you, what can you do with a daughter so absurd that she dreams of running water?"

Monsieur Pettigrat was a big, broad, uncommon man; he knew that he was uncommon, and dressed accordingly in a cloak and a brigand's hat; he saw what others did not, and spoke in a manner suitably impressive.

"I will tell you, madame, about your daughter," he said somberly. "To me she has a fated look."

Mrs. Thesiger was a little consoled to think that she had a daughter with a fated look.

"I wonder if others have noticed it," she said, cheerfully.

"No," replied Monsieur Pettigrat. "No others. Only I."

"There! That's just like Sylvia," cried Mrs. Thesiger, in exasperation. "She has a fated look and makes nothing of it."

But the secret of her discontent was just a woman's jealousy of a younger rival. Men were beginning to turn from her toward her daughter. That Sylvia never competed only made the sting the sharper. The grave face with its perfect oval, which smiled so rarely, but in so winning a way, its delicate color, its freshness, were points which she could not forgive her daughter. She felt faded and yellow beside her, she rouged more heavily on account of her, she looked with more apprehension at the crow's-feet which were beginning to show about the corners of her eyes, and the lines which were beginning to run from the nostrils to the corners of her mouth.

Sylvia reached the hotel in time for dinner, and as she sat with her mother, drinking her coffee in the garden afterward, Monsieur Pettigrat planted himself before the little iron table.

He shook his head, which was what his friends called "leonine."

"Mademoiselle," he said, in his most impressive voice, "I envy you."

Sylvia looked up at him with a little smile of mischief upon her lips.

"And why, monsieur?"

He waved his arm magnificently.

"I watched you at dinner. You are of the elect, mademoiselle, for whom the snow peaks have a message."

Sylvia's smile faded from her face.

"Perhaps so, monsieur," she said, gravely, and her mother interposed testily:

"A message! Ridiculous! There are only two words in the message, my dear. Cold-cream! and be sure you put it on your face before you go to bed."

Sylvia apparently did not hear her mother's comment. At all events she disregarded it, and Monsieur Pettigrat once again shook his head at Sylvia with a kindly magnificence.

"They have no message for me, mademoiselle," he said, with a sigh, as though he for once regretted that he was so uncommon. "I once went up there to see." He waved his hand generally to the chain of Mont Blanc and drifted largely away.

Mrs. Thesiger, however, was to hear more definitely of that message two days later. It was after dinner. She was sitting in the garden with her daughter on a night of moonlight; behind them rose the wall of mountains, silent and shadowed, in front were the lights of the little town, and the clatter of its crowded streets. Between the town and the mountains, at the side of the hotel this garden lay, a garden of grass and trees, where the moonlight slept in white brilliant pools of light, or dripped between the leaves of the branches. It partook alike of the silence of the hills and the noise of the town, for a murmur of voices was audible from this and that point, and under the shadows of the trees could be seen the glimmer of light-colored frocks and the glow of cigars waxing and waning. A waiter came across the garden with some letters for Mrs. Thesiger. There were none for Sylvia and she was used to none, for she had no girl friends, and though at times men wrote her letters she did not answer them.

A lamp burned near at hand. Mrs. Thesiger opened her letters and read them. She threw them on to the table when she had read them through. But there was one which angered her, and replacing it in its envelope, she tossed it so petulantly aside that it slid off the iron table and fell at Sylvia's feet. Sylvia stooped and picked it up. It had fallen face upward.

"This is from my father."

Mrs. Thesiger looked up startled. It was the first time that Sylvia had ever spoken of him to her. A wariness come into her eyes.

"Well?" she asked.

"I want to go to him."

Sylvia spoke very simply and gently, looking straight into her mother's face with that perplexing steadiness of gaze which told so very little of what thoughts were busy behind it. Her mother turned her face aside. She was rather frightened. For a while she made no reply at all, but her face beneath its paint looked haggard and old in the white light, and she raised her hand to her heart. When she did speak, her voice shook.

"You have never seen your father. He has never seen you. He and I parted before you were born."

"But he writes to you."

"Yes, he writes to me," and for all that she tried, she could not altogether keep a tone of contempt out of her voice. She added with some cruelty: "But he never mentions you. He has never once inquired after you, never once."

Sylvia looked very wistfully at the letter, but her purpose was not shaken.

"Mother, I want to go to him," she persisted. Her lips trembled a little, and with a choke of the voice, a sob half caught back, she added: "I am most unhappy here."

The rarity of a complaint from Sylvia moved her mother strangely. There was a forlornness, moreover, in her appealing attitude. Just for a moment Mrs. Thesiger began to think of early days of which the memory was at once a pain and a reproach. A certain little village underneath the great White Horse on the Dorsetshire Downs rose with a disturbing vividness before her eyes. She almost heard the mill stream babble by. In that village of Sutton Poyntz she had herself been born, and to it she had returned, caught back again for a little while by her own country and her youth, that Sylvia might be born there too. These months had made a kind of green oasis in her life. She had rested there in a farm-house, after a time of much turbulence, with the music of running water night and day in her ears, a high-walled garden of flowers and grass about her, and the downs with the shadow-filled hollows, and brown treeless slopes rising up from her very feet. She could not but think of that short time of peace, and her voice softened as she answered her daughter.

"We don't keep step, Sylvia," she said, with an uneasy laugh. "I know that. But, after all, would you be happier with your father, even if he wants to keep you! You have all you want here--frocks, amusement, companions. Try to be more friendly with people."

But Sylvia merely shook her head.

"I can't go on any longer like this," she said, slowly. "I can't, mother. If my father won't have me, I must see what I can do. Of course, I can't do much. I don't know anything. But I am too unhappy here. I cannot endure the life we are living without a home or--respect,--" Sylvia had not meant to use that word. But it had slipped out before she was aware. She broke off and turned her eyes again to her mother. They were very bright, for the moonlight glistened upon tears. But the softness had gone from her mother's face. She had grown in a moment hard, and her voice rang hard as she asked:

"Why do you think that your father and I parted? Come, let me hear!"

Sylvia turned her head away.

"I don't think about it," she said, gently. "I don't want to think about it. I just think that he left you, because you did not keep step either."

"Oh, he left me? Not I him? Then why does he write to me?"

The voice was growing harder with every word.

"I suppose because he is kind"; and at that simple explanation Sylvia's mother laughed with a bitter amusement. Sylvia sat scraping the gravel with her slipper.

"Don't do that!" cried her mother, irritably. Then she asked suddenly a question which startled her daughter.

"Did you meet any one last night on the mountain, at the inn?"

Sylvia's face colored, but the moonlight hid the change.

"Yes," she said.

"A man?"

"Yes."

"Who was it?"

"A Captain Chayne. He was at the hotel all last week. It was his friend who was killed on the Glacier des Nantillons."

"Were you alone at the inn, you and he?"

"Yes."

"Did he know your father?"

Sylvia stared at her mother.

"I don't know. I suppose not. How should he?"

"It's not impossible," replied Mrs. Thesiger. Then she leaned on the table. "It was he who put these ideas into your head about going away, about leaving me." She made an accusation rather than put a question, and made it angrily.

"No, mother," Sylvia replied. "He never spoke of you. The ideas have been growing in my mind for a long time, and to-day--" She raised her head, and turning slightly, looked up to where just behind her the ice-peaks of the Aiguilles du Midi and de Blaitiere soared into the moonlit sky. "To-day the end came. I became certain that I must go away. I am very sorry, mother."

"The message of the mountains!" said her mother with a sneer, and Sylvia answered quietly:

"Yes."

"Very well," said Mrs. Thesiger. She had been deeply stung by her daughter's words, by her wish to go, and if she delayed her consent, it was chiefly through a hankering to punish Sylvia. But the thought came to her that she would punish Sylvia more completely if she let her go. She smiled cruelly as she looked at the girl's pure and gentle face. And, after all, she herself would be free--free from Sylvia's unconscious rivalry, free from the competition of her freshness and her youth, free from the grave criticism of her eyes.

"Very well, you shall go to your father. But remember! You have made your choice. You mustn't come whining back to me, because I won't have you," she said, brutally. "You shall go to-morrow."

She took the letter from its envelope but she did not show it to her daughter.

"I don't use your father's name," she said. "I have not used it since"--and again the cruel smile appeared upon her lips--"since he left me, as you say. He is called Garratt Skinner, and he lives in a little house in Hobart Place. Yes, you shall start for your home to-morrow."

Sylvia stood up.

"Thank you," she said. She looked wistfully at her mother, asking her pardon with the look. But she did not approach her. She stood sadly in front of her. Mrs. Thesiger made no advance.

"Well?" she asked, in her hard, cold voice.

"Thank you, mother," Sylvia repeated, and she walked slowly to the door of the hotel. She looked up to the mountains. Needle spires of rock, glistening pinnacles of ice, they stood dreaming to the moonlight and the stars. The great step had been taken. She prayed for something of their calm, something of their proud indifference to storm and sunshine, solitude and company. She went up to her room and began to pack her trunks. And as she packed, the tears gathered in her eyes and fell.

Meanwhile, her mother sat in the garden. So Sylvia wanted a home; she could not endure the life she lived with her mother. Afar off a band played; the streets beyond were noisy as a river; beneath the trees of the garden here people talked quietly. Mrs. Thesiger sat with a little vindictive smile upon her face. Her rival was going to be punished. Mrs. Thesiger had left her husband, not he her. She read through the letter which she had received from him this evening. It was a pressing request for money. She was not going to send him money. She wondered how he would appreciate the present of a daughter instead.

CHAPTER IX
SYLVIA MAKES THE ACQUAINTANCE
OF HER FATHER

Sylvia left Chamonix the next afternoon. It was a Saturday, and she stepped out of her railway-carriage on to the platform of Victoria Station at seven o'clock on the Sunday evening. She was tired by her long journey, and she felt rather lonely as she waited for her trunks to be passed by the officers of the custom-house. It was her very first visit to London, and there was not one person to meet her. Other travelers were being welcomed on all sides by their friends. No one in all London expected her. She doubted if she had one single acquaintance in the whole town. Her mother, foreseeing this very moment, had with a subtlety of malice refrained from so much as sending a telegram to the girl's father; and Sylvia herself, not knowing him, had kept silence too. Since he did not expect her, she thought her better plan was to see him, or rather, since her thoughts were frank, to let him see her. Her mirror had assured her that her looks would be a better introduction than a telegram.

She had her boxes placed upon a cab and drove off to Hobart Place. The sense of loneliness soon left her. She was buoyed up by excitement. The novelty of the streets amused her. Moreover, she had invented her father, clothed him with many qualities as with shining raiment, and set him high among the persons of her dreams. Would he be satisfied with his daughter? That was her fear, and with the help of the looking-glass at the side of her hansom, she tried to remove the traces of travel from her young face.

The cab stopped at a door in a narrow wall between two houses, and she got out. Over the wall she saw the green leaves and branches of a few lime trees which rose from a little garden, and at the end of the garden, in the far recess between the two side walls, the upper windows of a little neat white house. Sylvia was charmed with it. She rang the bell, and a servant came to the door.

"Is Mr. Skinner in?" asked Sylvia.

"Yes," she said, doubtfully, "but--"

Sylvia, however, had made her plans.

"Thank you," she said. She made a sign to the cabman, and walked on through the doorway into a little garden of grass with a few flowers on each side against the walls. A tiled path led through the middle of the grass to the glass door of the house. Sylvia walked straight down, followed by the cabman who brought her boxes in one after the other. The servant, giving way before the composure of this strange young visitor, opened the door of a sitting-room upon the left hand, and Sylvia, followed by her trunks, entered and took possession.

"What name shall I say?" asked the servant in perplexity. She had had no orders to expect a visitor. Sylvia paid the cabman and waited until she heard the garden door close and the jingle of the cab as it was driven away. Then, and not till then, she answered the question.

"No name. Just please tell Mr. Skinner that some one would like to see him."

The servant stared, but went slowly away. Sylvia seated herself firmly upon one of the boxes. In spite of her composed manner, her heart was beating wildly. She heard a door open and the firm tread of a man along the passage. Sylvia clung to her box. After all she was in the house, she and her baggage. The door opened and a tall broad-shouldered man, who seemed to fill the whole tiny room, came in and stared at her. Then he saw her boxes, and he frowned in perplexity. As he appeared to Sylvia, he was a man of about forty-five, with a handsome, deeply-lined aquiline face. He had thick, dark brown hair, a mustache of a lighter brown and eyes of the color of hers--a man rather lean but of an athletic build. Sylvia watched him intently, but the only look upon his face was one of absolute astonishment. He saw a young lady, quite unknown to him, perched upon her luggage in a sitting-room of his house.

"You wanted to see me?" he asked.

"Yes," she replied, getting on to her feet. She looked at him gravely. "I am Sylvia," she said.

A smile, rather like her own smile, hesitated about his mouth.

"And--

"Who is Sylvia? What is she? Her trunks do not proclaim her!"

he said. "Beyond that Sylvia has apparently come to stay, I am rather in the dark."

"You are Mr. Garratt Skinner?"

"Yes."

"I am your daughter Sylvia."

"My daughter Sylvia!" he exclaimed in a daze. Then he sat down and held his head between his hands.

"Yes, by George. I *have* got a daughter Sylvia," he said, obviously recollecting the fact with surprise. "But you are at Chamonix."

"I was at Chamonix yesterday."

Garratt Skinner looked sharply at Sylvia.

"Did your mother send you to me?"

"No," she answered. "But she let me go. I came of my own accord. A letter came from you--"

"Did you see it?" interrupted her father. "Did she show it you?"

"No, but she gave me your address when I told her that I must come away."

"Did she? I think I recognize my wife in that kindly act," he said, with a sudden bitterness. Then he looked curiously at his daughter.

"Why did you want to come away?"

"I was unhappy. For a long time I had been thinking over this. I hated it all--the people we met, the hotels we stayed at, the life altogether. Then at Chamonix I went up a mountain."

"Oho," said her father, sitting up alertly. "So you went up a mountain? Which one?"

"The Aiguille d'Argentiere. Do you know it, father?"

"I have heard of it," said Garratt Skinner.

"Well, somehow that made a difference. It is difficult to explain. But I felt the difference. I felt something had happened to me which I had to recognize--a new thing. Climbing that mountain, staying for an hour upon its summit in the sunlight with all those great still pinnacles and ice-slopes about me--it was just like hearing very beautiful music." She was sitting now leaning forward with her hands clasped in front of her and speaking with great earnestness. "All the vague longings which had ever stirred within me, longings for something beyond, and beyond, came back upon me in a tumult. There was a place in shadow at my feet far below, the only place in shadow, a wall of black rock called the Col Dolent. It seemed to me that I was living in that cold shadow. I wanted to get up on the ridge, with the sunlight. So I came to you."

It seemed to Sylvia, that intently as she spoke, her words were and must be elusive to another, unless that other had felt what she felt or were moved by sympathy to feel it. Her father listened without ridicule, without a smile. Indeed, once or twice he nodded his head to her words. Was it comprehension, she wondered, or was it only patience?

"When I came down from that summit, I felt that what I had hated before was no longer endurable at all. So I came to you."

Her father got up from his chair and stood for a little while looking out of the window. He was clearly troubled by her words. He turned away with a shrug of his shoulders.

"But--but--what can I do for you here?" he cried. "Sylvia, I am a very poor man. Your mother, on the other hand, has some money."

"Oh, father, I shan't cost you much," she replied, eagerly. "I might perhaps by looking after things save you money. I won't cost you much."

Garratt Skinner looked at her with a rueful smile.

"You look to me rather an expensive person to keep up," he said.

"Mother dressed me like this. It's not my choice," she said. "I let her do as she wished. It did not seem to matter much. Really, if you will let me stay, you will find me useful," she said, in a pathetic appeal.

"Useful?" said Garratt Skinner, suddenly. He again took stock of her, but now with a scrutiny which caused her a vague discomfort. He seemed to be appraising her from the color of her hair and eyes to the prettiness of her feet, almost as though she was for sale, and he a doubtful purchaser. She looked down on the carpet and slowly her blood colored her neck and rose into her face. "Useful," he said, slowly. "Perhaps so, yes, perhaps so." And upon that he changed his tone. "We will see, Sylvia. You must stay here for the present, at all events. Luckily, there is a spare room. I have some friends here staying to supper--just a bachelor's friends, you know, taking pot-luck without any ceremony, very good fellows, not polished, perhaps, but sound of heart, Sylvia my girl, sound of heart." All his perplexity had vanished; he had taken his part; and he rattled along with a friendly liveliness which cleared the shadows from Sylvia's thoughts and provoked upon her face her rare and winning smile. He rang the bell for the housemaid.

"My daughter will stay here," he said, to the servant's astonishment. "Get the spare room ready at once. You will be hostess to-night, Sylvia, and sit at the head of the table. I become a family man. Well, well!"

He took Sylvia up-stairs and showed her a little bright room with a big window which looked out across the garden. He carried her boxes up himself. "We don't run to a butler," he said. "Got everything you want? Ring if you haven't. We have supper at eight and we shan't dress. Only--well, you couldn't look dowdy if you tried."

Sylvia had not the slightest intention to try. She put on a little frock of white lace, high at the throat, dressed her hair, and then having a little time to spare she hurriedly wrote a letter. This letter she gave to the servant and she ran down-stairs.

"You will be careful to have it posted, please!" she said, and at that moment her father came out into the passage, so quickly that he might have been listening for her approach.

She stopped upon the staircase, a few steps above him. The evening was still bright, and the daylight fell upon her from a window above the hall door.

"Shall I do?" she asked, with a smile.

The staircase was paneled with a dark polished wood, and she stood out from that somber background, a white figure, delicate and dainty and wholesome, from the silver buckle on her satin slipper to the white flower she had placed in her hair. Her face, with its remarkable gentleness, its suggestion of purity as of one unspotted by the world, was turned to him with a confident appeal. Her clear gray eyes rested quietly on his. Yet she saw his face change. It seemed that a spasm of pain or revolt shook him. Upon her face there came a blank look. Why was he displeased? But the spasm passed. He shrugged his shoulders and threw off his doubt.

"You are very pretty," he said.

Sylvia's smile just showed about the corners of her lips and her face cleared.

"Yes," she said, with satisfaction.

Garratt Skinner laughed.

"Oh, you know that?"

"Yes," she replied, nodding her head at him.

He led the way down the passage toward the back of the house, and throwing open a door introduced her to his friends.

"Captain Barstow," he said, and Sylvia found herself shaking hands with a little middle-aged man with a shiny bald head and a black square beard. He had an eyeglass screwed into his right eye, and that whole side of his face was distorted by the contraction of the muscles and drawn upward toward the eye. He did not look at her directly, but with an oblique and furtive glance he expressed his sense of the honor which the introduction conferred on him. However, Sylvia was determined not to be disappointed. She turned to the next of her father's guests.

"Mr. Archie Parminter."

He at all events looked her straight in the face. He was a man of moderate height, youthful in build, but old of face, upon which there sat always a smirk of satisfaction. He was of those whom no beauty in others, no grace, no sweetness, could greatly impress, so filled was he with self-complacency. He had no time to admire, since always he felt that he was being admired, and to adjust his pose, and to speak so that his words, carried to the right distance, occupied too much of his attention. He seldom spoke to the person he talked with but generally to some other, a woman for choice, whom he believed to be listening to the important sentences he uttered. For the rest, he had grown heavy in jaw and his face (a rather flat face in which were set a pair of sharp dark eyes) narrowed in toward the top of his head like a pear.

He bowed suavely to Sylvia, with the air of one showing to the room how a gentleman performed that ceremony, but took little note of her.

But Sylvia was determined not to be disappointed.

Her father took her by the elbow and turned her about.

"Mr. Hine."

Sylvia was confronted with a youth who reddened under her greeting and awkwardly held out a damp coarse hand, a poor creature with an insipid face, coarse hair, and manner of great discomfort. He was as tall as Parminter, but wore his good clothes with Sunday air, and having been introduced to Sylvia could find no word to say to her.

"Well, let us go in to supper," said her father, and he held open the door for her to pass.

Sylvia went into the dining-room across the narrow hall, where a cold supper was laid upon a round table. In spite of her resolve to see all things in a rosy light, she grew conscious, in spite of herself, that she was disappointed in her father's friends. She was perplexed, too. He was so clearly head and shoulders above his associates, that she wondered at their presence in his house. Yet he seemed quite content, and in a most genial mood.

"You sit here, Sylvia, my dear," he said, pointing to a chair. "Wallie"--this to the youth Hine--"sit beside my daughter and keep her amused. Barstow, you on the other side; Parminter next to me."

He sat opposite Sylvia and the rest took their places, Hine sidling timidly into his chair and tortured by the thought that he had to amuse this delicate being at his side.

"The supper is on the table," said Garratt Skinner. "Parminter, will you cut up this duck? Hine, what have you got in front of you? Really, this is so exceptional an occasion that I think--" he started up suddenly, as a man will with a new and happy idea--"I certainly think that for once in a way we might open a bottle of champagne."

Surprise and applause greeted this brilliant idea, and Hine cried out:

"I think champagne fine, don't you, Miss Skinner?"

He collapsed at his own boldness. Parminter shrugged his shoulders to show that champagne was an every-day affair with him.

"It's drunk a good deal at the clubs nowadays," he said.

Meanwhile Garratt Skinner had not moved. He stood looking across the table to his daughter.

"What do you say, Sylvia? It's an extravagance. But I don't have such luck every day. It's in your honor. Shall we? Yes, then!"

He did not wait for an answer, but opened the door of a cupboard in the sideboard, and there, quite ready, stood half a dozen bottles of champagne. A doubt flashed into Sylvia's mind--a doubt whether her father's brilliant idea was really the inspiration which his manner had suggested. Those bottles looked so obviously got in for the occasion. But Garratt Skinner turned to her apologetically, as though he divined her thought.

"We don't run to a wine cellar, Sylvia. We have to keep what little stock we can afford in here."

Her doubt vanished, but in an instant it returned again, for as her father came round the table with the bottle in his hand, she noticed that shallow champagne glasses were ready laid at every place. Garratt Skinner filled the glasses and returned to his place.

"Sylvia," he said, and, smiling, he drank to her. He turned to his companions. "Congratulate me!" Then he sat down.

The champagne thawed the tongues of the company, and as they spoke Sylvia's heart sank more and more. For in word and thought and manner her father's guests were familiar to her. She refused to acknowledge it, but the knowledge was forced upon her. She had thought to step out of a world which she hated, against which her delicacy and her purity revolted, and lo! she had stepped out merely to take a stride and step down into it again at another place.

The obsequious attentiveness of Captain Barstow, the vanity of Mr. Parminter and his affected voice, suggesting that he came out of the great world to this little supper party, really without any sense of condescension at all, and the behavior of Walter Hine, who, to give himself courage, gulped down his champagne--it was all horribly familiar. Her one consolation was her father. He sat opposite to her, his strong aquiline face a fine contrast to the faces of the others; he had an ease of man-ner which they did not possess; he talked with a quietude of his own, and he had a watchful eye and a ready smile for his daughter. Indeed, it seemed that what she felt his guests felt too. For they spoke to him with a certain deference, almost as if they spoke to their master. He alone apparently noticed no unsuitability in his guests. He sat at his ease, their bosom friend.

Meanwhile, plied with champagne by Archie Parminter, who sat upon the other side of him, "Wallie" Hine began to boast. Sylvia tried to check him, but he was not now to be stopped. His very timidity pricked him on to extravagance, and his boasting was that worst form of boasting--the vaunt of the innocent weakling anxious to figure as a conqueror of women. With a flushed face he dropped his fool-ish hints of Mrs. This and Lady That, with an eye upon Sylvia to watch the impres-sion which he made, and a wise air which said "If only I were to tell you all."

Garratt Skinner opened a fresh bottle of champagne--the supply by now was getting low--and came round the table with it. As he held the neck of the bottle to the brim of Hine's glass he caught an appealing look from his daughter. At once he lifted the bottle and left the glass unfilled. As he passed Sylvia, she said in a low voice:

"Thank you," and he whispered back:

"You are quite right, my dear. Interest him so that he doesn't notice that I have left his glass empty."

Sylvia set herself then to talk to Wallie Hine. But he was intent on making her understand what great successes had been his. He *would* talk, and it troubled her that all listened, and listened with an air of admiration. Even her father from his side of the table smiled indulgently. Yet the stories, or rather the hints of stories, were certainly untrue. For this her wanderings had taught her--the man of many successes never talks. It seemed that there was a conspiracy to flatter the wretched youth.

"Yes, yes. You have been a devil of a fellow among the women, Wallie," said

Captain Barstow. But at once Garratt Skinner interfered and sharply:

"Come, come, Barstow! That's no language to use before my daughter."

Captain Barstow presented at the moment a remarkable gradation of color. On the top was the bald head, very shiny and white, below that a face now everywhere a deep red except where the swollen veins stood out upon the surface of his cheeks, and those were purple, and this in its turn was enclosed by the black square beard. He bowed at once to Garratt Skinner's rebuke.

"I apologize. I do indeed, Miss Sylvia! But when I was in the service we still clung to the traditions of Wellington by--by George. And it's hard to break oneself of the habit. 'Red-hot,'" he said, with a chuckle. "That's what they called me in the regiment. Red-hot Barstow. I'll bet that Red-hot Barstow is still pretty well remembered among the boys at Cheltenham."

"Swearing's bad form nowadays," said Archie Parminter, superciliously. "They have given it up at the clubs."

Sylvia seized the moment and rose from the table. Her father sprang forward and opened the door.

"We will join you in a few minutes," he said.

Sylvia went down the passage to the room at the back of the house in which she had been presented by her father to his friends. She rang the bell at once and when the servant came she said:

"I gave you a letter to post this evening. I should like to have it back."

"I am sorry, miss, but it's posted."

"I am sorry, too," said Sylvia, quietly.

The letter had been written to Chayne, and gave him the address of this house as the place where he might find her if he called. She had no thought of going away. She had made her choice for good or ill and must abide by it. That she knew. But she was no longer sure that she wished Captain Chayne to come and find her there.

CHAPTER X
A LITTLE ROUND GAME OF CARDS

Sylvia sat down in a chair and waited. She waited impatiently, for she knew that she had almost reached the limits of her self-command, and needed the presence of others to keep her from breaking down. But her native courage came to her aid, and in half an hour she heard the steps of her father and his guests in the passage. She noticed that her father looked anxiously toward her as he came in.

"Do you mind if we bring in our cigars?" he asked.

"Not at all," said she; and he came in, carrying in his hand a box of cigars, which he placed in the middle of the table. Wallie Hine at once stumbled across the room to Sylvia; he walked unsteadily, his features were more flushed than before. She shrank a little from him. But he had not the time to sit down beside her, for Captain Barstow exclaimed jovially:

"I say, Garratt, I have an idea. There are five of us here. Let us have a little round game of cards."

Sylvia started. In her heart she knew that just some such proposal as this she had been dreading all the evening. Her sinking hopes died away altogether.

This poor witless youth, plied with champagne; the older men who flattered him with lies; the suggestion of champagne made as though it were a sudden inspiration, and the six bottles standing ready in the cupboard; and now the suggestion of a little round game of cards made in just the same tone! Sylvia had a feeling of horror. She had kept herself unspotted from her world, but not through ignorance. She knew it. She knew those little round games of cards and what came of them, sometimes merely misery and ruin, sometimes a pistol shot in the early morning. She turned very pale, but she managed to say:

"Thank you. I don't play cards."

And then she heard a sudden movement by her father, who at the moment when Barstow spoke had been lighting a fresh cigar. She looked up. Garratt Skinner was staring in astonishment at Captain Barstow.

"Cards!" he cried. "In my house? On a Sunday evening?"

With each question his amazement grew, and he ended in a tone of remonstrance.

"Come, Barstow, you know me too well to propose that. I am rather hurt. A friendly talk, and a smoke, yes. Perhaps a small whisky and soda. I don't say no. But cards on a Sunday evening! No indeed."

"Oh, I say, Skinner," objected Wallie Hine. "There's no harm in a little game."

Garratt Skinner shook his head at Hine in a grave friendly way.

"Better leave cards alone, Wallie, always. You are young, you know."

Hine flushed.

"I am old enough to hold my own against any man," he cried, hotly. He felt that Garratt Skinner had humiliated him, and before this wonderful daughter of his in whose good favors Mr. Hine had been making such inroads during supper. Barstow apologized for his suggestion at once, but Hine was now quite unwilling that he should withdraw it.

"There's no harm in it," he cried. "I really think you are too Puritanical, isn't he, Miss--Miss Sylvia?"

Hine had been endeavoring to pluck up courage to use her Christian name all the evening. His pride that he had actually spoken it was so great that he did not remark at all her little movement of disgust.

Garratt Skinner seemed to weaken in his resolution.

"Well, of course, Wallie," he said, "I want you to enjoy yourselves. And if you especially want it--"

Did he notice that Sylvia closed her eyes and really shivered? She could not tell. But he suddenly spoke in a tone of revolt:

"But card-playing on Sunday. Really no!"

"It's done nowadays at the West-End Clubs," said Archie Parminter.

"Oh, is it?" said Garratt Skinner, again grown doubtful. "Is it, indeed? Well, if they do it in the Clubs--" And then with an exclamation of relief--"I haven't got a pack of cards in the house. That settles the point."

"There's a public house almost next door," replied Barstow. "If you send out your servant, I am sure she could borrow one."

"No," said Garratt Skinner, indignantly. "Really, Barstow, your bachelor habits have had a bad effect on you. I would not think of sending a girl out to a public house on any consideration. It might be the very first step downhill for her, and I should be responsible."

"Oh well, if you are so particular, I'll go myself," cried Barstow, petulantly. He got up and walked to the door.

"I don't mind so much if you go yourself. Only please don't say you come from this house," said Garratt Skinner, and Barstow went out from the room. He came back in a very short time, and Sylvia noticed at once that he held two quite new and unopened packs of cards in his hand.

"A stroke of luck," he cried. "The landlord had a couple of new packs, for he was expecting to give a little party to-night. But a relation of his wife died rather suddenly yesterday, and he put his guests off. A decent-minded fellow, I think. What?"

"Yes. It's not every one who would have shown so much good feeling," said Garratt Skinner, seriously. "One likes to know that there are men about like that. One feels kindlier to the whole world"; and he drew up his chair to the table.

Sylvia was puzzled. Was this story of the landlord a glib lie of Captain Barstow's to account, with a detail which should carry conviction, for the suspiciously new pack of cards? And if so, did her father believe in its truth? Had the packs been waiting in Captain Barstow's coat pocket in the hall until the fitting moment for their appearance? If so, did her father play a part in the conspiracy? His face gave no sign. She was terribly troubled.

"Penny points," said Garratt Skinner. "Nothing more."

"Oh come, I say," cried Hine, as he pulled out a handful of sovereigns.

"Nothing more than penny points in my house. Put that money away, Wallie. We will use counters."

Garratt Skinner had a box of counters if he had no pack of cards.

"Penny points, a sixpenny ante and a shilling limit," he said. "Then no harm will be done to any one. The black counters a shilling, the red sixpence, and the white ones a penny. You have each a pound's worth," he said as he dealt them out.

Sylvia rose from her chair.

"I think I will go to bed."

Wallie Hine turned round in his chair, holding his counters in his hand. "Oh, don't do that, Miss Sylvia. Sit beside me, please, and bring me luck."

"You forget, Wallie, that my daughter has just come from a long journey. No doubt she is tired," said Garratt Skinner, with a friendly reproach in his voice. He got up and opened the door for his daughter. After she had passed out he followed her.

"I shall take a hand for a little while, Sylvia, to see that they keep to the stakes. I think young Hine wants looking after, don't you? He doesn't know any geography.

Good-night, my dear. Sleep well!"

He took her by the elbow and drew her toward him. He stooped to her, mean-ing to kiss her. Sylvia did not resist, but she drooped her head so that her forehead, not her lips, was presented to his embrace. And the kiss was never given. She re-mained standing, her face lowered from his, her attitude one of resignation and despondency. She felt her father's hand shake upon her arm, and looking up saw his eyes fixed upon her in pity. He dropped her arm quickly, and said in a sharp voice:

"There! Go to bed, child!"

He watched her as she went up the stairs. She went up slowly and without turning round, and she walked like one utterly tired out. Garratt Skinner waited until he heard her door close. "She should never have come," he said. "She should never have come." Then he went slowly back to his friends.

Sylvia went to bed, but she did not sleep. The excitement which had buoyed her up had passed; and her hopes had passed with it. She recalled the high anticipa-tions with which she had set out from Chamonix only yesterday--yes, only yester-day. And against them in a vivid contrast she set the actual reality, the supper party, Red-hot Barstow, Archie Parminter, and the poor witless Wallie Hine, with his twang and his silly boasts. She began to wonder whether there was any other world than that which she knew, any other people than those with whom she had lived. Her father was different--yes, but--but--Her father was too perplexing a problem to her at this moment. Why had he so clearly pitied her just now in the passage? Why had he checked himself from the kiss? She was too tired to reason it out. She was conscious that she was very wretched, and the tears gathered in her eyes; and in the darkness of her room she cried silently, pressing the sheet to her lips lest a sob should be heard. Were all her dreams mere empty imaginings? she asked. If so, why should they ever have come to her? she inquired piteously; why should she have found solace in them--why should they have become her real life? Did no one walk the earth of all that company which went with her in her fancies?

Upon that her thoughts flew to the Alps, to the evening in the Pavillon de Lo-gnan, the climb upon the rocks and the glittering ice-slope, the perfect hour upon the sunlit top of the Aiguille d'Argentiere. The memory of the mountains brought her consolation in her bad hour, as her friend had prophesied it would. Her tears ceased to flow, she lived that day--her one day--over again, jealous of every minute.

After all that had been real, and more perfect than any dream. Moreover, there had been with her through the day a man honest and loyal as any of her imagined company. She began to take heart a little; she thought of the Col Dolent with its broad ribbon of ice set in the sheer black rocks, and always in shadow. She thought of herself as going up some such hard, cold road in the shadow, and remembered that on the top of the Col one came out into sunlight and looked southward into Italy. So comforted a little, she fell asleep.

It was some hours before she woke. It was already day, and since she had raised her blinds before she had got into bed, the light streamed into the room. She thought for a moment that it was the light which had waked her. But as she lay she heard a murmur of voices, very low, and a sound of people moving stealthily. She looked out of the window. The streets were quite empty and silent. In the houses on the opposite side the blinds were drawn; a gray clear light was spread over the town; the sun had not yet risen. She looked at her watch. It was five o'clock. She listened again, gently opening her door for an inch or so. She heard the low voices more clearly now. Those who spoke were speaking almost in whispers. She thought that thieves had broken in. She hurried on a few clothes, cautiously opened her door wider, slipped through, and crept with a beating heart down the stairs.

Half way down the stairs she looked over the rail of the banister, turning her head toward the back part of the house whence the murmurs came. At the end of the passage was the little room in which the round game of cards was played the night before. The door stood open now, and she looked right into the room.

And this is what she saw:

Wallie Hine was sitting at the table. About him the carpet was strewn with crumpled pieces of paper. There was quite a number of them littered around his chair. He was writing, or rather, trying to write. For Archie Parminter leaning over the back of the chair held his hand and guided it. Captain Barstow stood looking intently on, but of her father there was no sign. She could not see the whole room, however. A good section of it was concealed from her. Wallie Hine was leaning forward on the table, with his head so low and his arms so spread that she could not see in what book he was writing. But apparently he did not write to the satisfaction of his companions. In spite of Parminter's care his pen spluttered. Sylvia saw Archie look at Barstow, and she heard Barstow answer "No, that won't do." Archie

Parminter dropped Hine's hand, tore a slip of paper out of the book, crumpled it, and threw it down with a gesture of anger on to the carpet.

"Try again, old fellow," said Barstow, eagerly, bending down toward Hine with a horrid smile upon his face, a smile which tried to conceal an intense exasperation, an intense desire to strike. Again Parminter leaned over the chair, again he took Wallie Hine's hand and guided the pen, very carefully lifting it from the paper at the end of an initial or a word, and spacing the letters. This time he seemed content.

"That will do, I think," he said, in a whisper.

Captain Barstow bent down and examined the writing carefully with his short-sighted eyes.

"Yes, that's all right."

Parminter tore the leaf out, but this time he did not crumple it. He blotted it carefully, folded it, and laid it on the mantle-shelf.

"Let us get him up," he said, and with Barstow's help they lifted Hine out of his chair. Sylvia caught a glimpse of his face. His mouth was loose, his eyes half shut, and the lids red; he seemed to be in a stupor. His head rolled upon his shoulders. He swayed as his companions held him up; his knees gave under him. He began incoherently to talk.

"Hush!" said Parminter. "You'll wake the house. You don't want that pretty girl to see you in this state, do you, Wallie? After the impression you made on her, too! Get his hat and coat out of the passage, Barstow."

He propped Hine against the table, and holding him upright turned to the door. He saw "the pretty girl" leaning over the banister and gazing with horror-stricken eyes into the room. Sylvia drew back on the instant. With a gesture of his hand, Archie Parminter stopped Barstow on his way to the door.

Sylvia leaned back against the wall of the staircase, holding her breath, and tightly pressing a hand upon her heart. Had they seen her? Would they come out into the passage? What would happen? Would they kill her? The questions raced through her mind. She could not have moved, she thought, had Death stood over her. But nothing happened. She could not now see into the room, and she heard no whisper, no footsteps creeping stealthily along the passage toward her, no sound at all. Presently she recovered her breath, and crept up-stairs. Once in her room, with great care she locked the door, and sank upon her bed, shaking and trembling. There she lay until the noise of the hall door closing very gently roused her. She crept along the wall till she was by the side of the window. Then she raised herself against the wall and peered out. She saw Barstow and Parminter supporting Hine along the street, each with an arm through his. A hansom-cab drove up, they lifted Hine into it, got in themselves, and drove off. As the cab turned, Archie Parminter glanced up to the windows of the house. But Sylvia was behind the curtains at the side. He could not have seen her. Sylvia leaned her head against the panels of the door and concentrated all her powers so that not a movement in the house might escape her ears. She listened for the sound of some one else moving in the room below, some one who had been left behind. She listened for a creak of the stairs, the brushing of a coat against the stair rail, the sound of some one going stealthily to his room. She stood at the door, with her face strangely set for a long while. Her mind was quite made up. If she heard her father moving from that room, she would just wait until he was asleep, and then she would go--anywhere. She could not go back to her mother, that she knew. She had no one to go to; nevertheless, she would go.

But no sound reached her. Her father was not in the room below. He must have gone to bed and left the others to themselves. The pigeon had been plucked that night, not a doubt of it, but her father had had no hand in the plucking. She laid herself down upon her bed, exhausted, and again sleep came to her. And in a moment the sound of running water was in her ears.

CHAPTER XI
SYLVIA'S FATHER MAKES A MISTAKE

Sylvia did not wake again until the maid brought in her tea and told her that it was eight o'clock. When she went down-stairs, her father was already in the dining-room. She scanned him closely, but his face bore no sign whatever of a late and tempestuous night; and a great relief enheartened her. He met her with an open smile.

"Did you sleep well, Sylvia?"

"Not very well, father," she answered, as she watched his face. "I woke up in the early morning."

But nothing could have been more easy or natural than his comment on her words.

"Yet you look like a good sleeper. A strange house, I suppose, Sylvia."

"Voices in the strange house," she answered.

"Voices?"

Garratt Skinner's face darkened.

"Did those fellows stay so late?" he asked with annoyance. "What time was it when they woke you up, Sylvia?"

"A little before five."

Garratt Skinner's annoyance increased.

"That's too bad," he cried. "I left them and went to bed. But they promised me faithfully only to stay another half-hour. I am very sorry, Sylvia." And as she poured out the tea, he continued: "I will speak pretty sharply to Barstow. It's altogether too bad."

Garratt Skinner breakfasted with an eye on the clock, and as soon as the hands pointed to five minutes to nine, he rose from the table.

"I must be off--business, my dear." He came round the table to her and gently laid a hand upon her shoulder. "It makes a great difference, Sylvia, to have a daughter, fresh and young and pretty, sitting opposite to me at the breakfast table--a very great difference. I shall cut work early to-day on account of it; I'll come home and fetch you, and we'll go out and lunch somewhere together."

He spoke with every sign of genuine feeling; and Sylvia, looking up into his face, was moved by what he said. He smiled down at her, with her own winning smile; he looked her in the face with her own frankness, her own good humor.

"I have been a lonely man for a good many years, Sylvia," he said, "too lonely. I am glad the years have come to an end"; and this time he did what yesterday night he had checked himself from doing. He stooped down and kissed her on the forehead. Then he went from the room, took his hat, and letting himself out of the house closed the door behind him. He called a passing cab, and, as he entered it, he said to the driver:

"Go to the London and County Bank in Victoria Street," and gaily waving his hand to his daughter, who stood behind the window, he drove off.

At one o'clock he returned in the same high spirits. Sylvia had spent the morning in removing the superfluous cherries and roses from her best hat and making her frock at once more simple and more suitable to her years. Garratt Skinner surveyed her with pride.

"Come on," he said. "I have kept the cab waiting."

For a poor man he seemed to Sylvia rather reckless. They drove to the Savoy Hotel and lunched together in the open air underneath the glass roof, with a bank of flowers upon one side of them and the windows of the grill-room on the other. The day was very hot, the streets baked in an arid glare of sunlight; a dry dust from the wood pavement powdered those who passed by in the Strand. Here, however, in this cool and shaded place the pair lunched happily together. Garratt Skinner had the tact not to ask any questions of his daughter about her mother, or how they had fared together. He talked easily of unimportant things, and pointed out from time to time some person of note or some fashionable actress who happened to pass in or out of the hotel. He could be good company when he chose, and he chose on this morning. It was not until coffee was set before them, and he had lighted a cigar, that he touched upon themselves, and then not with any paternal tone, but rather as one comrade conferring with another. There, indeed, was his great advantage with Sylvia. Her mother had either disregarded her or treated her as a child. She could not but be won by a father who laid bare his plans to her and asked for her criticism as well as her assent. Her suspicions of yesterday died away, or, at all events, slept so soundly that they could not have troubled her less had they been dead.

"Sylvia," he said, "I think London in August, and in such an August, is too hot. I don't want to see you grow pale, and for myself I haven't had a holiday for a long time. You see there is not much temptation for a lonely man to go away by himself."

For the second time that day he appealed to her on the ground of his loneliness; and not in vain. She began even to feel remorseful that she had left him to his loneliness so long. There rose up within her an almost maternal feeling of pity for her father. She did not stop to think that he had never sent for her; had never indeed shown a particle of interest in her until they had met face to face.

"But since you are here," he continued, "well--I have been doing fairly well in my business lately, and I thought we might take a little holiday together, at some quiet village by the sea. You know nothing of England. I have been thinking it all out this morning. There is no country more beautiful or more typical than Dorsetshire. Besides, you were born there. What do you say to three weeks or so in Dorsetshire? We will stay at an hotel in Weymouth for a few days and look about for a house."

"Father!" exclaimed Sylvia, leaning forward with shining eyes. "It will be splendid. Just you and I!"

"Well, not quite," he answered, slowly; and as he saw his daughter sink back with a pucker of disappointment on her forehead, he knocked the ash off his cigar and in his turn leaned forward over the table.

"Sylvia, I want to talk to you seriously," he said, and glanced around to make sure that no one overheard him. "I should very much like one person to come and stay with us."

Sylvia made no answer. Her face was grave and very still, her eyes dwelt quietly upon him and betrayed nothing of what she thought.

"You have guessed who the one person is?"

Again Sylvia did not answer.

"Yes. It is Wallie Hine," he continued.

Her suspicions were stirring again from their sleep. She waited in fear upon his words. She looked out, through the opening at the mouth of the court into the glare of the Strand. The bright prospect which her vivid fancies had pictured there a minute since, transforming the dusky street into fields of corn and purple heather, the omnibuses into wagons drawn by teams of great horses musical with bells, had all grown dark. A real horror was gripping her. But she turned her eyes quietly back upon her father's face and waited.

"His presence will spoil our holiday a little," Garratt Skinner continued with an easy assurance. "You saw, no doubt, what Wallie Hine is, last night--a weak, foolish youth, barely half-educated, awkward, with graces of neither mind nor body, and in the hands of two scoundrels."

Sylvia started, and she leaned forward with a look of bewilderment plain to see in her dark eyes.

"Yes, that's the truth, Sylvia. He has come into a little money, and he is in the hands of two scoundrels who are leading him by the nose. My poor girl," he cried, suddenly breaking off, "you must have found yourself in very strange and disappointing company last night. I was very sorry for you, and sorry for myself, too. All the evening I was saying to myself, 'I wonder what my little girl is thinking of me.' But I couldn't help it. I had not the time to explain. I had to sit quiet, knowing that you must be unhappy, certain that you must be despising me for the company I kept."

Sylvia blushed guiltily.

"Despising you? No, father," she said, in a voice of apology. "I saw how much above the rest you were."

"Blaming me, then," interrupted Garratt Skinner, with an easy smile. He was not at all offended. "Let us say blaming me. And it was quite natural that you should, judging by the surface. And there was nothing but the surface for you to judge by."

While in this way defending Sylvia against her own self-reproach, he only succeeded in making her feel still more that she had judged hastily where she should have held all judgment in abeyance, that she had lacked faith where by right she should have shown most faith. But he wished to spare her from confusion.

"I was so proud of you that I could not but suffer all the more. However, don't let us talk of it, my dear"; and waving with a gesture of the hand that little misunderstanding away forever, he resumed:

"Well, I am rather fond of Wallie Hine. I don't know why, perhaps because he is so helpless, because he so much stands in need of a steady mentor at his elbow. There is, after all, no accounting for one's likings. Logic and reason have little to do with them. As a woman you know that. And being rather fond of Wallie Hine, I have tried to do my best for him. It would not have been of any use to shut my door on Barstow and Archie Parminter. They have much too firm a hold on the poor youth. I should have been shutting it on Wallie Hine, too. No, the only plan was to welcome them all, to play Parminter's game of showing the youth about town, and Barstow's game of crude flattery, and gradually, if possible, to dissociate him from his companions, before they had fleeced him altogether. So you were let in, my dear, for that unfortunate evening. Of course I was quite sure that you would not attribute to me designs upon Wallie Hine, otherwise I should have turned them all out at once."

He spoke with a laugh, putting aside, as it were, a quite incredible suggestion. But he looked at her sharply as he laughed. Sylvia's face grew crimson, her eyes for once wavered from his face, and she lowered her head. Garratt Skinner, however, seemed not to notice her confusion.

"You remember," he continued, "that I tried to stop them playing cards at the beginning. I yielded in the end, because it became perfectly clear that if I didn't they would go away and play elsewhere, while I at all events could keep the points down in my own house. I ought to have stayed up, I suppose, until they went away. I blame myself there a little. But I had no idea they would stay so late. Are you sure it was their voices you heard and not the servants moving?"

He asked the question almost carelessly, but his eyes rather belied his tone, for they watched her intently.

"Quite sure," she answered.

"You might have made a mistake."

"No; for I saw them."

Garratt Skinner covered his mouth with his hand. It seemed to Sylvia that he smiled. A suspicion flashed across her mind, in spite of herself. Was he merely testing her to see whether she would speak the truth or not? Did he know that she had come down the stairs in the early morning? She thrust the suspicion aside, re-membering the self-reproach which suspicion had already caused her at this very luncheon table. If it were true that her father knew, why then Barstow or Par-minter must have told him this very morning. And if he had seen either of them this morning, all his talk to her in this cool and quiet place was a carefully prepared hypocrisy. No, she would not believe that.

"You saw them?" he exclaimed. "Tell me how."

She told him the whole story, how she had come down the staircase, what she had seen, as she leaned over the balustrade, and how Parminter had turned.

"Do you think he saw you?" asked her father.

Sylvia looked at him closely. But he seemed really anxious to know.

"I think he saw something," she answered. "Whether he knew that it was I whom he saw, I can't tell."

Garratt Skinner sat for a little while smoking his cigar in short, angry puffs.

"I wouldn't have had that happen for worlds," he said, with a frown. "I have no doubt whatever that the slips of paper on which poor Hine was trying to write were I.O.U's. Heaven knows what he lost last night."

"I know," returned Sylvia. "He lost L480 last night."

"Impossible," cried Garratt Skinner, with so much violence that the people lunching at the tables near-by looked up at the couple with surprise. "Oh, no! I'll not believe it, Sylvia." And as he lowered his voice, he seemed to be making an appeal to her to go back upon her words, so distressed was he at the thought that Wallie Hine should be jockeyed out of so much money at his house.

"Four hundred and eighty pounds," Sylvia repeated.

Garratt Skinner caught at a comforting thought.

"Well, it's only in I.O.U's. That's one thing. I can stop the redemption of them. You see, he has been robbed--that's the plain English of it--robbed."

"Mr. Hine was not writing an I.O.U. He was writing a check, and Mr. Parminter was guiding his hand as he wrote the signature."

Garratt Skinner fell back in his chair. He looked about him with a dazed air, as though he expected the world falling to pieces around him.

"Why, that's next door to forgery!" he whispered, in a voice of horror. "Guiding the hand of a man too drunk to write! I knew Archie Parminter was pretty bad, but I never thought that he would sink to that. I am not sure that he could not be laid by the heels for forgery." And then he recovered a little from the shock. "But you can't be sure, Sylvia! This is guesswork of yours--yes, guesswork."

"It's not," she answered. "I told you that the floor was littered with slips of the paper on which Mr. Hine had been trying to write."

"Yes."

There came an indefinable change in Garratt Skinner's face. He leaned forward with his mouth sternly set and his eyes very still. One might almost have believed that for the first time during that luncheon he was really anxious, really troubled.

"Well, this morning the carpet had been swept. The litter had gone. But just underneath the hearth-rug one of those crumpled slips of paper lay not quite hidden. I picked it up. It was a check."

"Have you got it? Sylvia, have you got it?" and Garratt Skinner's voice in steady quietude matched his face.

"Yes."

Sylvia opened the little bag which she carried at her wrist and took out the slip of paper. She unfolded it and spread it on the table before her. The inside was pink.

"A check for L480 on the London and County Bank, Victoria Street," she said.

Garrett Skinner looked over the table at the paper. There was Wallie Hine's wavering, unfinished signature at the bottom right-hand corner. Parminter had guided his hand as far as the end of the Christian name, before he tore the check out and threw it away. The amount of the body of the check had been filled in in Barstow's hand.

"You had better give it to me, Sylvia," he said, his fingers moving restlessly on the table-cloth. "That check would be a very dangerous thing if Parminter ever came to hear of it. Better give it to me."

He leaned over and took it gently from before her, and put it carefully away in his pocket.

"Now, you see, there's more reason ever why we should get Wallie Hine away from those two men. He is living a bad life here. Three weeks in the country may set his thoughts in a different grove. Will you make this sacrifice, Sylvia? Will you let me ask him? It will be a good action. You see he doesn't know any geography."

"Very well; ask him, father."

Garrett Skinner reached over the table and patted her hand.

"Thank you, my dear! Then that's settled. I propose that you and I go down this afternoon. Can you manage it? We might catch the four o'clock train from Water-loo if you go home now, pack up your traps and tell the housemaid to pack mine. I will just wind up my business and come home in time to pick you and the luggage up."

He rose from the table, and calling a hansom, put Sylvia into it. He watched the cab drive out into the Strand and turn the corner. Then he went back to the table and asked for his bill. While he waited for it, he lit a match and drawing from his pocket the crumpled check, he set fire to it. He held it by the corner until the flame burnt his fingers. Then he dropped it in his plate and pounded it into ashes with a fork.

"That was a bad break," he said to himself. "Left carelessly under the edge of the hearth-rug. A very bad break."

He paid his bill, and taking his hat, sauntered out into the Strand. The careless-ness which had left the check underneath the hearth-rug was not, however, the only bad break made in connection with this affair. At a certain moment during luncheon Garratt Skinner had unwisely smiled and had not quite concealed the smile with his hand. Against her every wish, that smile forced itself upon Sylvia's recollections as she drove home. She tried to interpret it in every pleasant sense, but it kept its true character in her thoughts, try as she might. It remained vividly a very hateful thing--the smile of the man who had gulled her.

CHAPTER XII
THE HOUSE OF THE RUNNING WATER

A week later, on a sunlit afternoon, Sylvia and her father drove northward out of Weymouth between the marshes and the bay. Sylvia was silent and looked about her with expectant eyes.

"I have been lucky, Sylvia," her father had said to her. "I have secured for our summer holiday the very house in which you were born. It cost me some trouble, but I was determined to get it if I could, for I had an idea that you would be pleased. However, you are not to see it until it is quite ready."

There was a prettiness and a delicacy in this thought which greatly appealed to Sylvia. He had spoken it with a smile of tenderness. Affection, surely, could alone have prompted it; and she thanked him very gratefully. They were now upon their way to take possession. A little white house set back under a hill and looking out across the bay from a thick cluster of trees caught Sylvia's eye. Was that the house, she wondered? The carriage turned inland and passed the white house, and half a mile further on turned again eastward along the road to Wareham, following the valley, which runs parallel to the sea. They ascended the long steep hill which climbs to Osmington, until upon their left hand a narrow road branched off be-tween hawthorn hedges to the downs. The road dipped to a little hollow and in the hollow a little village nestled. A row of deep-thatched white cottages with leaded window-panes opened on to a causeway of stone flags which was bordered with purple phlox and raised above the level of the road. Farther on, the roof of a mill rose high among trees, and an open space showed to Sylvia the black massive wheel against the yellow wall. And then the carriage stopped at a house on the left-hand side, and Garratt Skinner got out.

"Here we are," he said.

It was a small square house of the Georgian days, built of old brick, duskily red. You entered it at the side and the big level windows of the living rooms looked out upon a wide and high-walled garden whence a little door under a brick archway in the wall gave a second entrance on to the road. Into this garden Sylvia wandered. If she had met with but few people who matched the delicate company of her dreams, here, at all events, was a mansion where that company might have fitly gathered. Great elms and beeches bent under their load of leaves to the lawn; about the lawn, flowers made a wealth of color, and away to the right of the house twisted stems and branches, where the green of the apples was turning to red, stood evenly spaced in a great orchard. And the mill stream tunneling under the road and the wall ran swiftly between green banks through the garden and the orchard, singing as it ran. There lingered, she thought, an ancient grace about this old garden, some flavor of forgotten days, as in a room scented with potpourri; and she walked the lawn in a great contentment.

The house within charmed her no less. It was a place of many corners and quaint nooks, and of a flooring so unlevel that she could hardly pass from one room to another without taking a step up or a step down. Sylvia went about the house quietly and with a certain thoughtfulness. Here she had been born and a mystery of her life was becoming clear to her. On this summer evening the windows were set wide in every room, and thus in every room, as she passed up and down, she heard the liquid music of running water, here faint, like a whispered melody, there pleasant, like laughter, but nowhere very loud, and everywhere quite audible. In one of these rooms she had been born. In one of these rooms her mother had slept at nights during the weeks before she was born, with that music in her ears at the moment of sleep and at the moment of her waking. Sylvia understood now why she had always dreamed of running water. She wondered in which room she had been born. She tried to remember some corner of the house, some nook in its high-walled garden; and that she could not awoke in her a strange and almost eery feeling. She had come back to a house in which she had lived, to a scene on which her eyes had looked, to sounds which had murmured in her ears, and everything was as utterly new to her and unimagined as though now for the first time she had crossed the threshold. Yet these very surroundings to which her memory bore no testimony had assuredly modified her life, had given to her a particular possession, this dream of running water, and had made it a veritable element of her nature. She could not but reflect upon this new knowledge, and as she walked the garden in the darkness of the evening, she built upon it, as will be seen.

As she stepped back over the threshold into the library where her father sat, she saw that he was holding a telegram in his hand.

"Wallie Hine comes to-morrow, my dear," he said.

Sylvia looked at her father wistfully.

"It is a pity," she said, "a great pity. It would have been pleasant if we could have been alone."

The warmth of her gladness had gone from her; she walked once more in shadows; there was in her voice a piteous appeal for affection, for love, of which she had had too little in her life and for which she greatly craved. She stood by the door, her lips trembling and her dark eyes for a wonder glistening with tears. She had always, even to those who knew her to be a woman, something of the child in her appearance, which made a plea from her lips most difficult to refuse. Now she seemed a child on whom the world pressed heavily before her time for suffering had come; she had so motherless a look. Even Garratt Skinner moved uncomfortably in his chair; even that iron man was stirred.

"I, too, am sorry, Sylvia," he said, gently; "but we will make the best of it. Between us"--and he laughed gaily, setting aside from him his momentary compassion--"we will teach poor Wallie Hine a little geography, won't we?"

Sylvia had no smile ready for a reply. But she bowed her head, and into her face and her very attitude there came an expression of patience. She turned and opened the door, and as she opened it, and stood with her back toward her father, she said in a quiet and clear voice, "Very well," and so passed up the stairs to her room.

It might, after all, merely be kindness in her father which had led him to insist on Wallie Hine's visit. So she argued, and the more persistently because she felt that the argument was thin. He could be kind. He had been thoughtful for her during the past week in the small attentions which appeal so much to women. Because he saw that she loved flowers, he had engaged a new gardener for their stay; and he had shown, in one particular instance, a quite surprising thoughtfulness for a class of unhappy men with whom he could have had no concern, the convicts in Portland prison. That instance remained for a long time vividly in her mind, and at a later time she spoke of it with consequences of a far-reaching kind. She thought then, as she thought now, only of the kindness of her father's action, and for the first week of Hine's visit that thought remained with her. She was on the alert, but nothing occurred to arouse in her a suspicion. There were no cards, little wine was drunk, and early hours were kept by the whole household. Indeed, Garratt Skinner left entirely to his daughter the task of entertaining his guest; and although once he led them both over the great down to Dorchester and back, at a pace which tired his companions out, he preferred, for the most part, to smoke his pipe in a hammock in the garden with a novel at his side. The morning after that one expedition, he limped out into the garden, rubbing the muscles of his thigh.

"You must look after Wallie, my dear," he said. "Age is beginning to find me out. And after all, he will learn more of the tact and manners which he wants from you than from a rough man like me," and it did not occur to Sylvia, who was of a natural modesty of thought, that he had any other intention of throwing them thus together than to rid himself of a guest with whom he had little in common.

But a week later she changed her mind. She was driving Walter Hine one morning into Weymouth, and as the dog-cart turned into the road beside the bay, and she saw suddenly before her the sea sparkling in the sunlight, the dark battle-ships at their firing practice, and over against her, through a shimmering haze of heat, the crouching mass of Portland, she drew in a breath of pleasure. It seemed to her that her companion gave the same sign of enjoyment, and she turned to him with some surprise. But Walter Hine was looking to the wide beach, so black with holiday makers that it seemed at that distance a great and busy ant-heap.

"That's what I like," he said, with a chuckle of anticipation. "Lot's o' people. I've knocked about too long in the thick o' things, you see, Miss Sylvia, kept it up--I have--seen it right through every night till three o'clock in the morning, for months at a time. Oh, that's the real thing!" he broke off. "It makes you feel good."

Sylvia laughed.

"Then if you dislike the country," she said, and perhaps rather eagerly, "why did you come to stay with us at all?"

And suddenly Hine leered at her.

"Oh, you know!" he said, and almost he nudged her with his elbow. "I wouldn't have come, of course, if old Garratt hadn't particularly told me that you were agreeable." Sylvia grew hot with shame. She drew away, flicked the horse with her whip and drove on. Had she been used, she wondered, to lure this poor helpless youth to the sequestered village where they stayed?--and a chill struck through her even on that day of July. The plot had been carefully laid if that were so; she was to be hoodwinked no less than Wallie Hine. What sinister thing was then intended?

She tried to shake off the dread which encompassed her, pleading to herself that she saw perils in shadows like the merest child. But she had not yet shaken it off when Walter Hine cried out excitedly to her to stop.

"Look!" he said, and he pointed toward an hotel upon the sea-front which at that moment they were passing.

Sylvia looked, and saw obsequiously smirking upon the steps of the hotel, with his hat lifted from his shiny head, her old enemy, Captain Barstow. Fortunately she had not stopped. She drove quickly on, just acknowledging his salute. It needed but this meeting to confirm her fears. It was not coincidence which had brought Captain Barstow on their heels to Weymouth. He had come with knowledge and a definite purpose.

"Oh, I say," protested Wallie Hine, "you might have stopped, Miss Sylvia, and let me pass the time of day with old Barstow."

Sylvia stopped the trap at once.

"I am sorry," she said. "You will find your own way home. We lunch at half past one."

Hine looked doubtfully at her and then back toward the hotel.

"I didn't mean that I wanted to leave you, Miss Sylvia," he said. "Not by a long chalk."

"But you must leave me, Mr. Hine," she said, looking at him with serious eyes, "if you want to pass the time of day with your 'red-hot' friend."

There was no hint of a smile about her lips. She waited for his answer. It came accompanied with a smile which aimed at gallantry and was merely familiar.

"Of course I stay where I am. What do *you* think?"

Sylvia hurried over her shopping and drove homeward. She went at once to her father, who lay in the hammock in the shade of the trees, reading a book. She came up from behind him across the grass, and he was not aware of her approach until she spoke.

"Father!" she said, and he started up.

"Oh, Sylvia!" he said, and just for a second there was a palpable uneasiness in his manner. He had not merely started. He seemed also to her to have been startled. But he recovered his composure.

"You see, my dear, I have been thinking of you," he said, and he pointed to a man at work among the flower-beds. "I saw how you loved flowers, how you liked to have the rooms bright with them. So I hired a new gardener as a help. It is a great extravagance, Sylvia, but you are to blame, not I."

He smiled, confident of her gratitude, and had it been but yesterday he would have had it offered to him in full measure. To-day, however, all her thoughts were poisoned by suspicion. She knew it and was distressed. She knew how much happiness so simple a forethought would naturally have brought to her. She did not indeed suspect any new peril in her father's action. She barely looked toward the new gardener, and certainly neglected to note whether he worked skilfully or no. But the fears of the morning modified her thanks. Moreover the momentary uneasiness of her father had not escaped her notice and she was wondering upon its cause.

"Father," she resumed, "I saw Captain Barstow in Weymouth this morning."

Though her eyes were on his face, and perhaps because her eyes were resting there with so quiet a watchfulness, she could detect no self-betrayal now. Garratt Skinner stared at her in pure astonishment. Then the astonishment gave place to annoyance.

"Barstow!" he said angrily. He lay back in the hammock, looking up to the boughs overhead, his face wrinkled and perplexed. "He has found us out and followed us, Sylvia. I would not have had it happen for worlds. Did he see you?"

"Yes."

"And I thought that here, at all events, we were safe from him. I wonder how he found us out! Bribed the caretaker in Hobart Place, I suppose."

Sylvia did not accept this suggestion. She sat down upon a chair in a disconcerting silence, and waited. Garratt Skinner crossed his arms behind his head and deliberated.

"Barstow's a deep fellow, Sylvia," he said. "I am afraid of him."

He was looking up to the boughs overhead, but he suddenly glanced toward her and then quietly removed one of his hands and slipped it down to the book which was lying on his lap. Sylvia took quiet note of the movement. The book had been lying shut upon his lap, with its back toward her. Garratt Skinner did not alter its position; but she saw that his hand now hid from her the title on the back. It was a big, and had the appearance of an expensive, book. She noticed the binding--green cloth boards and gold lettering on the back. She was not familiar with the look of it, and it seemed to her that she might as well know--and as quickly as possible--what the book was and the subject with which it dealt.

Meanwhile Garratt Skinner repeated:

"A deep fellow--Captain Barstow," and anxiously Garratt Skinner debated how to cope with that deep fellow. He came at last to his conclusion.

"We can't shut our doors to him, Sylvia."

Even though she had half expected just that answer, Sylvia flinched as she heard it uttered.

"I understand your feelings, my dear," he continued in tones of commiseration, "for they are mine. But we must fight the Barstows with the Barstows' weapons. It would never do for us to close our doors. He has far too tight a hold of Wallie Hine as yet. He has only to drop a hint to Wallie that we are trying to separate him from his true friends and keep him to ourselves--and just think, my dear, what a horrible set of motives a mean-minded creature like Barstow could impute to us! Let us be candid, you and I," cried Garratt Skinner, starting up, as though carried away by candor. "Here am I, a poor man--here are you, my daughter, a girl with the charm and the beauty of the spring, and here's Wallie Hine, rich, weak, and susceptible. Oh, there's a story for a Barstow to embroider! But, Sylvia, he shall not so much as hint at the story. For your sake, my dear, for your sake," cried Garratt Skinner, with all the emphasis of a loving father. He wiped his forehead with his handkerchief.

"I was carried away by my argument," he went on in a calmer voice. Sylvia for her part had not been carried away at all, and no doubt her watchful composure helped him to subdue as ineffective the ardor of his tones. "Barstow has only to drop this hint to Wallie Hine, and Wallie will be off like a rabbit at the sound of a gun.

And there's our chance gone of helping him to a better life. No, we must welcome Barstow, if he comes here. Yes, actually welcome him, however repugnant it may be to our feelings. That's what we must do, Sylvia. He must have no suspicion that we are working against him. We must lull him to sleep. That is our only way to keep Wallie Hine with us. So that, Sylvia, must be our plan of campaign."

The luncheon bell rang as he ended his oration. He got out of the hammock quickly, as if to prevent discussion of his plan; and the book which he was carrying caught in the netting of the hammock and fell to the ground. Sylvia could read the title now. She did read it, hastily, as Garratt Skinner stooped to pick it up. It was entitled "The Alps in 1864."

She knew the book by repute and was surprised to find it in her father's hands. She was surprised still more that he should have been at so much pains to conceal the title from her notice. After all, what could it matter? she wondered.

Sylvia lay deep in misery that night. Her father had failed her utterly. All the high hopes with which she had set out from Chamonix had fallen, all the rare qualities with which her dreams had clothed him as in shining raiment must now be stripped from him. She was not deceived. Parminter, Barstow, Garratt Skinner-- there was one "deep fellow" in that trio, but it was neither Barstow nor Parminter. It was her father. She had but to set the three faces side by side in her thoughts, to remember the differences of manner, mind and character. Garratt Skinner was the master in the conspiracy, the other two his mere servants. It was he who to some dark end had brought Barstow down from London. He loomed up in her thoughts as a relentless and sinister figure, unswayed by affection, yet with the power to counterfeit it, long-sighted for evil, sparing no one--not even his daughter. She recalled their first meeting in the little house in Hobart Place, she remembered the thoughtful voice with which, as he had looked her over, he had agreed that she might be "useful." She thought of his caresses, his smile of affection, his comrade- ship, and she shuddered. Walter Hine's words had informed her to-day to what use her father had designed her. She was his decoy.

She lay upon her bed with her hands clenched, repeating the word in hor- ror. His decoy! The moonlight poured through the open window, the music of the stream filled the room. She was in the house in which she had been born, a place mystically sacred to her thoughts; and she had come to it to learn that she was her father's decoy in a vulgar conspiracy to strip a weakling of his money. The stream sang beneath her windows, the very stream of which the echo had ever been rippling through her dreams. Always she had thought that it must have some particular meaning for her which would be revealed in due time. She dwelt bitterly upon her folly. There was no meaning in its light laughter.

In a while she was aware of a change. There came a grayness in the room. The moonlight had lost its white brilliance, the night was waning. Sylvia rose from her bed, and slowly like one very tired she began to gather together and pack into a bag such few clothes as she could carry. She had made up her mind to go, and to go silently before the house waked. Whither she was to go, and what she was to do once she had gone, she could not think. She asked herself the questions in vain, feeling very lonely and very helpless as she moved softly about the room by the light of her candle. Her friend might write to her and she would not receive his letter. Still she must go. Once or twice she stopped her work, and crouching down upon the bed allowed her tears to have their way. When she had finished her preparations she blew out her candle, and leaning upon the sill of the open window, gave her face to the cool night air.

There was a break in the eastern sky; already here and there a blackbird sang in the garden boughs, and the freshness, the quietude, swept her thoughts back to the Chalet de Lognan. With a great yearning she recalled that evening and the story of the great friendship so quietly related to her in the darkness, beneath the stars. The world and the people of her dreams existed; only there was no door of entrance into that world for her. Below her the stream sang, even as the glacier stream had sung, though without its deep note of thunder. As she listened to it, certain words spoken upon that evening came back to her mind and gradually began to take on a particular application.

"What you know, that you must do, if by doing it you can save a life or save a soul."

That was the law. "If you can save a life or save a soul." And she *did* know. Sylvia raised herself from the window and stood in thought.

Garratt Skinner had made a great mistake that day. He had been misled by the gentleness of her ways, the sweet aspect of her face, and by a look of aloofness in her eyes, as though she lived in dreams. He had seen surely that she was innocent, and since he believed that knowledge must needs corrupt, he thought her ignorant as well. But she was not ignorant. She had detected his trickeries. She knew of the conspiracy, she knew of the place she filled in it herself; and furthermore she knew that as a decoy she had been doing her work. Only yesterday, Walter Hine had been forced to choose between Barstow and herself and he had let Barstow go. It was a small matter, no doubt. Still there was promise in it. What if she stayed, strengthened her hold on Walter Hine and grappled with the three who were ranged against him?

Walter Hine was, of course, and could be, nothing to her. He was the mere puppet, the opportunity of obedience to the law. It was of the law that she was thinking--and of the voice of the man who had uttered it. She knew--by using her knowledge, she could save a soul. She did not think at this time that she might be saving a life too.

Quietly she undressed and slipped into her bed. She was comforted. A smile had come upon her lips. She saw the face of her friend in the darkness, very near to her. She needed sleep to equip herself for the fight, and while thinking so she slept. The moonlight faded altogether, and left the room dark. Beneath the window the stream went singing through the lawn. After all, its message had been revealed to her in its due season.

CHAPTER XIII
CHAYNE RETURNS

"Hullo," cried Captain Barstow, as he wandered round the library after luncheon. "Here's a scatter-gun."

He took the gun from a corner where it stood against the wall, opened the breech, shut it again, and turning to the open window lifted the stock to his shoulder.

"I wonder whether I could hit anything nowadays," he said, taking careful aim at a tulip in the garden. "Any cartridges, Skinner?"

"I don't know, I am sure," Garratt Skinner replied, testily. The newspapers had only this moment been brought into the room, and he did not wish to be disturbed. Sylvia had never noticed that double-barreled gun before; and she won-dered whether it had been brought into the room that morning. She watched Cap-tain Barstow bustle into the hall and back again. Finally he pounced upon an oblong card-box which lay on the top of a low book-case. He removed the lid and pulled out a cartridge.

"Hullo!" said he. "No. 6. The very thing! I am going to take a pot at the starlings, Skinner. There are too many of them about for your fruit-trees."

"Very well," said Garratt Skinner, lazily lifting his eyes from his newspaper and looking out across the lawn. "Only take care you don't wing my new gardener."

"No fear of that," said Barstow, and filling his pockets with cartridges he took the gun in his hand and skipped out into the garden. In a moment a shot was heard, and Walter Hine rose from his chair and walked to the window. A second shot fol-lowed.

"Old Barstow can't shoot for nuts," said Hine, with a chuckle, and in his turn he stepped out into the garden. Sylvia made no attempt to hinder him, but she took his place at the window ready to intervene. A flight of starlings passed straight and swift over Barstow's head. He fired both barrels and not one of the birds fell. Hine spoke to him, and the gun at once changed hands. At the next flight Hine fired and one of the birds dropped. Barstow's voice was raised in jovial applause.

"That was a good egg, Wallie. A very good egg. Let me try now!" and so alter-nately they shot as the birds darted overhead across the lawn. Sylvia waited for the moment when Barstow's aim would suddenly develop a deadly precision, but that moment did not come. If there was any betting upon this match, Hine would not be the loser. She went quietly back to a writing-desk and wrote her letters. She had no wish to rouse in her father's mind a suspicion that she had guessed his design and was setting herself to thwart it. She must work secretly, more secretly than he did himself. Meanwhile the firing continued in the garden; and unobserved by Sylvia, Garratt Skinner began to take in it a stealthy interest. His chair was so placed that, without stirring, he could look into the garden and at the same time keep an eye on Sylvia; if she moved an elbow or raised her head, Garratt Skinner was at once reading his paper with every appearance of concentration. On the other hand, her back was turned toward him, so that she saw neither his keen gaze into the garden nor the good-tempered smile of amusement with which he turned his eyes upon his daughter.

In this way perhaps an hour passed; certainly no more. Sylvia had, in fact, almost come to the end of her letters, when Garratt Skinner suddenly pushed back his chair and stood up. At the noise, abrupt as a startled cry, Sylvia turned swiftly round. She saw that her father was gazing with a look of perplexity into the garden, and that for the moment he had forgotten her presence. She crossed the room quickly and noiselessly, and standing just behind his elbow, saw what he saw. The blood flushed her throat and mounted into her cheeks, her eyes softened, and a smile of welcome transfigured her grave face. Her friend Hilary Chayne was standing under the archway of the garden door. He had closed the door behind him, but he had not moved thereafter, and he was not looking toward the house. His attention was riveted upon the shooting-match. Sylvia gave no thought to his attitude at the moment. He had come--that was enough. And Garratt Skinner, turning about, saw the light in his daughter's face.

"You know him!" he cried, roughly.

"Yes."

"He has come to see you?"

"Yes."

"You should have told me," said Garratt Skinner, angrily. "I dislike secrecies." Sylvia raised her eyes and looked her father steadily in the face. But Garratt Skinner was not so easily abashed. He returned her look as steadily.

"Who is he?" he continued, in a voice of authority.

"Captain Hilary Chayne."

It seemed for a moment that the name was vaguely familiar to Garratt Skinner, and Sylvia added:

"I met him this summer in Switzerland."

"Oh, I see," said her father, and he looked with a new interest across the garden to the door. "He is a great friend."

"My only friend," returned Sylvia, softly; and her father stepped forward and called aloud, holding up his hand:

"Barstow! Barstow!"

Sylvia noticed then, and not till then, that the coming of her friend was not the only change which had taken place since she had last looked out upon the garden.

The new gardener was now shooting alternately with Walter Hine, while Captain Barstow, standing a few feet behind them, recorded the hits in a little book. He looked up at the sound of Garratt Skinner's voice and perceiving Chayne at once put a stop to the match. Garratt Skinner turned again to his daughter, and spoke now without any anger at all. There was just a hint of reproach in his voice, but as though to lessen the reproof he laid his hand affectionately upon her arm.

"Any friend of yours is welcome, of course, my dear. But you might have told me that you expected him. Let us have no secrets from each other in the future? Now bring him in, and we will see if we can give him a cup of tea."

He rang the bell. Sylvia did not think it worth while to argue that Chayne's coming was a surprise to her as much as to her father. She crossed the garden toward her friend. But she walked slowly and still more slowly. Her memories had flown back to the evening when they had bidden each other good-by on the little platform in front of the Chalet de Lognan. Not in this way had she then planned that they should meet again, nor in such company. The smile had faded from her lips, the light of gladness had gone from her eyes. Barstow and Walter Hine were moving toward the house. It mortified her exceedingly that her friend should find her amongst such companions. She almost wished that he had not found her out at all. And so she welcomed him with a great restraint.

"It was kind of you to come," she said. "How did you know I was here?"

"I called at your house in London. The caretaker gave me the address," he replied. He took her hand and, holding it, looked with the careful scrutiny of a lover into her face.

"You have needed those memories of your one day to fall back upon," he said, regretfully. "Already you have needed them. I am very sorry."

Sylvia did not deny the implication of the words that "troubles" had come. She turned to him, grateful that he should so clearly have remembered what she had said upon that day.

"Thank you," she answered, gently. "My father would like to know you. I wrote to you that I had come to live with him."

"Yes."

"You were surprised?" she asked.

"No," he answered, quietly. "You came to some important decision on the very top of the Aiguille d'Argentiere. That I knew at the time, for I watched you. When I got your letter, I understood what the decision was."

To leave Chamonix--to break completely with her life--it was just to that decision she would naturally have come just on that spot during that one sunlit hour. So much his own love of the mountains taught him. But Sylvia was surprised at his insight; and what with that and the proof that their day together had remained vividly in his thoughts, she caught back something of his comradeship. As they crossed the lawn to the house her embarrassment diminished. She drew comfort, besides, from the thought that whatever her friend might think of Captain Barstow and Walter Hine, her father at all events would impress him, even as she had been impressed. Chayne would see at once that here was a man head and shoulders above his companions, finer in quality, different in speech.

But that afternoon her humiliation was to be complete. Her father had no fancy for the intrusion of Captain Chayne into his quiet and sequestered house. The flush of color on his daughter's face, the leap of light into her eyes, had warned him. He had no wish to lose his daughter. Chayne, too, might be inconveniently watchful. Garratt Skinner desired no spy upon his little plans. Consequently he set himself to play the host with an offensive geniality which was calculated to disgust a man with any taste for good manners. He spoke in a voice which Sylvia did not know, so coarse it was in quality, so boisterous and effusive; and he paraded Walter Hine and Captain Barstow with the pride of a man exhibiting his dearest friends.

"You must know 'red-hot' Barstow, Captain Chayne," he cried, slapping the little man lustily on the back. "One of the very best. You are both brethren of the sword."

Barstow sniggered obsequiously and screwed his eye-glass into his eye.

"Delighted, I am sure. But I sheathed the sword some time ago, Captain Chayne."

"And exchanged it for the betting book," Chayne added, quietly.

Barstow laughed nervously.

"Oh, you refer to our little match in the garden," he said. "We dragged the gardener into it."

"So I saw," Chayne replied. "The gardener seemed to be a remarkable shot. I think he would be a match for more than one professional."

And turning away he saw Sylvia's eyes fixed upon him, and on her face an expression of trouble and dismay so deep that he could have bitten off his tongue for speaking. She had been behind him while he had spoken; and though he had spoken in a low voice, she had heard every word. She bent her head over the tea-table and busied herself with the cups. But her hands shook; her face burned, she was tortured with shame. She had set herself to do battle with her father, and already in the first skirmish she had been defeated. Chayne's indiscreet words had laid bare to her the elaborate conspiracy. The new gardener, the gun in the corner, the cartridges which had to be looked for, Barstow's want of skill, Hine's superiority which had led Barstow so naturally to offer to back the gardener against him--all was clear to her. It was the little round game of cards all over again; and she had not possessed the wit to detect the trick! And that was not all. Her friend had witnessed it and understood!

She heard her father presenting Walter Hine, and with almost intolerable pain she realized that had he wished to leave Chayne no single opportunity of misap-prehension, he would have spoken just these words and no others.

"Wallie is the grandson--and indeed the heir--of old Joseph Hine. You know his name, no doubt. Joseph Hine's Chateau Marlay, what? A warm man, Joseph Hine. I don't know a man more rich. Treats his grandson handsomely into the bar-gain, eh, Wallie?"

Sylvia felt that her heart would break. That Garrett Skinner's admission was boldly and cunningly deliberate did not occur to her. She simply understood that here was the last necessary piece of evidence given to Captain Chayne which would convince him that he had been this afternoon the witness of a robbery and swin-dle.

She became aware that Chayne was standing beside her. She did not lift her face, for she feared that it would betray her. She wished with all her heart that he would just replace his cup upon the tray and go away without a word. He could not want to stay; he could not want to return. He had no place here. If he would go away quietly, without troubling to take leave of her, she would be very grateful and do justice to him for his kindness.

But though he had the mind to go, it was not without a word.

"I want you to walk with me as far as the door," he said, gently.

Sylvia rose at once. Since after all there must be words, the sooner they were spoken the better. She followed him into the garden, making her little prayer that they might be very few, and that he would leave her to fight her battle and to hide her shame alone.

They crossed the lawn without a word. He held open the garden door for her and she passed into the lane. He followed and closed the door behind them. In the lane a hired landau was waiting. Chayne pointed to it.

"I want you to come away with me now," he said, and since she looked at him with the air of one who does not understand, he explained, standing quietly beside her with his eyes upon her face. And though he spoke quietly, there was in his eyes a hunger which belied his tones, and though he stood quietly, there was a tension in his attitude which betrayed extreme suspense. "I want you to come away with me, I want you never to return. I want you to marry me."

The blood rushed into her cheeks and again fled from them, leaving her very white. Her face grew mutinous like an angry child's, but her eyes grew hard like a resentful woman's.

"You ask me out of pity," she said, in a low voice.

"That's not true," he cried, and with so earnest a passion that she could not but believe him. "Sylvia, I came here meaning to ask you to marry me. I ask you something more now, that is all. I ask you to come to me a little sooner--that is all. I want you to come with me now."

Sylvia leaned against the wall and covered her face with her hands.

"Please!" he said, making his appeal with a great simplicity. "For I love you, Sylvia."

She gave him no answer. She kept her face still hid, and only her heaving breast bore witness to her stress of feeling. Gently he removed her hands, and holding them in his, urged his plea.

"Ever since that day in Switzerland, I have been thinking of you, Sylvia, remembering your looks, your smile, and the words you spoke. I crossed the Col Dolent the next day, and all the time I felt that there was some great thing wanting. I said to myself, 'I miss my friend.' I was wrong, Sylvia. I missed you. Something ached in me--has ached ever since. It was my heart! Come with me now!"

Sylvia had not looked at him, though she made no effort to draw her hands away, and still not looking at him, she answered in a whisper:

"I can't, I can't."

"Why?" he asked, "why? You are not happy here. You are no happier than you were at Chamonix. And I would try so very hard to make you happy. I can't leave you here--lonely, for you are lonely. I am lonely too; all the more lonely because I carry about with me--you--you as you stood in the chalet at night looking through the open window, with the candle-light striking upward on your face, and with your reluctant smile upon your lips--you as you lay on the top of the Aiguille d'Argentiere with the wonder of a new world in your eyes--you as you said good-by in the sunset and went down the winding path to the forest. If you only knew, Sylvia!"

"Yes, but I don't know," she answered, and now she looked at him. "I suppose that, if I loved, I should know, I should understand."

Her hands lay in his, listless and unresponsive to the pressure of his. She spoke slowly and thoughtfully, meeting his gaze with troubled eyes.

"Yet you were glad to see me when I came," he urged.

"Glad, yes! You are my friend, my one friend. I was very glad. But the gladness passed. When you asked me to come with you across the garden, I was wanting you to go away."

The words hurt him. They could not but hurt him. But she was so plainly unconscious of offence, she was so plainly trying to straighten out her own tangled position, that he could feel no anger.

"Why?" he asked; and again she frankly answered him.

"I was humbled," she replied, "and I have had so much humiliation in my life."

The very quietude of her voice and the wistful look upon the young tired face hurt him far more than her words had done.

"Sylvia," he cried, and he drew her toward him. "Come with me now! My dear, there will be an end of all humiliation. We can be married, we can go down to my home on the Sussex Downs. That old house needs a mistress, Sylvia. It is very lonely." He drew a breath and smiled suddenly. "And I would like so much to show you it, to show you all the corners, the bridle-paths across the downs, the woods, and the wide view from Arundel to Chichester spires. Sylvia, come!"

Just for a moment it seemed that she leaned toward him. He put his arm about her and held her for a moment closer. But her head was lowered, not lifted up to his; and then she freed herself gently from his clasp.

She faced him with a little wrinkle of thought between her brows and spoke with an air of wisdom which went very prettily with the childlike beauty of her face.

"You are my friend," she said, "a friend I am very grateful for, but you are not more than that to me. I am frank. You see, I am thinking now of reasons which would not trouble me if I loved you. Marriage with me would do you no good, would hurt you in your career."

"No," he protested.

"But I am thinking that it would," she replied, steadily, "and I do not believe that I should give much thought to it, if I really loved you. I am thinking of something else, too--" and she spoke more boldly, choosing her words with care--"of a plan which before you came I had formed, of a task which before you came I had set myself to do. I am still thinking of it, still feeling that I ought to go on with it. I do not think that I should feel that if I loved. I think nothing else would count at all except that I loved. So you are still my friend, and I cannot go with you."

Chayne looked at her for a moment sadly, with a mist before his eyes.

"I leave you to much unhappiness," he said, "and I hate the thought of it."

"Not quite so much now as before you came," she answered. "I am proud, you know, that you asked me," and putting her troubles aside, she smiled at him bravely, as though it was he who needed comforting. "Good-by! Let me hear of you through your success."

So again they said good-by at the time of sunset. Chayne mounted into the landau and drove back along the road to Weymouth. "So that's the end," said Sylvia. She opened the door and passed again into the garden. Through the window of the library she saw her father and Walter Hine, watching, it seemed, for her appearance. It was borne in upon her suddenly that she could not meet them or speak with them, and she ran very quickly round the house to the front door, and escaped unaccosted to her room.

In the library Hine turned to Garratt Skinner with one of his rare flashes of shrewdness.

"She didn't want to meet us," he said, jealously. "Do you think she cares for him?"

"I think," replied Garratt Skinner with a smile, "that Captain Chayne will not trouble us with his company again."

CHAPTER XIV
AN OLD PASSION BETRAYS A NEW SECRET

Garratt Skinner, however, was wrong. He was not aware of the great revolution which had taken place in Chayne; and he misjudged his tenacity. Chayne, like many another man, had mapped out his life only to find that events would happen in a succession different to that which he had ordained. He had arranged to devote his youth and the earlier part of his manhood entirely to his career, if the career were not brought to a premature end in the Alps. That possibility he had always foreseen. He took his risks with full knowledge, setting the gain against them, and counting them worth while. If then he lived, he proposed at some indefinite time, in the late thirties, to fall in love and marry. He had no parents living; there was the empty house upon the Sussex Downs; and the small estate which for generations had descended from father to son. Marriage was thus a recognized event. Only it was thrust away into an indefinite future. But there had come an evening which he had not foreseen, when, sorely grieved by the loss of his great friend, he had fallen in with a girl who gave with open hands the sympathy he needed, and claimed, by her very reticence and humility, his sympathy in return. A day had followed upon that evening; and thenceforth the image of Sylvia standing upon the snow-ridge of the Aiguille d'Argentiere, with a few strips of white cloud sailing in a blue sky overhead, the massive pile of Mont Blanc in front, freed to the sunlight which was her due, remained fixed and riveted in his thoughts. He began in imagination to refer matters of moment to her judgment; he began to save up little events of interest that he might remember to tell them to her. He understood that he had a companion, even when he was alone, a condition which he had not anticipated even for his late thirties. And he came to the conclusion that he had not that complete ordering of his life on which he had counted. He was not, however, disappointed. He seized upon the good thing which had come to him with a great deal of wonder and a very thankful heart; and he was not disposed to let it lightly go.

Thus the vulgarity which Garratt Skinner chose to assume, the unattractive figure of "red-hot" Barstow, and the obvious swindle which was being perpetrated on Walter Hine, had the opposite effect to that which Skinner expected. Chayne, instead of turning his back upon so distasteful a company, frequented it in the resolve to take Sylvia out of its grasp. It did not need a lover to see that she slept little of nights and passed distressful days. She had fled from her mother's friends at Chamonix, only to find herself helpless amongst a worse gang in her father's house. Very well. She must be released. He had proposed to take her away then and there. She had refused. Well, he had been blunt. He would go about the business in the future in a more delicate way. And so he came again and again to the little house under the hill where the stream babbled through the garden, and every day the apples grew redder upon the boughs.

But it was disheartening work. His position indeed became difficult, and it needed all his tenacity to enable him to endure it. The difficulty became very evident one afternoon early in August, and the afternoon was, moveover, remarkable in that Garratt Skinner was betrayed into a revelation of himself which was to bear consequences of gravity in a future which he could not foresee. Chayne rode over upon that afternoon, and found Garratt Skinner alone and, according to his habit, stretched at full-length in his hammock with a cigar between his lips. He received Captain Chayne with the utmost geniality. He had long since laid aside his ineffectual vulgarity of manner.

"You must put up with me, Captain Chayne," he said. "My daughter is out. However, she--I ought more properly to say, they--will be back no doubt before long."

"They being--"

"Sylvia and Walter Hine."

Chayne nodded his head. He had known very well who "they" must be, but he had not been able to refrain from the question. Jealousy had hold of him. He knew nothing of Sylvia's determination to acquire a power greater than her father's over the vain and defenceless youth. The words with which she had hinted her plan to him had been too obscure to convey their meaning. He was simply aware that

Sylvia more and more avoided him, more and more sought the companionship of Walter Hine; and such experience as he had, taught him that women were as apt to be blind in their judgment of men as men in their estimation of women.

He sought now to enlist Garratt Skinner on his side, and drawing a chair nearer to the hammock he sat down.

"Mr. Skinner," he said, speaking upon an impulse, "you have no doubt in your mind, I suppose, as to why I come here so often."

Garratt Skinner smiled.

"I make a guess, I admit."

"I should be very glad if your daughter would marry me," Chayne continued, "and I want you to give me your help. I am not a poor man, Mr. Skinner, and I should certainly be willing to recognize that in taking her away from you I laid myself under considerable obligations."

Chayne spoke with some natural hesitation, but Garratt Skinner was not in the least offended.

"I will not pretend to misunderstand you," he replied. "Indeed, I like your frankness. Please take what I say in the same spirit. I cannot give you any help, Captain Chayne."

"Why?"

Garratt Skinner raised himself upon his elbow, and fixing his eyes upon his companion's face, said distinctly and significantly:

"Because Sylvia has her work to do here."

Chayne in his turn made no pretence to misunderstand. He was being told clearly that Sylvia was in league with her father and Captain Barstow to pluck Walter Hine. But he was anxious to discover how far Garratt Skinner's cynicism would carry him.

"Will you define the work?" he asked.

"If you wish it," replied Garratt Skinner, falling back in his hammock. "I should have thought it unnecessary myself. The work is the reclaiming of Wallie Hine from the very undesirable company in which he has mixed. Do you understand?"

"Quite," said Chayne. He understood very well. He had been told first the real design--to pluck Walter Hine--and then the excuse which was to cloak it. He understood, too, the reason why this information had been given to him with so cynical a frankness. He, Chayne, was in the way. Declare the swindle and persuade him that Sylvia was a party to it--what more likely way could be discovered for getting rid of Captain Chayne? He looked at his smiling companion, took note of his strong aquiline face, his clear and steady eyes. He recognized a redoubtable antagonist, but he leaned forward and said with a quiet emphasis:

"Mr. Skinner, I have, nevertheless, not lost heart."

Garratt Skinner laughed in a friendly way.

"I suppose not. It is only in the wisdom of middle age that we lose heart. In youth we lose our hearts--a very different thing."

"I propose still to come to this house."

"As often as you will, Captain Chayne," said Garratt Skinner, gaily. "My doors are always open to you. I am not such a fool as to give you a romantic interest by barring you out."

Garratt Skinner had another reason for his hospitality which he kept to himself. He was inclined to believe that a few more visits from Captain Chayne would settle his chances without the necessity of any interference. It was Garratt Skinner's business, as that of any other rogue, to play with simple artifices upon the faults and vanities of men. He had, therefore, cultivated a habit of observation; he had become naturally attentive to trifles which others might overlook; and he was aware that he needed to go very warily in the delicate business on which he was now engaged. He was fighting Sylvia for the possession of Walter Hine--that he had recognized--and Chayne for the possession of Sylvia. It was a three-cornered contest, and he had in consequence kept his eyes alert. He had noticed that Chayne was growing importunate, and that his persistence was becoming troublesome to Sylvia. She gave him a less warm welcome each time that he came to the house. She made plans to prevent herself being left alone with him, and if by chance the plans failed she listened rather than talked and listened almost with an air of boredom.

"Come as often as you please!" consequently said Garratt Skinner from his hammock. "And now let us talk of something else."

He talked of nothing for a while. But it was plain that he had a subject in his thoughts. For twice he turned to Chayne and was on the point of speaking; but each time he thought silence the better part and lay back again. Chayne waited and at last the subject was broached, but in a queer, hesitating, diffident way, as though

Garratt Skinner spoke rather under a compulsion of which he disapproved.

"Tell me!" he said. "I am rather interested. A craze, an infatuation which so masters people must be interesting even to the stay-at-homes like myself. But I am wrong to call it a craze. From merely reading books I think it a passion which is easily intelligible. You are wondering what I am talking about. My daughter tells me that you are a famous climber. The Aiguille d'Argentiere, I suppose, up which you were kind enough to accompany her, is not a very difficult mountain."

"It depends upon the day," said Chayne, "and the state of the snow."

"Yes, that is what I have gathered from the books. Every mountain may become dangerous."

"Yes."

"Each mountain," said Garratt Skinner, thoughtfully, "may reward its conquerors with death"; and for a little while he lay looking up to the green branches interlaced above his head. "Thus each mountain on the brightest day holds in its recesses mystery, and also death."

There had come a change already in the manner of the two men. They found themselves upon neutral ground. Their faces relaxed from wariness; they were no longer upon their guard. It seemed that an actual comradeship had sprung up between them.

"There is a mountain called the Grepon," said Skinner. "I have seen pictures of it--a strange and rather attractive pinnacle, with its knife-like slabs of rock, set on end one above the other--black rock splashed with red--and the overhanging boulder on the top. Have you climbed it?"

"Yes."

"There is a crack, I believe--a good place to get you into training."

Chayne laughed with the enjoyment of a man who recollects a stiff difficulty overcome.

"Yes, to the right of the Col between the Grepon and the Charmoz. There is a step half way up--otherwise there is very little hold and the crack is very steep."

They talked of other peaks, such as the Charmoz, where the first lines of ascent had given place to others more recently discovered, of new variations, new ascents and pinnacles still unclimbed; and then Garratt Skinner said:

"I saw that a man actually crossed the Col des Nantillons early this summer. It used to be called the Col de Blaitiere. He was killed with his guide, but after the real dangers were passed. That seems to happen at times."

Chayne looked at Garratt Skinner in surprise.

"It is strange that you should have mentioned John Lattery's death," he said, slowly.

"Why?" asked Garratt Skinner, turning quietly toward his companion. "I read of it in 'The Times.'"

"Oh, yes. No doubt it was described. What I meant was this. John Lattery was my great friend, and he was a distant kind of cousin to your friend Walter Hine, and indeed co-heir with him to Joseph Hine's great fortune. His death, I suppose, has doubled your friend's inheritance."

Garratt Skinner raised himself up on his elbow. The announcement was really news to him.

"Is that so?" he asked. "It is true, then. The mountains hold death too in their recesses--even on the clearest day--yes, they hold death too!" And letting himself fall gently back upon his cushions, he remained for a while with a very thoughtful look upon his face. Twice Chayne spoke to him, and twice he did not hear. He lay absorbed. It seemed that a new and engrossing idea had taken possession of his mind, and when he turned his eyes again to Chayne and spoke, he appeared to be speaking with reference to that idea rather than to any remarks of his companion.

"Did you ever ascend Mont Blanc by the Brenva route?" he asked. "There's a thin ridge of ice--I read an account in Moore's 'Journal'--you have to straddle across the ridge with a leg hanging down either precipice."

Chayne shook his head.

"Lattery and I meant to try it this summer. The Dent du Requin as well."

"Ah, that is one of the modern rock scrambles, isn't it? The last two or three hundred feet are the trouble, I believe."

And so the talk went on and the comradeship grew. But Chayne noticed that always Garratt Skinner came back to the great climbs of the earlier mountaineers, the Brenva ascent of Mont Blanc, the Col Dolent, the two points of the Aiguille du Dru and the Aiguille Verte.

"But you, too, have climbed," Chayne cried at length.

"On winter nights by my fireside," replied Garratt Skinner, with a smile. "I have a lame leg which would hinder me."

"Nevertheless, you left Miss Sylvia and myself behind when you led us over the hills to Dorchester."

It was Walter Hine who interrupted. He had come across the grass from behind, and neither of the two men had noticed his approach. But the moment when he did interrupt marked a change in their demeanor. The comradeship which had so quickly bloomed as quickly faded. It was the flower of an idle moment. Antagonism preceded and followed it. Thus, one might imagine, might sentries at the outposts of opposing armies pile their arms for half an hour and gossip of their homes or their children, or of something dear to both of them and separate at the bugle sound. Garratt Skinner swung himself out of his hammock.

"Where's Sylvia, Wallie?"

"She went up to her room."

Chayne waited for ten minutes, and for another ten, and still Sylvia did not appear. She was avoiding him. She could spend the afternoon with Walter Hine, but she must run to her room when he came upon the scene. Jealousy flamed up in him. Every now and then a whimsical smile of amusement showed upon Garratt Skinner's face and broadened into a grin. Chayne was looking a fool, and was quite conscious of it. He rose abruptly from his chair.

"I must be going," he said, over loudly, and Garratt Skinner smiled.

"I'm afraid she won't hear that," he said softly, measuring with his eyes the distance between the group and the house. "But come again, Captain Chayne, and sit it out."

Chayne flushed with anger. He said, "Thank you," and tried to say it jauntily and failed. He took his leave and walked across the lawn to the garden, trying to assume a carriage of indifference and dignity. But every moment he expected to hear the two whom he had left laughing at his discomfiture. Neither, however, did laugh. Walter Hine was, indeed, indignant.

"Why did you ask him to come again?" he asked, angrily, as the garden door closed upon Chayne.

Garratt Skinner laid his hand on Walter Hine's arm.

"Don't you worry, Wallie," he said, confidentially. "Every time Chayne comes here he loses ten marks. Give him rope! He does not, after all, know a great deal of geography."

CHAPTER XV
KENYON'S JOHN LATTERY

Chayne returned to London on the following day, restless and troubled. Jealousy, he knew, was the natural lot of the lover. But that he should have to be jealous of a Walter Hine--there was the sting. He asked the old question over and over again, the old futile question which the unrewarded suitor puts to himself with amazement and a despair at the ridiculous eccentricities of human nature. "What in the world can she see in the fellow?" However, he did not lose heart. It was not in his nature to let go once he had clearly set his desires upon a particular goal. Sooner or later, people and things would adjust themselves to their proper proportions in Sylvia's eyes. Meanwhile there was something to be done--a doubt to be set at rest, perhaps a discovery to be made.

His conversation with Garratt Skinner, the subject which Garratt Skinner had chosen, and the knowledge with which he had spoken, had seemed to Chayne rather curious. A man might sit by his fireside and follow with interest, nay almost with the passion of the mountaineer, the history of Alpine exploration and adventure. That had happened before now. And very likely Chayne would have troubled himself no more about Garratt Skinner's introduction of the theme but for one or two circumstances which the more he reflected upon them became the more significant. For instance: Garratt Skinner had spoken and had asked questions about the new ascents made, the new passes crossed within the last twenty years, just as a man would ask who had obtained his knowledge out of books. But of the earlier ascents he had spoken differently, though the difference was subtle and hard to define. He seemed to be upon more familiar ground. He left in Chayne's mind a definite suspicion that he was speaking no longer out of books, but from an intimate personal knowledge, the knowledge of actual experience. The suspicion had grown up gradually, but it had strengthened almost into a conviction.

It was to the old climbs that Garratt Skinner's conversation perpetually recurred--the Aiguille Verte, the Grand and the Petit Dru and the traverse between them, the Col Dolent, the Grandes Jorasses and the Brenva route--yes, above all, the Brenva route up Mont Blanc. Moreover, how in the world should he know that those slabs of black granite on the top of the Grepon were veined with red--splashed with red as he described them? Unless he had ascended them, or the Aiguille des Charmoz opposite--how should he know? The philosophy of his guide Michel Revailloud flashed across Chayne's mind. "One needs some one with whom to exchange one's memories."

Had Garratt Skinner felt that need and felt it with so much compulsion that he must satisfy it in spite of himself? Yet why should he practise concealment at all? There certainly had been concealment. Chayne remembered how more than once Garratt Skinner had checked himself before at last he had yielded. It was in spite of himself that he had spoken. And then suddenly as the train drew up at Vauxhall Station for the tickets to be collected, Chayne started up in his seat. On the rocks of the Argentiere, beside the great gully, as they descended to the glacier, Sylvia's guide had spoken words which came flying back into Chayne's thoughts. She had climbed that day, though it was her first mountain, as if knowledge of the craft had been born in her. How to stand upon an ice-slope, how to hold her ax--she had known. On the rocks, too! Which foot to advance, with which hand to grasp the hold--she had known. Suppose that knowledge *had* been born in her! Why, then those words of her guide began to acquire significance. She had reminded him of some one--some one whose name he could not remember--but some one with whom years ago he had climbed. And then upon the rocks, some chance movement of Sylvia's, some way in which she moved from ledge to ledge, had revealed to him the name--Gabriel Strood.

Was it possible, Chayne asked? If so, what dark thing was there in the record of Strood's life that he must change his name, disappear from the world, and avoid the summer nights, the days of sunshine and storm on the high rock-ledges and the ice-slope?

Chayne was minded to find an answer to that question. Sylvia was in trouble; that house under the downs was no place for her. He himself was afraid of what was being planned there. It might help him if he knew something more of Garratt Skinner than he knew at present. And it seemed to him that there was just a chance of acquiring that knowledge.

He dined at his club, and at ten o'clock walked up St. James' Street. The street was empty. It was a hot starlit night of the first week in August, and there came upon him a swift homesickness for the world above the snow-line. How many of his friends were sleeping that night in mountain huts high up on the shoulders of the mountains or in bivouacs open to the stars with a rock-cliff at their backs and a fire of pine wood blazing at their feet. Most likely amongst those friends was the one he sought to-night.

"Still there's a chance that I may find him," he pleaded, and crossing Piccadilly passed into Dover Street. Half way along the street of milliners, he stopped before a house where a famous scholar had his lodging.

"Is Mr. Kenyon in London?" he asked, and the man-servant replied to his great relief:

"Yes, sir, but he is not yet at home."

"I will wait for him," said Chayne.

He was shown into the study and left there with a lighted lamp. The room was lined with books from floor to ceiling. Chayne mounted a ladder and took down from a high corner some volumes bound simply in brown cloth. They were volumes of the "Alpine Journal." He had chosen those which dated back from twenty years to a quarter of a century. He drew a chair up beside the lamp and began eagerly to turn over the pages. Often he stopped, for the name of which he was in search often leaped to his eyes from the pages. Chayne read of the exploits in the Alps of Gabriel Strood. More than one new expedition was described, many variations of old ascents, many climbs already familiar. It was clear that the man was of the true brotherhood. A new climb was very well, but the old were as good to Gabriel Strood, and the climb which he had once made he had the longing to repeat with new companions. None of the descriptions were written by Strood himself but all by companions whom he had led, and most of them bore testimony to an unusual endurance, an unusual courage, as though Strood triumphed perpetually over a difficulty which his companions did not share and of which only vague hints were given. At last Chayne came to that very narrative which Sylvia had been reading on her way to Chamonix--and there the truth was bluntly told for the first time.

Chayne started up in that dim and quiet room, thrilled. He had the proof now, under his finger--the indisputable proof. Gabriel Strood suffered from an affection of the muscles in his right thigh, and yet managed to out-distance all his rivals. Hine's words drummed in Chayne's ears:

"Nevertheless he left us all behind."

Garratt Skinner: Gabriel Strood. Surely, surely! He replaced the volumes and took others down. In the first which he opened--it was the autumn number of nineteen years ago--there was again mention of the man; and the climb described was the ascent of Mont Blanc from the Brenva Glacier. Chayne leaned back in his chair fairly startled by this confirmation. It was to the Brenva route that Garratt Skinner had continually harked back. The Aiguille Verte, the Grandes Jorasses, the Charmoz, the Blaitiere--yes, he had talked of them all, but ever he had come back, with an eager voice and a fire in his eyes, to the ice-arete of the Brenva route. Chayne searched on through the pages. But there was nowhere in any volume on which he laid his hands any further record of his exploits. Others who followed in his steps mentioned his name, but of the man himself there was no word more. No one had climbed with him, no one had caught a glimpse of him above the snow-line. For five or six seasons he had flashed through the Alps. Arolla, Zermatt, the Montanvert, the Concordia hut--all had known him for five or six seasons, and then just under twenty years ago he had come no more.

Chayne put back the volumes in their places on the shelf, and sat down again in the arm-chair before the empty grate. It was a strange and a haunting story which he was gradually piecing together in his thoughts. Men like Gabriel Strood *always* come back to the Alps. They sleep too restlessly at nights, they needs must come. And yet this man had stayed away. There must have been some great impediment. He fell into another train of thought. Sylvia was eighteen, nearly nineteen. Had Gabriel Strood married just after that last season when he climbed from the Brenva Glacier to the Calotte. The story was still not unraveled, and while he perplexed his fancies over the unraveling, the door opened, and a tall, thin man with a pointed beard stood upon the threshold. He was a man of fifty years; his shoulders were just learning how to stoop; and his face, fine and delicate, yet lacking nothing of strength, wore an aspect of melancholy, as though he lived much alone--until he smiled. And in the smile there was much companionship and love. He smiled now as he stretched out his long, finely-molded hand.

"I am very glad to see you, Chayne," he said, in a voice remarkable for its gentleness, "although in another way I am sorry. I am sorry because, of course, I know why you are in England and not among the Alps."

Chayne had risen from his chair, but Kenyon laid a hand upon his shoulder and forced him down again with a friendly pressure. "I read of Lattery's death. I am grieved about it--for you as much as for Lattery. I know just what that kind of loss means. It means very much," said he, letting his deep-set eyes rest with sympathy upon the face of the younger man. Kenyon put a whisky and soda by Chayne's elbow, and setting the tobacco jar on a little table between them, sat down and lighted his pipe.

"You came back at once?" he asked.

"I crossed the Col Dolent and went down into Italy," replied Chayne.

"Yes, yes," said Kenyon, nodding his head. "But you will go back next year, or the year after."

"Perhaps," said Chayne; and for a little while they smoked their pipes in silence. Then Chayne came to the object of his visit.

"Kenyon," he asked, "have you any photographs of the people who went climbing twenty to twenty-five years ago? I thought perhaps you might have some groups taken in Switzerland in those days. If you have, I should like to see them."

"Yes, I think I have," said Kenyon. He went to his writing-desk and opening a drawer took out a number of photographs. He brought them back, and moving the green-shaded lamp so that the light fell clear and strong upon the little table, laid them down.

Chayne bent over them with a beating heart. Was his suspicion to be confirmed or disproved?

One by one he took the photographs, closely examined them, and laid them aside while Kenyon stood upright on the other side of the table. He had turned over a dozen before he stopped. He held in his hand the picture of a Swiss hotel, with an open space before the door. In the open space men were gathered. They were talking in groups; some of them leaned upon ice-axes, some carried **Ruecksacks** upon their backs, as though upon the point of starting for the hills. As he held the photograph a little nearer to the lamp, and bent his head a little lower, Kenyon made a slight uneasy movement. But Chayne did not notice. He sat very still, with his eyes fixed upon the photograph. On the outskirts of the group stood Sylvia's father.

Younger, slighter of build, with a face unlined and a boyish grace which had long since gone--but undoubtedly Sylvia's father.

The contours of the mountains told Chayne clearly enough in what valley the hotel stood.

"This is Zermatt," he said, without lifting his eyes.

"Yes," replied Kenyon, quietly, "a Zermatt you are too young to know," and then Chayne's forefinger dropped upon the figure of Sylvia's father.

"Who is this?" he asked.

Kenyon made no answer.

"It is Gabriel Strood," Chayne continued.

There was a pause, and then Kenyon confirmed the guess.

"Yes," he said, and some hint of emotion in his voice made Chayne lift his eyes. The light striking upward through the green shade gave to Kenyon's face an extraordinary pallor. But it seemed to Chayne that not all the pallor was due to the lamp.

"For six seasons," Chayne said, "Gabriel Strood came to the Alps. In his first season he made a great name."

"He was the best climber I have ever seen," replied Kenyon.

"He had a passion for the mountains. Yet after six years he came back no more. He disappeared. Why?"

Kenyon stood absolutely silent, absolutely still. Perhaps the trouble deepened a little on his face; but that was all. Chayne, however, was bent upon an answer. For Sylvia's sake alone he must have it, he must know the father into whose clutches she had come.

"You knew Gabriel Strood. Why?"

Kenyon leaned forward and gently took the photograph out of Chayne's hand. He mixed it with the others, not giving to it a single glance himself, and then re-placed them all in the drawer from which he had taken them. He came back to the table and at last answered Chayne:

"John Lattery was your friend. Some of the best hours of your life were passed in his company. You know that now. But you will know it still more surely when you come to my age, whatever happiness may come to you between now and then. The camp-fire, the rock-slab for your floor and the black night about you for walls, the hours of talk, the ridge and the ice-slope, the bad times in storm and mist, the good times in the sunshine, the cold nights of hunger when you were caught by the darkness, the off-days when you lounged at your ease. You won't forget John Lattery."

Kenyon spoke very quietly but with a conviction, and, indeed, a certain solemnity, which impressed his companion.

"No," said Chayne, gently, "I shall not forget John Lattery." But his question was still unanswered, and by nature he was tenacious. His eyes were still upon Kenyon's face and he added: "What then?"

"Only this," said Kenyon. "Gabriel Strood was my John Lattery," and moving round the table he dropped his hand upon Chayne's shoulder. "You will ask me no more questions," he said, with a smile.

"I beg your pardon," said Chayne.

He had his answer. He knew now that there was something to conceal, that there was a definite reason why Gabriel Strood disappeared.

"Good-night," he said; and as he left the room he saw Kenyon sink down into his arm-chair. There seemed something sad and very lonely in the attitude of the older man. Once more Michel Revailloud's warning rose up within his mind.

"When it is all over, and you go home, take care that there is a lighted lamp in the room and the room not empty. Have some one to share your memories when life is nothing but memories."

At every turn the simple philosophy of Michel Revailloud seemed to obtain an instance and a confirmation. Was that to be his own fate too? Just for a moment he was daunted. He closed the door noiselessly, and going down the stairs let himself out into the street. The night was clear above his head. How was it above the Downs of Dorsetshire, he wondered. He walked along the street very slowly. Garratt Skinner was Gabriel Strood. There was clearly a dark reason for the metamorphosis. It remained for Chayne to discover that reason. But he did not ponder any more upon that problem to-night. He was merely thinking as he walked along the street that Michel Revailloud was a very wise man.

CHAPTER XVI
AS BETWEEN GENTLEMEN

"Between gentlemen," said Wallie Hine. "Yes, between gentlemen."

He was quoting from a letter which he held in his hand, as he sat at the breakfast table, and, in his agitation, he had quoted aloud. Garratt Skinner looked up from his plate and said:

"Can I help you, Wallie?"

Hine flushed red and stammered out: "No, thank you. I must run up to town this morning--that's all."

"Sylvia will drive you into Weymouth in the dog-cart after breakfast," said Garratt Skinner, and he made no further reference to the journey. But he glared at the handwriting of the letter, and then with some perplexity at Walter Hine. "You will be back this evening, I suppose?"

"Rather," said Walter Hine, with a smile across the table at Sylvia; but his agitation got the better of his gallantry, and as she drove him into Weymouth, he spoke as piteously as a child appealing for protection. "I don't want to go one little bit, Miss Sylvia. But between gentlemen. Yes, I mustn't forget that. Between gentlemen." He clung to the phrase, finding some comfort in its reiteration.

"You have given me your promise," said Sylvia. "There will be no cards, no bets."

Walter Hine laughed bitterly.

"I shan't break it. I have had my lesson. By Jove, I have."

Walter Hine traveled to Waterloo and drove straight to the office of Mr. Jarvice.

"I owe some money," he began, bleating the words out the moment he was ushered into the inner office.

Mr. Jarvice grinned.

"This interview is concluded," he said. "There's the door."

"I owe it to a friend, Captain Barstow," Hine continued, in desperation. "A thousand pounds. He has written for it. He says that debts of honor between gentlemen--" But he got no further, for Mr. Jarvice broke in upon his faltering explanations with a snarl of contempt.

"Barstow! You poor little innocent. I have something else to do with my money than to pour it into Barstow's pockets. I know the man. Send him to me to-morrow, and I'll talk to him--as between gentlemen."

Walter Hine flushed. He had grown accustomed to deference and flatteries in the household of Garratt Skinner. The unceremonious scorn of Mr. Jarvice stung his vanity, and vanity was the one strong element of his character. He was in the mind hotly to defend Captain Barstow from Mr. Jarvice's insinuations, but he refrained.

"Then Barstow will know that I draw my allowance from you, and not from my grandfather," he stammered. There was the trouble for Walter Hine. If Barstow knew, Garratt Skinner would come to know. There would be an end to the deference and the flatteries. He would no longer be able to pose as the favorite of the great millionaire, Joseph Hine. He would sink in Sylvia's eyes. At the cost of any humiliation that downfall must be avoided.

His words, however, had an immediate effect upon Mr. Jarvice, though for quite other reasons.

"Why, that's true," said Mr. Jarvice, slowly, and in a voice suddenly grown smooth. "Yes, yes, we don't want to mix up my name in the affair at all. Sit down, Mr. Hine, and take a cigar. The box is at your elbow. Young men of spirit must have some extra license allowed to them for the sake of the promise of their riper years. I was forgetting that. No, we don't want my name to appear at all, do we?"

Publicity had no charms for Mr. Jarvice. Indeed, on more than one occasion he had found it quite a hindrance to the development of his little plans. To go his own quiet way, unheralded by the press and unacclaimed of men--that was the modest ambition of Mr. Jarvice.

"However, I don't look forward to handing over a thousand pounds to Captain Barstow," he continued, softly. "No, indeed. Did you lose any of your first quarter's allowance to him besides the thousand?"

Walter Hine lit his cigar and answered reluctantly:

"Yes."

"All of it?"

"Oh no, no, not all of it."

Jarvice did not press for the exact amount. He walked to the window and stood there with his hands in his pockets and his back toward his visitor. Walter Hine watched his shoulders in suspense and apprehension. He would have been greatly surprised if he could have caught a glimpse at this moment of Mr. Jarvice's face. There was no anger, no contempt, expressed in it at all. On the contrary, a quiet smile of satisfaction gave to it almost a merry look. Mr. Jarvice had certain plans for Walter Hine's future--so he phrased it with a smile for the grim humor of the phrase--and fate seemed to be helping toward their fulfilment.

"I can get you out of this scrape, no doubt," said Jarvice, turning back to his table. "The means I must think over, but I can do it. Only there's a condition. You need not be alarmed. A little condition which a loving father might impose upon his only son," and Mr. Jarvice beamed paternally as he resumed his seat.

"What is the condition?" asked Walter Hine.

"That you travel for a year, broaden your mind by visiting the great countries and capitals of Europe, take a little trip perhaps into the East and return a cultured gentleman well equipped to occupy the high position which will be yours when your grandfather is in due time translated to a better sphere."

Mr. Jarvice leaned back in his chair, and with a confident wave of his desk ruler had the air of producing the startling metamorphosis like some heavy but benevolent fairy. Walter Hine, however, was not attracted by the prospect.

"But--" he began, and at once Mr. Jarvice interrupted him.

"I anticipate you," he said, with a smile. "Standing at the window there, I foresaw your objection. But--it would be lonely. Quite true. Why should you be lonely? And so I am going to lay my hands on some pleasant and companionable young fellow who will go with you for his expenses. An Oxford man, eh? Fresh from Alma Mater with a taste for pictures and statuettes and that sort of thing! Upon my word, I envy you, Mr. Hine. If I were young, bless me, if I wouldn't throw my bonnet over the mill, as after a few weeks in La Ville Lumiere you will be saying, and go with you. You will taste life--yes, life."

And as he repeated the word, all the jollity died suddenly out of the face of Mr. Jarvice. He bent his eyes somberly upon his visitor and a queer inscrutable smile played about his lips. But Walter Hine had no eyes for Mr. Jarvice. He was nerving himself to refuse the proposal.

"I can't go," he blurted out, with the ungracious stubbornness of a weak mind which fears to be over-persuaded. Afraid lest he should consent, he refused aggressively and rudely.

Mr. Jarvice repressed an exclamation of anger. "And why?" he asked, leaning forward on his elbows and fixing his bright, sharp eyes on Walter Hine's face.

Walter Hine shifted uncomfortably in his chair but did not answer.

"And why can't you go?" he repeated.

"I can't tell you."

"Oh, surely," said Mr. Jarvice, with a scarcely perceptible sneer. "Come now! Between gentlemen! Well?"

Walter Hine yielded to Jarvice's insistence.

"There's a girl," he said, with a coy and odious smile.

Mr. Jarvice beat upon his desk with his fists in a savage anger. His carefully calculated plan was to be thwarted by a girl.

"She's a dear," cried Walter Hine. Having made the admission, he let himself go. His vanity pricked him to lyrical flights. "She's a dear, she's a sob, she would never let me go, she's my little girl."

Such was Sylvia's reward for engaging in a struggle which she loathed for the salvation of Walter Hine. She was jubilantly claimed by him as his little girl in a money-lender's office. Mr. Jarvice swore aloud.

"Who is she?" he asked, sternly.

A faint sense of shame came over Walter Hine. He dimly imagined what Sylvia would have thought and said, and what contempt her looks would have betrayed, had she heard him thus boast of her goodwill.

"You are asking too much, Mr. Jarvice," he said.

Mr. Jarvice waved the objection aside.

"Of course I ask it as between gentlemen," he said, with an ironical politeness.

"Well, then, as between gentlemen," returned Walter Hine, seriously. "She is the daughter of a great friend of mine, Mr. Garratt Skinner. What's the matter?" he cried; and there was reason for his cry.

It had been an afternoon of surprises for Mr. Jarvice, but this simple mention of the name of Garratt Skinner was more than a surprise. Mr. Jarvice was positively startled. He leaned back in his chair with his mouth open and his eyes staring at Walter Hine. The high color paled in his face and his cheeks grew mottled. It seemed that fear as well as surprise came to him in the knowledge that Garratt Skinner was a friend of Walter Hine.

"What is the matter?" repeated Hine.

"It's nothing," replied Mr. Jarvice, hastily. "The heat, that is all." He crossed the room, and throwing up the window leaned for a few moments upon the sill. Yet even when he spoke again, there was still a certain unsteadiness in his voice. "How did you come across Mr. Garratt Skinner?" he asked.

"Barstow introduced me. I made Barstow's acquaintance at the Criterion Bar, and he took me to Garratt Skinner's house in Hobart Place."

"I see," said Mr. Jarvice. "It was in Garratt Skinner's house that you lost your money, I suppose."

"Yes, but he had no hand in it," exclaimed Walter Hine. "He does not know how much I lost. He would be angry if he did."

A faint smile flickered across Jarvice's face.

"Quite so," he agreed, and under his deft cross-examination the whole story was unfolded. The little dinner at which Sylvia made her appearance and at which Walter Hine was carefully primed with drink; the little round game of cards which Garratt Skinner was so reluctant to allow in his house on a Sunday evening, and from which, being an early riser, he retired to bed, leaving Hine in the hands of Captain Barstow and Archie Parminter; the quiet secluded house in the country; the new gardener who appeared for one day and shot with so surprising an accuracy, when Barstow backed him against Walter Hine, that Hine lost a thousand pounds; the incidents were related to Mr. Jarvice in their proper succession, and he interpreted them by his own experience. Captain Barstow, who was always to the fore, counted for nothing in the story as Jarvice understood it. He was the mere creature, the servant. Garratt Skinner, who was always in the background, prepared the swindle and pocketed the profits.

"You are staying at the quiet house in Dorsetshire now, I suppose. Just you and Garratt Skinner and the pretty daughter, with occasional visits from Barstow?"

"Yes," answered Hine. "Garratt Skinner does not care to see much company."

Once more the smile of amusement played upon Mr. Jarvice's face.

"No, I suppose not," he said, quietly. There were certain definite reasons of which he was aware, to account for Garratt Skinner's reluctance to appear in a general company. He turned back from the window and returned to his table. He had taken his part. There was no longer either unsteadiness or anger in his voice.

"I quite understand your reluctance to leave your new friends," he said, with the utmost friendliness. "I recognize that the tour abroad on which I had rather set my heart must be abandoned. But I have no regrets. For I think it possible that the very object which I had in mind when proposing that tour may be quite as easily effected in the charming country house of Garratt Skinner."

He spoke in a quiet matter-of-fact voice, looking benevolently at his visitor. If the words were capable of another and a more sinister meaning than they appeared to convey, Walter Hine did not suspect it. He took them in their obvious sense.

"Yes, I shall gain as much culture in Garratt Skinner's house as I should by seeing picture-galleries abroad," he said eagerly, and then Mr. Jarvice smiled.

"I think that very likely," he said. "Meanwhile, as to Barstow and his thousand pounds. I must think the matter over. Barstow will not press you for a day or two. Just leave me your address--the address in Dorsetshire."

He dipped a pen in the ink and handed it to Hine. Hine took it and drew a sheet of paper toward him. But he did not set the pen to the paper. He looked suddenly up at Jarvice, who stood over against him at the other side of the table.

"Garratt Skinner's address?" he said, with one of his flashes of cunning.

"Yes, since you are staying there. I shall want to write to you."

Walter Hine still hesitated.

"You won't peach to Garratt Skinner about the allowance, eh?"

"My dear fellow!" said Mr. Jarvice. He was more hurt than offended. "To put it on the lowest ground, what could I gain?"

Walter Hine wrote down the address, and at once the clerk appeared at the door and handed Jarvice a card.

"I will see him," said Jarvice, and turning to Hine: "Our business is over, I think."

Jarvice opened a second door which led from the inner office straight down a little staircase into the street. "Good-by. You shall hear from me," he said, and Walter Hine went out.

Jarvice closed the door and turned back to his clerk.

"That will do," he said.

There was no client waiting at all. Mr. Jarvice had an ingenious contrivance for getting rid of his clients at the critical moment after they had come to a decision and before they had time to change their minds. By pressing a particular button in the leather covering of the right arm of his chair, he moved an indicator above the desk of his clerk in the outer office. The clerk thereupon announced a visitor, and the one in occupation was bowed out by the private staircase. By this method Walter Hine had been dismissed.

Jarvice had the address of Garratt Skinner. But he sat with it in front of him upon his desk for a long time before he could bring himself to use it. All the amiability had gone from his expression now that he was alone. He was in a savage mood, and every now and then a violent gesture betrayed it. But it was with himself that he was angry. He had been a fool not to keep a closer watch on Walter Hine.

"I might have foreseen," he cried in his exasperation. "Garratt Skinner! If I had not been an ass, I *should* have foreseen."

For Mr. Jarvice was no stranger to Walter Hine's new friend. More than one young buck fresh from the provinces, heir to the great factory or the great estate, had been steered into this inner office by the careful pilotage of Garratt Skinner. In all the army of the men who live by their wits, there was not one to Jarvice's knowledge who was so alert as Garratt Skinner to lay hands upon the new victim or so successful in lulling his suspicions. He might have foreseen that Garratt Skinner would throw his net over Walter Hine. But he had not, and the harm was done.

Mr. Jarvice took the insurance policy from his safe and shook his head over it sadly. He had seen his way to making in his quiet fashion, and at comparatively little cost, a tidy little sum of one hundred thousand pounds. Now he must take a partner, so that he might not have an enemy. Garratt Skinner with Barstow for his jackal and the pretty daughter for his decoy was too powerful a factor to be lightly regarded. Jarvice must share with Garratt Skinner--unless he preferred to abandon his scheme altogether; and that Mr. Jarvice would not do.

There was no other way. Jarvice knew well that he could weaken Garratt Skinner's influence over Walter Hine by revealing to the youth certain episodes in the new friend's life. He might even break the acquaintanceship altogether. But Garratt Skinner would surely discover who had been at work. And then? Why, then,

Mr. Jarvice would have upon his heels a shrewd and watchful enemy; and in this particular business, such an enemy Mr. Jarvice could not afford to have. Jarvice was not an impressionable man, but his hands grew cold while he imagined Garratt Skinner watching the development of his little scheme--the tour abroad with the pleasant companion, the things which were to happen on the tour--watching and waiting until the fitting moment had come, when all was over, for him to step in and demand the price of his silence and hold Mr. Jarvice in the hollow of his hand for all his life. No, that would never do. Garratt Skinner must be a partner so that also he might be an accessory.

Accordingly, Jarvice wrote his letter to Garratt Skinner, a few lines urging him to come to London on most important business. Never was there a letter more innocent in its appearance than that which Jarvice wrote in his inner office on that summer afternoon. Yet even at the last he hesitated whether he should seal it up or no. The sun went down, shadows touched with long cool fingers the burning streets; shadows entered into that little inner office of Mr. Jarvice. But still he sat undecided at his desk.

The tour upon the Continent must be abandoned, and with it the journey under canvas to the near East--a scheme so simple, so sure, so safe. Still Garratt Skinner might confidently be left to devise another. And he had always kept faith. To that comforting thought Mr. Jarvice clung. He sealed up his letter in the end, and stood for a moment or two with the darkness deepening about him. Then he rang for his clerk and bade him post it, but the voice he used was one which the clerk did not know, so that he pushed his head forward and peered through the shadows to make sure that it was his master who spoke.

Two days afterward Garratt Skinner paid a long visit to Mr. Jarvice, and that some agreement was reached between the two men shortly became evident. For Walter Hine received a letter from Captain Barstow which greatly relieved him.

"Garratt Skinner has written to me," wrote the 'red-hot' Captain, "that he has discovered that the gardener, whom he engaged for a particular job, is notorious as a poacher and a first-class shot. Under these circumstances, my dear old fellow, the red-hot one cannot pouch your pennies. As between gentlemen, the bet must be considered o-p-h."

CHAPTER XVII
SYLVIA TELLS MORE THAN SHE KNOWS

Hilary Chayne stayed away from Dorsetshire for ten complete days; and though the hours crept by, dilatory as idlers at a street corner, he obtained some poor compensation by reflecting upon his fine diplomacy. In less than a week he would surely be missed; by the time that ten days had passed the sensation might have become simply poignant. So for ten days he wandered about the Downs of Sussex with an aching heart, saying the while, "It serves her right." On the morning of the eleventh he received a letter from the War Office, bidding him call on the following afternoon.

"That will just do," he said. "I will go down to Weymouth to-day, and I will return to London to-morrow." And with an unusual lightness of spirit, which he as- cribed purely to his satisfaction that he need punish Sylvia no longer, he started off upon his long journey. He reached the house of the Running Water by six o'clock in the evening; and at the outset it seemed that his diplomacy had been sagacious.

He was shown into the library, and opposite to him by the window Sylvia stood alone. She turned to him a white terror-haunted face, gazed at him for a second like one dazed, and then with a low cry of welcome came quickly toward him. Chayne caught her outstretched hands and all his joy at her welcome lay dead at the sight of her distress. "Sylvia!" he exclaimed in distress. He was hurt by it as he had never thought to be hurt.

"I am afraid!" she said, in a trembling whisper. He drew her toward him and she yielded. She stood close to him and very still, touching him, leaning to him like a frightened child. "Oh, I am afraid," she repeated; and her voice appealed piteously for sympathy and a little kindness.

In Chayne's mind there was suddenly painted a picture of the ice-slope on the Aiguille d'Argentiere. A girl had moved from step to step, across that slope, looking down its steep glittering incline without a tremor. It was the same girl who now leaned to him and with shaking lips and eyes tortured with fear cried, "I am afraid." By his recollection of that day upon the heights Chayne measured the greatness of her present trouble.

"Why, Sylvia? Why are you afraid?"

For answer she looked toward the open window. Chayne followed her glance and this was what he saw: The level stretch of emerald lawn, the stream running through it and catching in its brown water the red light of the evening sun, the great beech trees casting their broad shadows, the high garden walls with the dusky red of their bricks glowing amongst fruit trees, and within that enclosure pacing up and down, in and out among the shadows of the trees, Garratt Skinner and Walter Hine. Yet that sight she must needs have seen before. Why should it terrify her beyond reason now?

"Do you see?" Sylvia said in a low troubled voice. For once distress had mastered her and she spoke without her usual reticence. "There can be no friendship between those two. No real friendship! You have but to see them side by side to be sure of it. It is pretence."

Yet that too she must have known before. Why then should the pretence now so greatly trouble her? Chayne watched the two men pacing in the garden. Certainly he had never seen them in so intimate a comradeship. Garratt Skinner had passed his arm through Walter Hine's and held him so, plying him with stories, bending down his keen furrowed aquiline face toward him as though he had no thought in the world but to make him his friend and bind him with affection; and Walter Hine looked up and listened and laughed, a vain, weak wisp of a creature, flattered to the skies and defenceless as a rabbit.

"Why the pretence?" said Sylvia. "Why the linked arms? The pretence has grown during these last days. What new thing is intended?" Her eyes were on the garden, and as she looked it seemed that her terror grew. "My father went away a week ago. Since he has returned the pretence has increased. I am afraid! I am afraid!"

Garratt Skinner turned in his walk and led Walter Hine back toward the house. Sylvia shrank from his approach as from something devilish. When he turned again, she drew her breath like one escaped from sudden peril.

"Sylvia! Of what are you afraid?"

"I don't know!" she cried. "That's just the trouble. I don't know!" She clenched her hands together at her breast. Chayne caught them in his and was aware that in one shut palm she held something which she concealed. Her clasp tightened upon it as his hands touched hers. Sylvia had more reason for her fears than she had disclosed. Barstow came no more. There were no more cards, no more bets; and this change taken together with Garratt Skinner's increased friendship added to her apprehensions. She dreaded some new plot more sinister, more terrible than that one of which she was aware.

"If only I knew," she cried. "Oh, if only I knew!"

Archie Parminter had paid one visit to the house, had stayed for one night; and he and Garratt Skinner and Walter Hine had sat up till morning, talking together in the library. Sylvia waking up from a fitful sleep, had heard their voices again and again through the dark hours; and when the dawn was gray, she had heard them coming up to bed as on the first night of her return; and as on that night there was one who stumbled heavily. It was since that night that terror had distracted her.

"I have no longer any power," she said. "Something has happened to destroy my power. I have no longer any influence. Something was done upon that night," and she shivered as though she guessed; and she looked at her clenched hand as though the clue lay hidden in its palm. There lay her great trouble. She had lost her influence over Walter Hine. She had knowledge of the under side of life--yes, but her father had a greater knowledge still. He had used his greater knowledge. Craftily and with a most ingenious subtlety he had destroyed her power, he had blunted her weapons. Hine was attracted by Sylvia, fascinated by her charm, her looks, and the gentle simplicity of her manner. Very well. On the other side Garratt Skinner had held out a lure of greater attractions, greater fascination; and Sylvia was powerless.

"He has changed," Sylvia went on, with her eyes fixed on Walter Hine. "Oh, not merely toward me. He has changed physically. Can you understand? He has grown nervous, restless, excitable, a thing of twitching limbs. Oh, and that's not all. I will tell you. This morning it seemed to me that the color of his eyes had changed."

Chayne stared at her. "Sylvia!" he exclaimed.

"Oh, I have not lost my senses," she answered, and she resumed: "I only noticed that there was an alteration at first. I did not see in what the alteration lay. Then I saw. His eyes used to be light in color. This morning they were dark. I looked carefully to make sure, and so I understood. The pupils of his eyes were so dilated that they covered the whole eyeball. Can you think why?" and even as she asked, she looked at that clenched hand of hers as though the answer to that question as well lay hidden there. "I am afraid," she said once more; and upon that Chayne committed the worst of the many indiscretions which had signalized his courtship.

"You are afraid? Sylvia! Then let me take you away!"

At once Sylvia drew back. Had Chayne not spoken, she would have told him all that there was to tell. She was in the mood at this unguarded moment. She would have told him that during these last days Walter Hine had taken to drink once more. She would have opened that clenched fist and showed the thing it hid, even though the thing condemned her father beyond all hope of exculpation. But Chayne had checked her as surely as though he had laid the palm of his hand upon her lips. He would talk of love and flight, and of neither had she any wish to hear. She craved with a great yearning for sympathy and a little kindness. But Chayne was not content to offer what she needed. He would add more, and what he added marred the whole gift for Sylvia. She shook her head, and looking at him with a sad and gentle smile, said:

"Love is for the happy people."

"That is a hard saying, Sylvia," Chayne returned, "and not a true one."

"True to me," said Sylvia, with a deep conviction, and as he advanced to her she raised her hand to keep him off. "No, no," she cried, and had he listened, he might have heard a hint of exasperation in her voice. But he would not be warned.

"You can't go on, living here, without sympathy, without love, without even kindness. Already it is evident. You are ill, and tired. And you think to go on all your life or all your father's life. Sylvia, let me take you away!"

And each unwise word set him further and further from his aim. It seemed to her that there was no help anywhere. Chayne in front of her seemed to her almost as much her enemy as her father, who paced the lawn behind her arm in arm with Walter Hine. She clasped her hands together with a quick sharp movement.

"I will not let you take me away," she cried. "For I do not love you"; and her voice had lost its gentleness and grown cold and hard. Chayne began again, but whether it was with a renewal of his plea, she did not hear. For she broke in upon him quickly:

"Please, let me finish. I am, as you said, a little over-wrought! Just hear me out and leave me to bear my troubles by myself. You will make it easier for me"; she saw that the words hurt her lover. But she did not modify them. She was in the mood to hurt. She had been betrayed by her need of sympathy into speaking words which she would gladly have recalled; she had been caught off her guard and almost un-awares; and she resented it. Chayne had told her that she looked ill and tired; and she resented that too. No wonder she looked tired when she had her father with his secret treacheries on one side and an importunate lover upon the other! She thought for a moment or two how best to put what she had still to stay:

"I have probably said to you," she resumed, "more than was right or fair--I mean fair to my father. I have no doubt exaggerated things. I want you to forget what I have said. For it led you into a mistake."

Chayne looked at her in perplexity.

"A mistake?"

"Yes," she answered. She was standing in front of him with her forehead wrinkled and a somber, angry look in her eyes. "A mistake which I must correct. You said that I was living here without kindness. It is not true. My father is kind!" And as Chayne raised his eyes in a mute protest, she insisted on the word. "Yes, kind and thoughtful--thoughtful for others besides myself." A kind of obstinacy forced her on to enlarge upon the topic. "I can give you an instance which will surprise you."

"There is no need," Chayne said, gently, but Sylvia was implacable.

"But there is need," she returned. "I beg you to hear me. When my father and I were at Weymouth we drove one afternoon across the neck of the Chesil beach to Portland."

Chayne looked at Sylvia quickly.

"Yes?" he said, and there was an indefinable change in his voice. He had consented to listen, because she wished it. Now he listened with a keen attention. For a strange thought had crept into his mind.

"We drove up the hill toward the plateau at the top of the island, but as we passed through the village--Fortune's Well I think they call it--my father stopped the carriage at a tobacconist's, and went into the shop. He came out again with some plugs of tobacco--a good many--and got into the carriage. You won't guess why he bought them. I didn't."

"Well?" said Chayne, and now he spoke with suspense. Suspense, too, was visible in his quiet attitude. There was a mystery which for Sylvia's sake he wished to unravel. Why did Gabriel Strood now call himself Garratt Skinner? That was the mystery. But he must unravel it without doing any hurt to Sylvia. He could not go too warily--of that he had been sure, ever since Kenyon had refused to speak of it. There might be some hidden thing which for Sylvia's sake must not be brought to light. Therefore he must find out the truth without help from any one. He wondered whether unconsciously Sylvia herself was going to give him the clue. Was she to tell him what she did not know herself--why Gabriel Strood was now Garratt Skinner? "Well?" he repeated.

"As we continued up the hill," she resumed, "my father cut up the tobacco into small pieces with his pocket knife. 'Why are you doing that?' I asked, and he laughed and said, 'Wait, you will see.' At the top of the hill we got out of the carriage and walked across the open plateau. In front of us, rising high above a little village, stood out a hideous white building. My father asked if I knew what it was. I said I guessed."

"It was the prison," Chayne interrupted, quickly.

"Yes."

"You went to it?"

Upon the answer to the question depended whether or no Chayne was to unravel his mystery, to-day.

"No," replied Sylvia, and Chayne drew a breath. Had she answered "Yes," the suspicion which had formed within his mind must needs be set aside, as clearly and finally disproved. Since she answered "No," the suspicion gathered strength. "We went, however, near to it. We went as close to it as the quarries. It was five o'clock in the afternoon, and as we came to the corner of the wall which surrounds the quarries, my father said, 'They have stopped work now.'"

"He knew that?" asked Chayne.

"Yes. We turned into a street which runs down toward the prison. On one side are small houses, on the other the long wall of the Government quarries. The street was empty; only now and then--very seldom--some one passed along it. On the top of the wall, there were sentry-boxes built at intervals, for the warders to overlook the convicts. But these were empty too. The wall is not high; I suppose--in fact my father said--the quarry was deep on the other side."

"Yes," said Chayne, quietly. "And then?"

"Then we walked slowly along the street, and whenever there was no one near, my father threw some tobacco over the wall. 'I don't suppose they have a very enjoyable time,' he said. 'They will be glad to find the tobacco there to-morrow.' We walked up the street and turned and came back, and when we reached the corner he said with a laugh, 'That's all, Sylvia. My pockets are empty.' We walked back to the carriage and drove home again to Weymouth."

Sylvia had finished her story, and the mystery was clear to Chayne. She had told him the secret which she did not know herself. He was sure now why Gabriel Strood had changed his name; he knew now why Gabriel Strood no longer climbed the Alps; and why Kenyon would answer no question as to the disappearance of his friend.

"I have told you this," said Sylvia, "because you accused my father of unkindness and want of thought. Would you have thought of those poor prisoners over there in the quarries? If you had, would you have taken so much trouble just to give them a small luxury? I think they must have blessed the unknown man who thought for them and showed them what so many want--a little sympathy and a little kindness."

Chayne bowed his head.

"Yes," he said, gently. "I was unjust."

Indeed even to himself he acknowledged that Garratt Skinner had shown an unexpected kindness, although he was sure of the reason for the act. He had no doubt that Garratt Skinner had labored in those quarries himself, and perhaps had himself picked up in bygone days, as he stooped over his work, tobacco thrown over the walls by some more fortunate man.

"I am glad you acknowledge that," said Sylvia, but her voice did not relent from its hostility. She stood without further word, expecting him to take his leave. Chayne recollected with how hopeful a spirit he had traveled down from London. His fine diplomacy had after all availed him little. He had gained certainly some unexpected knowledge which convinced him still more thoroughly that the sooner he took Sylvia away from her father and his friends the better it would be. But he was no nearer to his desire. It might be that he was further off than ever.

"You are returning to London?" she asked.

"Yes. I have to call at the War Office to-morrow."

Sylvia had no curiosity as to that visit. She took no interest in it whatever, he noticed with a pang.

"And then?" she asked slowly, as she crossed the hall with him to the door. "You will go home?"

Chayne smiled rather bitterly.

"Yes, I suppose so."

"Into Sussex?"

"Yes."

She opened the door, and as he came out on to the steps she looked at him with a thoughtful scrutiny for a few moments. But whether her thoughts portended good or ill for him, he could not tell.

"When I was a boy," he said abruptly, "I used to see from the garden of my house, far away in a dip of the downs, a dark high wall standing up against the sky. I never troubled myself as to how it came to have been built there. But I used to wonder, being a boy, whether it could be scaled or no. One afternoon I rode my pony over to find out, and I discovered--What do you think?--that my wall was a mere hedge just three feet high, no more."

"Well!" said Sylvia.

"Well, I have not forgotten--that's all," he replied.

"Good-by," she said, and he learned no more from her voice than he had done from her looks. He walked away down the lane, and having gone a few yards he looked back. Sylvia was still standing in the doorway, watching him with grave and thoughtful eyes. But there was no invitation to him to return, and turning away again he walked on.

Sylvia went up-stairs to her room. She unclenched her hand at last. In its palm there lay a little phial containing a colorless solution. But there was a label upon the phial, and on the label was written "cocaine." It was that which had struck at her influence over Walter Hine. It was to introduce this drug that Archie Parminter had been brought down from London and the West End clubs.

"It's drunk a good deal in a quiet way," Archie had said, as he made a pretence himself to drink it.

"You leave such drugs to the aristocracy, Walter," Garratt Skinner had chimed in. "Just a taste if you like. But go gently."

Sylvia had not been present. But she conjectured the scene, and her conjecture was not far from the truth. But why? she asked, and again fear took hold of her. "What was to be gained?" There were limits to Sylvia's knowledge of the under side of life. She did not guess.

She turned to her mirror and looked at herself. Yes, she looked tired, she looked ill. But she was not grateful for having the fact pointed out to her. And while she still looked, she heard her father's voice calling her. She shivered, as though her fear once more laid hold on her. Then she locked the bottle of cocaine away in a drawer and ran lightly down the stairs.

CHAPTER XVIII
BOTH SIDES OF THE QUESTION

Chayne's house stood high upon a slope of the Sussex Downs. Built of stone two centuries ago, it seemed gradually to have taken on the brown color of the hill behind it, subduing itself to the general scheme, even as birds and animals will do; so that strangers who searched for it in the valley discovered it by the upward swirl of smoke from its wide chimneys. On its western side and just beneath the house, there was a cleft in the downs through which the high road ran and in the cleft the houses of a tiny village clustered even as at the foot of some old castle in Picardy. On the east the great ridge with its shadow-holding hollows, its rounded gorse-strewn slopes of grass, rolled away for ten miles and then dipped suddenly to the banks of the River Arun. The house faced the south, and from its high-terraced garden, a great stretch of park and forest land was visible, where amidst the green and russet of elm and beach, a cluster of yews set here and there gave the illusion of a black and empty space. Beyond the forest land a lower ridge of hills rose up, and over that ridge one saw the spires of Chichester and the level flats of Selsea reaching to the sea.

Into this garden Chayne came on the next afternoon, and as he walked along its paths alone he could almost fancy that his dead father paced with the help of his stick at his side, talking, as had been his wont, of this or that improvement needed by the farms, pointing out to him a meadow in the hollow beneath which might soon be coming into the market, and always ending up with the same plea.

"Isn't it time, Hilary, that you married and came home to look after it all your-self?"

Chayne had turned a deaf ear to that plea, but it made its appeal to him to-night. Wherever his eyes rested, he recaptured something of his boyhood; the country-side was alive with memories. He looked south, and remembered how the perished cities of history had acquired reality for him by taking on the aspect of Chichester lying low there on the flats; and how the spires of the fabled towns of his storybooks had caught the light of the setting sun, just as did now the towers of the cathedral. Eastward, in the dip between the shoulder of the downs, and the trees of Arundel Park, a long black hedge stood out with a remarkable definition against the sky--the hedge of which he had spoken to Sylvia--the great dark wall of brambles guarding the precincts of the Sleeping Beauty. He recalled the adventurous day when he had first ridden alone upon his pony along the great back of the downs and had come down to it through a sylvan country of silence and ferns and open spaces; and had discovered it to be no more than a hedge waist-high. The dusk came upon him as he loitered in that solitary garden; the lights shone out in cottage and farm-house; and more closely still his memories crowded about him weaving spells. Some one to share them with! Chayne had no need to wait for old age before he learnt the wisdom of Michel Revailloud. For his heart leaped now, as he dreamed of exploring once more with Sylvia at his side the enchanted country of his boyhood; gallops in the quiet summer mornings along that still visible track across the downs, by which the Roman legions had marched in the old days from London straight as a die to Chichester; winter days with the hounds; a rush on windy afternoons in a sloop-rigged boat down the Arun to Littlehampton. Chayne's heart leaped with a passion-ate longing as he dreamed, and sank as he turned again to the blank windows of the empty house.

He dined alone, and while he dined evoked Sylvia's presence at the table, set-ting her, not at the far end, but at the side and close, so that a hand might now and then touch hers; calling up into her face her slow hesitating smile; seeing her still gray eyes grow tender; in a word watching the Madonna change into the woman. He went into the library where, since the night had grown chilly, a fire was lit. It was a place of comfort, with high bookshelves, deep-cushioned chairs, and dark curtains. But, no less than the dining-room it needed another presence, and lacking that lacked everything. It needed the girl with the tired and terror-haunted face. Here, surely the fear would die out of her soul, the eyes would lose their shadows, the feet regain the lightness of their step.

Chayne took down his favorite books, but they failed him. Between the pages and his eyes one face would shape itself. He looked into the fire and sought as of old to picture in the flames some mountain on which his hopes were set and to discover the right line for its ascent. But even that pastime brought no solace for his discontent. The house oppressed him. It was empty, it was silent. He drew aside the curtains and looking down into the valley through the clear night air watched the lights in cottage and farm with the envy born of his loneliness.

In spite of the brave words he had used, he wondered to-night whether the three-foot hedge was not after all to prove the unassailable wall. And it was important that he should know. For if it were so, why then he had not called at the War Office in vain. A proposal had been made to him--that he should join a commission for the delimitation of a distant frontier. A year's work and an immediate departure--those were the conditions. Within two days he must make up his mind--within ten days he must leave England.

Chayne pondered over the decision which he must make. If he had lost Sylvia, here was the mission to accept. For it meant complete severance, a separation not to be measured by miles alone, but by the nature of the work, and the comrades, and even the character of the vegetation. He went to bed in doubt, thinking that the morning might bring him counsel. It brought him a letter from Sylvia instead.

The letter was long; it was written in haste, it was written in great distress, so that words which were rather unkind were written down. But the message of the letter was clear. Chayne was not to come again to the House of the Running Water; nor to the little house in London when she returned to it. They were not to meet again. She did not wish for it.

Chayne burnt the letter as soon as he had read it, taking no offence at the hasty words. "I seem to have worried her more than I thought," he said to himself with a wistful smile. "I am sorry," and again as the sparks died out from the black ashes of the letter he repeated: "Poor little girl. I am very sorry."

So the house would always be silent and empty.

Sylvia had written the letter in haste on the very evening of Chayne's visit, and had hurried out to post it in fear lest she might change her mind in the morning. But in the morning she was only aware of a great lightness of spirit. She could now devote herself to the work of her life; and for two long tiring days she kept Walter Hine at her side. But now he sought to avoid her. The little energy he had ever had was gone, he alternated between exhilaration and depression; he preferred, it seemed, to be alone. For two days, however, Sylvia persevered, and on the third her lightness of spirit unaccountably deserted her.

She drove with Walter Hine that morning, and something of his own irritability seemed to have passed into her; so that he turned to her and asked:

"What have I done? Aren't you pleased with me? Why are you angry?"

"I am not angry," she replied, turning her great gray eyes upon him. "But if you wish to know, I miss something."

So much she owned. She missed something, and she knew very well what it was that she missed. Even as Chayne in his Sussex home had ached to know that the house lacked a particular presence, so it began to be with Sylvia in Dorsetshire.

"Yet he has been absent for a longer time," she argued with herself, "and I have not missed him. Indeed, I have been glad of his absence." And the answer came quickly from her thoughts.

"At any time you could have called him to your side, and you knew it. Now you have sent him away for always."

During the week the sense of loss, the feeling that everything was unbearably incomplete, grew stronger and stronger within her. She had no heart for the losing battle in which she was engaged. A dangerous question began to force itself forward in her mind whenever her eyes rested upon Walter Hine. "Was he worth while?" she asked herself: though as yet she did not define all that the "while" connoted. The question was most prominent in her mind on the seventh day after the letter had been sent. She had persuaded Walter Hine to mount with her on to the down behind the house; they came to the great White Horse, and Hine, pleading fatigue, a plea which during these last days had been ever on his lips, flung himself down upon the grass. For a little time Sylvia sat idly watching the great battle ships at firing-practice in the Bay. It was an afternoon of August; a light haze hung in the still air softening the distant promontories; and on the waveless sparkling sea the great ships, coal-black to the eye, circled about the targets, with now and then a roar of thunder and a puff of smoke, like some monstrous engines of heat--heat stifling and oppressive. By sheer contrast, Sylvia began to dream of the cool glaciers; and the Chalet de Lognan suddenly stood visible before her eyes. She watched the sunlight die off the red rocks of the Chardonnet, the evening come with silent feet across the snow, and the starlit night follow close upon its heels; night fled as she dreamed. She saw the ice-slope on the Aiguille d'Argentiere, she could almost hear the chip-chip of the axes as the steps were cut and the perpetual hiss as the ice-fragments streamed down the slope. Then she looked toward Walter Hine with the speculative inquiry which had come so often into her eyes of late. And as she looked, she saw him furtively take from a pocket a tabloid or capsule and slip it secretly into his mouth.

"How long have you been taking cocaine?" she asked, suddenly.

Walter Hine flushed scarlet and turned to her with a shrinking look.

"I don't," he stammered.

"Yet you left a bottle of the drug where I found it."

"That was not mine," said he, still more confused. "That was Archie Parminter's. He left it behind."

"Yes," said Sylvia, finding here a suspicion confirmed. "But he left it for you?"

"And if I did take it," said Hine, turning irritably to her, "what can it matter to you? I believe that what your father says is true."

"What does he say?"

"That you care for Captain Chayne, and that it's no use for any one else to think of you."

Sylvia started.

"Oh, he says that!"

She understood now one of the methods of the new intrigue. Sylvia was in love with Chayne; therefore Walter Hine may console himself with cocaine. It was not Garratt Skinner who suggested it. Oh, no! But Archie Parminter is invited for the night, takes the drug himself, or pretends to take it, praises it, describes how the use of it has grown in the West End and amongst the clubs, and then conveniently leaves the drug behind, and no doubt supplies it as it is required.

Sylvia began to dilate upon its ill-effects, and suddenly broke off. A great disgust was within her and stopped her speech. She got to her feet. "Let us go home," she said, and she went very quickly down the hill. When she came to the house she ran up-stairs to her room, locked the door and flung herself upon her bed. Walter Hine, her father, their plots and intrigues, were swept clean from her mind as of no account. Her struggle for the mastery became unimportant in her thoughts--a folly, a waste. For what her father had said was true; she cared for Chayne. And what she herself had said to Chayne when first he came to the House of the Running Water was no less true. "If I loved, I think nothing else would count at all except that I loved."

She had judged herself aright. She knew that, as she lay prone upon her bed, plunged in misery, while the birds called upon the boughs in the garden and the mill stream filled the room with its leaping music. In a few minutes a servant knocked upon the door and told her that tea was ready in the library; but she returned no answer. And in a few minutes more--or so it seemed, but meanwhile the dusk had come--there came another knock and she was told that dinner had been served. But to that message again she returned no answer. The noises of the busy day ceased in the fields, the birds were hushed upon the branches, quiet and darkness took and refreshed the world. Only the throbbing music of the stream beat upon the ears, and beat with a louder significance, since all else was still. Sylvia lay staring wide-eyed into the darkness. To the murmur of this music, in perhaps this very room, she had been born. "Why," she asked piteously, "why?" Of what use was it that she must suffer?

Of all the bad hours of her life, these were the worst. For the yearning for happiness and love throbbed and cried at her heart, louder and louder, just as the music of the stream swelled to importance with the coming of the night. And she learned that she had had both love and happiness within her grasp and that she had thrown them away for a shadow. She thought of the letter which she had written, recalling its phrases with a sinking heart.

"No man could forgive them. I must have been mad," she said, and she huddled herself upon her bed and wept aloud.

She ran over in her mind the conversations which she and Hilary Chayne had exchanged, and each recollection accused her of impatience and paid a tribute to his gentleness. On the very first day he had asked her to go with him and her heart cried out now:

"Why didn't I go?"

He had been faithful and loyal ever since, and she had called his faithfulness importunity and his loyalty a humiliation. She struck a match and looked at her watch and by habit wound it up. And she drearily wondered on how many, many nights she would have to wind it up and speculate in ignorance what he, her lover, was doing and in what corner of the world, before the end of her days was reached. What would become of her? she asked. And she raised the corner of a curtain and glanced at the bright picture of what might have been. And glancing at it, the demand for happiness raised her in revolt.

She lit her candle and wrote another letter, of the shortest. It contained but these few words:

"Oh, please forgive me! Come back and forgive. Oh, you must!--SYLVIA."

And having written them, Sylvia stole quietly down-stairs, let herself out at the door and posted them.

Two nights afterward she leaned out of her window at midnight, wondering whether by the morrow's post she would receive an answer to her message. And while she wondered she understood that the answer would not come that way. For suddenly in the moonlit road beneath her, she saw standing the one who was to send it. Chayne had brought his answer himself. For a moment she distrusted her own eyes, believing that her thoughts had raised this phantom to delude her. But the figure in the road moved beneath her window and she heard his voice call to her:

"Sylvia! Sylvia!"

CHAPTER XIX
THE SHADOW IN THE ROOM

Sylvia raised her hand suddenly, enjoining silence, and turned back into the room. She had heard a door slam violently within the house; and now from the hall voices rose. Her father and Walter Hine were coming up early to-night from the library, and it seemed in anger. At all events Walter Hine was angry. His voice rang up the stairway shrill and violent.

"Why do you keep it from me? I will have it, I tell you. I am not a child," and an oath or two garnished the sentences.

Sylvia heard her father reply with the patronage which never failed to sting the vanity of his companion, which was the surest means to provoke a quarrel, if a quarrel he desired.

"Go to bed, Wallie! Leave such things to Archie Parminter! You are too young."

His voice was friendly, but a little louder than he generally used, so that Sylvia clearly distinguished every word; so clearly indeed, that had he wished her to hear, thus he would have spoken. She heard the two men mount the stairs, Hine still protesting with the violence which had grown on him of late; Garratt Skinner seeking apparently to calm him, and apparently oblivious that every word he spoke inflamed Walter Hine the more. She had a fear there would be blows--blows struck, of course, by Hine. She knew the reason of the quarrel. Her father was depriving Hine of his drug. They passed up-stairs, however, and on the landing above she heard their doors close. Then coming back to the window she made a sign to Chayne, slipped a cloak about her shoulders and stole quietly down the dark stairs to the door. She unlocked the door gently and went out to her lover. Upon the threshold she hesitated, chilled by a fear as to how he would greet her. But he turned to her and in the moonlight she saw his face and read it. There was no anger there. She ran toward him.

"Oh, my dear," she cried, in a low, trembling voice, and his arms enclosed her. As she felt them hold her to him, and knew indeed that it was he, her lover, whose lips bent down to hers, there broke from her a long sigh of such relief and such great uplifting happiness as comes but seldom, perhaps no more than once, in the life of any man or woman. Her voice sank to a whisper, and yet was very clear and, to the man who heard it, sweet as never music was.

"Oh, my dear, my dear! You have come then?" and she stroked his face, and her hands clung about his neck to make very sure.

"Were you afraid that I wouldn't come, Sylvia?" he asked, with a low, quiet laugh.

She lifted her face into the moonlight, so that he saw at once the tears bright in her eyes and the smile trembling upon her lips.

"No," she said, "I rather thought that you would come," and she laughed as she spoke. Or did she sob? He could hardly tell, so near she was to both. "Oh, but I could not be sure! I wrote with so much unkindness," and her eyes dropped from his in shame.

"Hush!" he said, and he held her close.

"Have you forgiven me? Oh, please forgive me!"

"Long since," said he.

But Sylvia was not reassured.

"Ah, but you won't forget," she said, ruefully. "One can forgive, but one can't forget what one forgives," and then since, even in her remorse, hope was uppermost with her that night, she cried, "Oh, Hilary, do you think you ever will forget what I wrote to you?"

And again Chayne laughed quietly at her fears.

"What does it matter what you wrote a week ago, since to-night we are here, you and I--together, in the moonlight, for all the world to see that we are lovers."

She drew him quickly aside into the shadow of the wall.

"Are you afraid we should be seen?" he asked.

"No, but afraid we may be interrupted," she replied, with a clear trill of laughter which showed to her lover that her fears had passed.

"The whole village is asleep, Sylvia," he said in a whisper; and as he spoke a blind was lifted in an upper story of the house, a window was flung wide, and the light streamed out from it into the moonlit air and spread over their heads like a great, yellow fan. Walter Hine leaned his elbows on the sill and looked out.

Sylvia moved deeper into the shadow.

"He cannot see us," said Chayne, with a smile, and he set his arm about her waist; and so they stood very quietly.

The house was built a few yards back from the road, and on each side of it the high wall of the garden curved in toward it, making thus an open graveled space in front of its windows. Sylvia and her lover stood at one of the corners where the wall curved in; the shadow reached out beyond their feet and lay upon the white road in a black triangle; they could hardly be seen from any window of the house, and certainly they could not be recognized. But on the other hand they could see. From behind Walter Hine the light streamed out clear. The ceiling of the room was visible and the shadow of the lamp upon it, and even the top part of the door in the far corner.

"We will wait until he turns back into the room," Sylvia whispered; and for a little while they stood and watched. Then she felt Chayne's arm tighten about her and hold her still.

"Do you see?" he cried, in a low, quick voice. "Sylvia, do you see?"

"What?"

"The door. Look! Behind him! The door!" And Sylvia, looking as he bade her, started, and barely stifled the cry which rose to her lips. For behind Walter Hine, the door in the far corner of the room was opening--very slowly, very stealthily, as though the hand which opened it feared to be detected. So noiselessly had the latch been loosed that Walter Hine did not so much as turn his head. Nor did he turn it now. He heard nothing. He leaned from the window with his elbows on the sill, and behind him the gap between the door and the wall grew wider and wider. The door opened into the room and toward the window, so that the two people in the shadow below could see nothing of the intruder. But the secrecy of his coming had something sinister and most alarming. Sylvia joined her hands above her lover's arm, holding her breath.

"Shout to him!" she whispered. "Cry out that there's danger."

"Not yet!" said Chayne, with his eyes fixed upon the lighted room; and then, in spite of herself, a low and startled cry broke from Sylvia's lips. A great shadow had been suddenly flung upon the ceiling of the room, the shadow of a man, bloated and made monstrous by the light. The intruder had entered the room; and with so much stealth that his presence was only noticed by the two who watched in the road below. But even they could not see who the intruder was, they only saw the shadow on the ceiling.

Walter Hine, however, heard Sylvia's cry, faint though it was. He leaned forward from the window and peered down.

"Now!" said Sylvia. "Now!"

But Chayne did not answer. He was watching with an extraordinary suspense. He seemed not to hear. And on the ceiling the shadow moved, and changed its shape, now dwindling, now growing larger again, now disappearing altogether as though the intruder stooped below the level of the lamp; and once there was flung on the white plaster the huge image of an arm which had something in its hand. Was the arm poised above the lamp, on the point of smashing it with the thing it held? Chayne waited, with a cry upon his lips, expecting each moment that the room would be plunged in darkness. But the cry was not uttered, the arm was withdrawn. It had not been raised to smash the lamp, the thing which the hand held was for some other purpose. And once more the shadow appeared moving and changing as the intruder crept nearer to the window. Sylvia stood motionless. She had thought to cry out, now she was fascinated. A spell of terror constrained her to silence. And then, suddenly, behind Walter Hine there stood out clearly in the light the head and shoulders of Garratt Skinner.

"My father," said Sylvia, in relief. Her clasp upon Chayne's arm relaxed; her terror passed from her. In the revulsion of her feelings she laughed quietly at her past fear. Chayne looked quickly and curiously at her. Then as quickly he looked again to the window. Both men in the room were now lit up by the yellow light; their attitudes, their figures were very clear but small, like marionettes upon the stage of some tiny theater. Chayne watched them with no less suspense now that he knew who the intruder was. Unlike Sylvia he had betrayed no surprise when he had seen Garratt Skinner's head and shoulders rise into view behind Walter Hine; and unlike Sylvia, he did not relax his vigilance. Suddenly Garratt Skinner stepped forward, very quickly, very silently. With one step he was close behind his friend; and then just as he was about to move again--it seemed to Sylvia that he was raising his arm, perhaps to touch his friend upon the shoulder--Chayne whistled--whistled sharply, shrilly and with a kind of urgency which Sylvia did not understand.

Walter Hine leaned forward out of the window. That was quite natural. But on the other hand Garratt Skinner did nothing of the kind. To Sylvia's surprise he stepped back, and almost out of sight. Very likely he thought that he was out of sight. But to the watchers in the road his head was just visible. He was peering over Walter Hine's shoulder.

Again Chayne whistled and, not content with whistling, he cried out in a feigned bucolic accent:

"I see you."

At once Garratt Skinner's head disappeared altogether.

Walter Hine peered down into the darkness whence the whistle came, curving his hands above his forehead to shut out the light behind him; and behind him once more the shadow appeared upon the ceiling and the wall. A third time Chayne whistled; and Walter Hine cried out:

"What is it?"

And behind him the shadow vanished from the ceiling and the door began to close, softly and stealthily, just as softly and stealthily as it had been opened.

Again, Hine cried out:

"Who's there? What is it?"

And Chayne laughed aloud derisively, as though he were some yokel practising a joke. Hine turned back into the room. The room was empty, but the door was unlatched. He disappeared from the window, and the watchers below saw the door slammed to, heard the sound of the slamming and then another sound, the sound of a key turning in the lock.

It seemed almost that Chayne had been listening for that sound. For he turned at once to Sylvia.

"We puzzled them fairly, didn't we?" he said, with a smile. But the smile somehow seemed hardly real, and his face was very white.

"It's the moonlight," he explained. "Come!"

They walked quietly through the silent village where the thick eaves of the cottages threw their black shadows on the white moonlit road, past the mill and the running water, to a gate which opened on the down. They unlatched the gate noiselessly and climbed the bare slope of grass. Half way up Chayne turned and looked down upon the house. There was no longer any light in any window. He turned to Sylvia and slipped his arm through hers.

"Come close," said he, and now there was no doubt the smile was real. "Shall we keep step, do you think?"

"If we go always like this, we might," said Sylvia, with a smile.

"At times there will be a step to be cut, no doubt," said he.

"You once said that I could stand firm while the step was being cut," she answered. Always at the back of both their minds, evident from time to time in some such phrase as this, was the thought of the mountain upon which their friendship had been sealed. Friendship had become love here in the quiet Dorsetshire village, but in both their thoughts it had another background--ice-slope and rock-spire and the bright sun over all.

CHAPTER XX
ON THE DOWN

Sylvia led the way to a little hollow just beneath the ridge of the downs, a sheltered spot open to the sea. On the three other sides bushes grew about it and dry branches and leaves deeply carpeted the floor. Here they rested and were silent. Upon Sylvia's troubled heart there had fallen a mantle of deep peace. The strife, the fears, the torturing questions had become dim like the small griefs of childhood. Even the incident of the lighted window vexed her not at all.

"Hilary," she said softly, lingering on the name, since to frame it and utter it and hear her lips speaking it greatly pleased her, "Hilary," and her hand sought his, and finding it she was content.

It was a warm night of August. Overhead the moon sailed in a cloudless summer sky, drowning the stars. To the right, far below, the lamps of Weymouth curved about the shore; and in front the great bay shimmered like a jewel. Seven miles across it the massive bluff of Portland pushed into the sea; and even those rugged cliffs were subdued to the beauty of the night. Beneath them the riding-lights shone steady upon the masts of the battle ships. Sylvia looked out upon the scene with an overflowing heart. Often she had gazed on it before, and she marveled now how quickly she had turned aside. Her eyes were now susceptible to beauty as they had never been. There was a glory upon land and sea, a throbbing tenderness in the warm air of which she had not known till now. It seemed to her that she had lived until this night in a prison. Once the doors had been set ajar for a little while--just for a night and a day in the quiet of the High Alps. But only now had they been opened wide. Only to-night had she passed through and looked forth with an unhindered vision upon the world; and she discovered it to be a place of wonders and sweet magic.

"They were true, then," she said, with a smile on her lips.

"Of what do you speak?" asked Chayne.

"My dreams," Sylvia answered, knowing that she was justified of them. "For I have come awake into the land of my dreams, and I know it at last to be a real land, even to the sound of running water."

For from the hollow at her feet the music of the mill stream rose to her ears through the still night, very clear and with a murmur of laughter. Sylvia looked down toward it. She saw it flashing like a riband of silver in the garden of the dark quiet house. There was no breath of wind in that garden, and all the great trees were still. She saw the intricate pattern of their boughs traced upon the lawn in black and silver.

"In that house I was born," she said softly, "to the noise of that stream. I am very glad to know that in that house, too, my great happiness has come to me."

Chayne leaned forward, and sitting side by side with Sylvia, gazed down upon it with rapture. Oh, wonderful house where Sylvia was born! How much the world owed to it!

"It was there!" he said with awe.

"Yes," replied Sylvia. She was not without a proper opinion of herself, and it seemed rather a wonderful house to her, too.

"Perhaps on some such night as this," he said, and at once took the words back. "No! You were born on a sunny morning of July and the blackbirds on the branches told the good news to the blackbirds on the lawn, and the stream took up the message and rippled it out to the ships upon the sea. There were no wrecks that day."

Sylvia turned to him, her face made tender by a smile, her dark eyes kind and bright.

"Hilary!" she whispered. "Oh, Hilary!"

"Sylvia!" he replied, mimicking her tone. And Sylvia laughed with the clear melodious note of happiness. All her old life was whirled away upon those notes of laughter. She leaned to her lover with a sigh of contentment, her hair softly touching his cheek; her eyes once more dropped to the still garden and the dark square house at the down's foot.

"There you asked me to marry you, to go away with you," she said, and she caught his hand and held it close against her breast.

"Yes, there I first asked you," he said, and some distress, forgotten in these first perfect moments, suddenly found voice. "Sylvia, why didn't you come with me then? Oh, my dear, if you only had!"

But Sylvia's happiness was as yet too fresh, too loud at her throbbing heart for her to mark the jarring note.

"I did not want to then," she replied lightly, and then tightening her clasp upon his hand. "But now I do. Oh, Hilary, I do!"

"If only you had wanted then!"

Though he spoke low, the anguish of his voice was past mistaking. Sylvia looked at him quickly and most anxiously; and as quickly she looked away.

"Oh, no," she whispered hurriedly.

Her happiness could not be so short-lived a thing. Her heart stood still at the thought. It could not be that she had set foot actually within the dreamland, to be forthwith cast out again. She thought of the last week, its aching lonely hours. She needed her lover at her side, longed for him with a great yearning, and would not let him go.

"I'll not listen, Hilary," she said stubbornly. "I will not hear! No"; and Chayne drew her close to his side.

"There is bad news, Sylvia."

The outcry died away upon her lips. The words crushed the rebellion in her heart, they were so familiar. It seemed to her that all her life bad news had been brought to her by every messenger. She shivered and was silent, looking straight out across the moonlit sea. Then in a small trembling voice, like a child's, she pleaded, still holding her face averted:

"Don't go away from me, Hilary! Oh, please! Don't go away from me now!"

Her voice, her words, went to Chayne's heart. He knew that pride and a certain reticence were her natural qualities. That she should throw aside the one, break through the other, proved to him indeed how very much she cared, how very much she needed him.

"Sylvia," he cried, "it will only be for a little while"; and again silence followed upon his words.

Since bad news was to be imparted, strength was needed to bear it; and habit had long since taught Sylvia that silence was the best nurse of strength. She did not turn her face toward her lover; but she drooped her head and clenched her hands tightly together upon her knees, nerving herself for the blow. The movement, slight though it was, stirred Chayne to pity and hurt him with an intolerable pain. It betrayed so unmistakably the long habit of suffering. She sat silent, motionless, with the dumb patience of a wounded animal.

"Oh, Sylvia, why did you not come with me on that first day?" he cried.

"Tell me your bad news, dear," she replied, gently.

"I cannot help it," he began in broken tones. "Sylvia, you will see that there is no escape, that I must go. An appointment was offered to me--by the War Office. It was offered to me, pressed on me, the day after I last came here, the day after we were together in the library. I did not know what to do. I did not accept it. But it seemed to me that each time I came to see you we became more and more estranged. I was given two days to make up my mind, and within the two days, my dear, your letter came, telling me you did not wish to see me any more."

"Oh, Hilary!" she whispered.

"I accepted the appointment at once. There were reasons why I welcomed it. It would take me abroad!"

"Abroad!" she cried.

"Yes, I welcomed that. To be near you and not to see you--to be near you and know that others were talking with you, any one, every one except me--to be near you and know that you were unhappy and in trouble, and that I could not even tell you how deeply I was sorry--I dreaded that, Sylvia. And yet I dreaded one thing more. Here, in England, at each turn of the street, I should think to come upon you suddenly. To pass you as a stranger, or almost as a stranger. No! I could not do it!"

"Oh, Hilary!" she whispered, and lifting his hand she laid it against her cheek.

"So for a week I was glad. But this morning I received your second letter, Sylvia. It came too late, my dear. There was no time to obtain a substitute."

Sylvia turned to him with a startled face.

"When do you go?"

"Very soon."

"When?"

The words had to be spoken.

"To-morrow morning. I catch the first train from Weymouth to Southampton. We sail from Southampton at noon."

Habit came again to her assistance. She turned away from him so that he might not see her face, and he went on:

"Had there been more time, I could have made arrangements. Some one else could have gone. As it is--" He broke off suddenly, and bending toward her cried: "Sylvia, say that I must go."

But she could not bring herself to that. She was minded to hold with both hands the good thing which had come to her this night. She shook her head. He sought to turn her face to his, but she looked stubbornly away.

"And when will you return?" she asked.

"In a few months, Sylvia."

"When?"

"In June." And she counted off the months upon her fingers.

"So after to-night," she said, in a low voice, "I shall not see you any more for all these months. The winter must pass, and the spring, too. Oh, Hilary!" and she turned to him with a quivering face and whispered piteously: "Don't go, my dear. Don't go!"

"Say that I must go!" he insisted, and she laughed with scorn. Then the laughter ceased and she said:

"There will be danger?"

"None," he cried.

"Yes--from sickness, and--" her voice broke in a sob--"I shall not be near."

"I will take great care, Sylvia. Be sure of that," he answered. "Now that I have you, I will take great care," and leaning toward her, as she sat with her hands clasped upon her knees, he touched her hair with his lips very tenderly.

"Oh, Hilary, what will I do? Till you come back to me! What will I do?"

"I have thought of it, Sylvia. I thought this. It might be better if, for these months--they will not pass quickly, my dear, either for you or me. They will be long slow months for both of us. That's the truth, my dear. But since they must be got through, I thought it might be better if you went back to your mother."

Sylvia shook her head.

"It would be better," he urged, with a look toward the house.

"I can't do that. Afterward, in a year's time--when we are together, I should like very much for us both to go to her. But my mother forbade it when I went away from Chamonix. I was not to come whining back to her, those were her words. We parted altogether that night."

She spoke with an extreme simplicity. There was neither an appeal for pity nor a hint of any bitterness in her voice. But the words moved Chayne all the more on that account. He would be leaving a very lonely, friendless girl to battle through the months of his absence by herself; and to battle with what? He was not sure. But he had not taken so lightly the shadow on the ceiling and the opening door.

"If only you had come with me on that first day," he cried.

"I will have to-night to look back upon, my dear," she said. "That will be something. Oh, if I had not asked you to come back! If you had gone away and said nothing! What would I have done then? As it is, I will know that you are thinking of me--" and suddenly she turned to him, and held him away from her in a spasm of fear while her eyes searched his face. But in a moment they melted and a smile made her lips beautiful. "Oh, yes, I can trust you," she said, and she nestled against him contentedly like a child.

For a little while they sat thus, and then her eyes sought the garden and the house at her feet. It seemed that the sinister plot was not, after all, to develop in that place of quiet and old peace without her for its witness. It seemed that she was to be kept by some fatality close-fettered to the task, the hopeless task, which she would now gladly have foregone. And she wondered whether, after all, she was in some way meant to watch the plot, perhaps, after all, to hinder it.

"Hilary," she said, "you remember that evening at the Chalet de Lognan?"

"Do I remember it?"

"You explained to me a law--that those who know must use their knowledge, if by using it they can save a soul, or save a life."

"Yes," he said, vaguely remembering that he had spoken in this strain.

"Well, I have been trying to obey that law. Do you understand? I want you to understand. For when I have been unkind, as I have been many times, it was, I think, because I was not obeying it with very much success. And I should like you to believe and know that. For when you are away, you will remember, in spite of yourself, the times when I was bitter."

Her words made clear to him many things which had perplexed him during these last weeks. Her friendship for Walter Hine became intelligible, and as though to leave him no shadow of doubt, she went on.

"You see, I knew the under side of things, and I seemed to see the opportunity to use the knowledge. So I tried to save"; and whether it was life or soul, or both, she did not say. She did not add that so far she had tried in vain; she did not mention the bottle of cocaine, or the dread which of late had so oppressed her. She was careful of her lover. Since he had to go, since he needs must be absent, she would spare him anxieties and dark thoughts which he could do nothing to dispel. But even so, he obtained a clearer insight into the distress which she had suffered in that house, and the bravery with which she had borne it.

"Sylvia," he said, "I had no thought, no wish, that what I said should stay with you."

"Yet it did," she answered, "and I was thankful. I am thankful even now. For though I would gladly give up all the struggle now, if I had you instead; since I have not you, I am thankful for the law. It was your voice which spoke it, it came from you. It will keep you near to me all through the black months until you come back. Oh, Hilary!" and the brave argument spoken to enhearten herself and him ended suddenly in a most wistful cry. Chayne caught her to him.

"Oh, Sylvia!" and he added: "The life is not yet saved!"

"Perhaps I am given to the summer," she answered, and then, with a whimsical change of humor, she laughed tenderly. "Oh, but I wish I wasn't. You will write? Letters will come from you."

"As often as possible, my dear. But they won't come often."

"Let them be long, then," she whispered, "very long," and she leaned her head against his shoulder.

"Lie close, my dear," said he. "Lie close!"

For a while longer they talked in low voices to one another, the words which lovers know and keep fragrant in their memories. The night, warm and clear, drew on toward morning, and the passage of the hours was unremarked. For both of them there was a glory upon the moonlit land and sea which made of it a new world. And into this new world both walked for the first time--walked in their youth and hand in hand. Each for the first time knew the double pride of loving and being loved. In spite of their troubles they were not to be pitied, and they knew it. The gray morning light flooded the sky and turned the moon into a pale white disk.

"Lie close, my dear," said he. "It is not time."

In the trees in the garden below the blackbirds began to bustle amongst the leaves, and all at once their clear, sweet music thrilled upward to the lovers in the hollow of the down.

"Lie close, my dear," he repeated.

They watched the sun leap into the heavens and flash down the Channel in golden light.

"The night has gone," said Chayne.

"Nothing can take it from us while we live," answered Sylvia, very softly. She raised herself from her couch of leaves.

Then from one of the cottages in the tiny village a blue coil of smoke rose into the air.

"It is time," said Chayne, and they rose and hand in hand walked down the slope of the hill to the house. Sylvia unlatched the door noiselessly and went in. Chayne stepped in after her; and in the silent hall they took farewell of one another.

"Good-by, my dear," she whispered, with the tears in her eyes and in her voice, and she clung to him a little and so let him go. She held the door ajar until the sound of his footsteps had died away--and after that. For she fancied that she heard them still, since, she so deeply wished to hear them. Then with a breaking heart she went up the stairs to her room.

CHAPTER XXI
CHAYNE COMES TO CONCLUSIONS

"Six weeks ago I said good-by to the French Commission on the borders of a great lake in Africa. A month ago I was still walking to the rail head through the tangle of a forest's undergrowth," said Chayne, and he looked about the little restaurant in King Street, St. James', as though to make sure that the words he spoke were true. The bright lights, the red benches against the walls, the women in their delicate gowns of lace, and the jingle of harness in the streets without, made their appeal to one who for the best part of a year had lived within the dark walls of a forest. June had come round again, and Sylvia sat at his side.

"You shall tell me how these months have gone with you while we dine," said he. "Your letters told me nothing of your troubles."

"I did not mean them to," replied Sylvia.

"I guessed that, my dear. It was like you. Yet I would rather have known."

Only a few hours before he had stood upon the deck of the Channel packet and had seen the bows swing westward of Dover Castle and head toward the pier. Would Sylvia be there, he had wondered, as he watched the cluster of atoms on the quay, and in a little while he had seen her, standing quite alone, at the very end of the breakwater that she might catch the first glimpse of her lover. Others had traveled with them in the carriage to London and there had been no opportunity of speech. All that he knew was that she had been alone now for some weeks in the little house in Hobart Place.

"One thing I see," he said. "You are not as troubled as you were. The look of fear--that has gone from your eyes. Sylvia, I am glad!"

"There, were times," she answered--and as she thought upon them, terror once more leapt into her face--"times when I feared more than ever, when I needed you very much. But they are past now, Hilary," and her hand dropped for a moment upon his, and her eyes brightened with a smile. As they dined she told the story of those months.

"We returned to London very suddenly after you had gone away," she began. "We were to have stayed through September. But my father said that business called him back, and I noticed that he was deeply troubled."

"When did you notice that?" asked Chayne, quickly. "When did you first notice it?"

Sylvia reflected for a moment.

"The day after you had gone."

"Are you sure?" asked Chayne, with a certain intensity.

"Quite."

Chayne nodded his head.

"I did not understand the reason of the hurry. And I was perplexed--and also a little alarmed. Everything which I did not understand frightened me in those days." She spoke as if "those days" and all their dark events belonged to some dim period of which no consequence could reach her now. "Our departure had almost the look of a flight."

"Yes," said Chayne. For his part he was not surprised at their flight. He had passed more than one wakeful night during the last few months arguing and arguing again whether or no he should have disclosed to Sylvia the meaning of that softly opening door and the shadow on the ceiling as he read it. He might have been wrong; if so, he would have added to Sylvia's burden of troubles yet another, and one more terrible than all the rest. He might have been right; and if so, he might have enabled Sylvia to avert a tragedy. Thus the argument had revolved in a circle and left him always in the same doubt. Now he understood that his explanation of the incident had been confirmed. The loud whistle from the darkness of the road, the yokel's cry, which had driven Garratt Skinner from the room, as noiselessly as he had entered it, had done more than that--they had driven him from the neighborhood altogether. Some one had seen him--had seen him standing just behind Walter Hine in the lighted room--and on the next day he had fled!

"I was right," he said, absently, "right to keep silent." For here was Sylvia at his side and the dreaded peril unfulfilled. "Well, you returned to London?" he added, hastily.

"Yes. There is something of which I did not tell you, that night when we were together on the downs. Walter Hine had begun to take cocaine."

Chayne started.

"Cocaine!" he cried.

"Yes. My father taught him to take it."

"Your father," said Chayne, slowly, trying to fit this new and astounding fact in with the rest. "But why?"

"I think I can tell you," said Sylvia. "My father knew quite well that he had me working against him, trying to rescue Walter Hine out of his hands. And I was beginning to get some power. He understood that, and destroyed it. I was no match for him. I thought that I knew something of the under side of life. But he knew more, ever so much more, and my knowledge was of no avail. He taught Walter Hine the craving for cocaine, and he satisfied the craving--there was his power. He provided the drug. I do not know--I might perhaps have fought against my father and won. But against my father and a drug I was helpless. My father obtained it in sufficient quantity, withheld it at times, gave it at other times, played with him, tantalized him, gratified him. You can understand there was only one possible result. Walter Hine became my father's slave, his dog. I no longer counted in his thoughts at all. I was nothing."

"Yes," said Chayne.

The device was subtle, diabolically subtle. But he wondered whether it was only to counterbalance and destroy Sylvia's influence that Garratt Skinner had introduced cocaine to Hine's notice; whether he had not had in view some other end, even still more sinister.

"I saw very little of Mr. Hine after our return to London," she continued. "He did not come often to the house, but when he did come, each time I saw that he had changed. He had grown nervous and violent of temper. Even before we left Dorsetshire the violence had become noticeable."

"Oh!" said Chayne, looking quickly at Sylvia. "Before you left Dorsetshire?"

"Yes; and my father seemed to me to provoke it, though I could not guess why. For instance--"

"Yes?" said Chayne. "Tell me!"

He spoke quietly enough, but once again there was audible a certain intensity in his voice. There had been an occasion when Sylvia had given to him more news of Garratt Skinner than she had herself. Was she to do so once more? He leaned forward with his eyes on hers.

"The night when you came back to me. Do you remember, Hilary?" and a smile lightened his face.

"I shall forget no moment of that night, sweetheart, while I live," he whispered; and blushes swept prettily over her face, and in a sweet confusion she smiled back at him.

"Oh, Hilary!" she said.

"Oh, Sylvia!" he mimicked; and as they laughed together, it seemed there was a danger that the story of the months of separation would never be completed. But Chayne brought her back to it.

"Well? On that night when I came back?"

"I saw you in the road from my window, and then motioning you to be silent, I disappeared from the window."

"Yes, I remember," said Chayne, eagerly. He began to think that the cocaine was after all going to fit in with the incidents of that night.

"Walter Hine and my father were going up to bed. I heard them on the stairs. They were going earlier than usual."

"You are sure?" interrupted Chayne. "Think well!"

"Much earlier than usual, and they were quarreling. At least, Walter Hine was quarreling; and my father was speaking to him as if he were a child. That hurt his vanity and made him worse."

"Your father was provoking him?"

Sylvia's forehead puckered.

"I could not say that, and be sure of it. But I can say this. If my father had wished to provoke him to a greater anger, it's in that way that he would have done it."

"Yes. I see."

"They were speaking loudly--even my father was--more loudly than usual--especially at that time. For when they went up-stairs, they usually went very quietly"; and again Chayne interrupted her.

"Your father might have wanted you to hear the quarrel?" he suggested.

Sylvia turned to him curiously.

"Why should he wish that?" she asked, and considered the point. "He might have. Only, on the other hand, they were earlier than usual. They would not be so careful to go quietly; I was likely to be still awake."

"Exactly," said Chayne.

For in the probability that Sylvia would be still awake, would hear the violent words of Hine, and would therefore be an available witness afterward, Chayne found the reason both of the loudness of Garratt Skinner's tones and his early retirement for the night.

"Did you hear what was said? Can you repeat the words?" he asked.

"Yes. My father was keeping something from Mr. Hine which he wanted. I have no doubt it was the cocaine," and she repeated the words.

"Yes," said Chayne. "Yes," in the tone of one who is satisfied. The incident of the lighted room and the shadow on the ceiling were clear to him now. A quarrel of which there was a witness, a quarrel all to the credit of Garratt Skinner since it arose from his determination to hinder Walter Hine from poisoning himself with drugs--at least, that is how the evidence would work out; the quarrel continued in Walter Hine's bedroom, whither Garratt Skinner had accompanied his visitor, a struggle begun for the possession of the drug, begun by a man half crazy for want of it, a blow in self-defence delivered by Garratt Skinner, perhaps a fall from the window--that is how Chayne read the story of that night, as fashioned by the ingenuity of Garratt Skinner.

But on one point he was still perplexed. The story had not been told out to its end that night: there had come an unexpected shout, which had interrupted it, and indeed forever had prevented its completion on that spot. But why had it not been completed afterward, during the next few months, somewhere else? It had not been completed. For here was Sylvia with all her fears allayed, continuing the story of those months.

"But violence was not the only change in Walter Hine. There were some physical alterations which frightened me. Mr. Hine, as I say, came very seldom to our house, though my father saw a great deal of him. Otherwise I should have noticed them before. But early this year he came and--you remember he was fair--well, his skin had grown dark, quite dark, his complexion had changed altogether. And there was something else which shocked me. His tongue was black, really black. I asked him what was the matter? He grew restless and angry and lied to me, and then he broke down and told me he could not sleep. He slept for a few minutes only at a time. He really was ill--very ill."

Was this the explanation, Chayne asked himself? Having failed at the quick process, the process of the lighted room and the open window, had Garratt Skinner left the drug to do its work slowly and surely?

"He was so weak, so broken in appearance, that I was alarmed. My father was not in the house. I sent for a cab and I took Mr. Hine myself to a doctor. The doctor knew at once what was amiss. For a time Mr. Hine said 'No,' but he gave in at the last. He was in the habit of taking thirty grains of cocaine a day."

"Thirty grains!" exclaimed Chayne.

"Yes. Of course it could not go on. Death or insanity would surely follow. He was warned of it, and for a while he went into a home. Then he got better, and he determined to go abroad and travel."

"Who suggested that?" asked Chayne.

"I do not know. I know only that he refused to go without my father, and that my father consented to accompany him."

Chayne was startled.

"They are away together now?" he cried. A look of horror in his eyes betrayed his fear. He stared at Sylvia. Had she no suspicion--she who knew something of the under side of life? But she quietly returned his look.

"I took precautions. I told my father what I knew--not merely that Mr. Hine had acquired the habit of taking cocaine, but who had taught him the habit. Yes, I did that," she said simply, answering his look of astonishment. "It was difficult, my dear, and I would very much have liked to have had you there to help me through with it. But since you were not there, since I was alone, I did it alone. I thought of you, Hilary, while I was saying what I had to say. I tried to hear your voice speaking again outside the Chalet de Lognan. 'What you know, that you must do.' I warned my father that if any harm came to Walter Hine from taking the drug again, any harm at all which I traced to my father, I would not keep silent."

Chayne leaned back in his seat.

"You said that--to Garratt Skinner, Sylvia!" and the warmth of pride and admiration in his voice brought the color to her cheeks and compensated her for that bad hour. "You stood up alone and braved him out! My dear, if I had only been there! And you never wrote to me a word of it!"

"It would only have troubled you," she answered. "It would not have helped me to know that you were troubled!"

"And he--your father?" he asked. "How did he receive it?"

Sylvia's face grew pale, and she stared at the table-cloth as though she could not for the moment trust her voice. Then she shuddered and said in a low and shaking voice--so vivid was still the memory of that hour:

"I thought that I should never see you again."

She said no more. From those few words, and from the manner in which she uttered them, Chayne had to build up the terrible scene which had taken place between Sylvia and her father in the little back room of the house in Hobart Place. He looked round the lighted room, listened to the ripple of light voices, and watched the play of lively faces and bright eyes. There was an incongruity between these surroundings and the words which he had heard which shocked him.

"My dear, I'll make it up to you," he said. "Trust me, I will! There shall be good hours, now. I'll watch you, till I know surely without a word from you what you are thinking and feeling and wanting. Trust me, dearest!"

"With all my heart and the rest of my life," she answered, a smile responding to his words, and she resumed her story:

"I extracted from my father a promise that every week he should write to me and tell me how Mr. Hine was and where they both were. And to that--at last--he consented. They have been away together for two months, and every week I have heard. So I think there is no danger."

Chayne did not disagree. But, on the other hand, he did not assent.

"I suppose Mr. Hine is very rich?" he said, doubtfully.

"No," replied Sylvia. "That's another reason why--I am not afraid." She chose the words rather carefully, unwilling to express a deliberate charge against her father. "I used to think that he was--in the beginning when Captain Barstow won so much from him. But when the bets ceased and no more cards were played--I used to puzzle over why they ceased last year. But I think I have hit upon the explanation. My father discovered then what I only found out a few weeks ago. I wrote to Mr. Hine's grandfather, telling him that his grandson was ill, and asking him whether he would not send for him. I thought that would be the best plan."

"Yes, well?"

"Well, the grandfather answered me very shortly that he did not know his grandson, that he did not wish to know him, and that they had nothing to do with one another in any way. It was a churlish letter. He seemed to think that I wanted to marry Mr. Hine," and she laughed as she spoke, "and that I was trying to find out what we should have to live upon. I suppose that it was natural he should think so. And I am so glad that I wrote. For he told me that although Mr. Hine must eventually have a fortune, it would not be until he himself died and that he was a very healthy man. So you see, there could be no advantage to any one--" and she did not finish the sentence.

But Chayne could finish it for himself. There could be no advantage to any one if Walter Hine died. But then why the cocaine? Why the incident of the lighted window?

"Yes," he said, in perplexity, "I can corroborate that. It happened that my friend

John Lattery, who was killed in Switzerland, was also connected with Joseph Hine. He also would have inherited; and I knew from him that the old man did not recognize his heirs. But--but Walter Hine had money--some money, at all events. And he earned none. From whom did he get it?"

Sylvia shook her head.

"I do not know."

"Had he no other relations, no friends?"

"None who would have made him an allowance."

Chayne pondered over that question. For in the answer to it he was convinced he would find the explanation of the mystery. If money was given to Walter Hine, who had apparently no rich relations but his grandfather, and certainly no rich friends, it would have been given with some object. To discover the giver and his object--that was the problem.

"Think! Did he never speak of any one?"

Sylvia searched her memories.

"No," she said. "He never spoke of his private affairs. He always led us to understand that he drew an allowance from his grandfather."

"But your father found that that was untrue when you were in Dorsetshire, ten months ago. For the card-playing and the bets ceased."

"Yes," Sylvia agreed thoughtfully. Then her face brightened. "I remember a morning when Mr. Hine was in trouble. Wait a moment! He had a letter. We were at breakfast and the letter came from Captain Barstow. There was some phrase in the letter which Mr. Hine repeated. 'As between gentlemen'--that was it! I remember thinking at the time what in the world Captain Barstow could know about gentlemen; and wondering why the phrase should trouble Mr. Hine. And that morning Mr. Hine went to London."

"Oh, did he?" cried Chayne. "'As between gentlemen.' Had Hine been losing money lately to Captain Barstow?"

"Yes, on the day when you first came."

"The starlings," exclaimed Chayne in some excitement. "That's it--Walter Hine owes money to Captain Barstow which he can't pay. Barstow writes for it--a debt of honor between gentlemen--one can imagine the letter. Hine goes up to London. Well, what then?"

Sylvia started.

"My father went to London two days afterward."

"Are you sure?"

It seemed to Chayne that they were getting hot in their search.

"Quite sure. For I remember that after his return his manner changed. What I thought to be the new plot was begun. The cards disappeared, the bets ceased, Mr. Parminter was brought down with the cocaine. I remember it all clearly. For I always associated the change with my father's journey to London. You came one evening--do you remember? You found me alone and afraid. My father and Walter Hine were walking arm-in-arm in the garden. That was afterward."

"Yes, you were afraid because there was no sincerity in that friendship. Now let me get this right!"

He remained silent for a little while, placing the events in their due order and interpreting them, one by the other.

"This is what I make of it," he said at length. "The man in London who supplies Walter Hine with money finds that Walter Hine is spending too much. He therefore puts himself into communication with Garratt Skinner, of whom he has doubtless heard from Walter Hine. Garratt Skinner travels to London, has an interview, and a concerted plan of action is agreed upon, which Garratt Skinner proceeds to put in action."

He spoke so gravely that Sylvia turned anxiously toward him.

"What do you infer, then?" she asked.

"That we are in very deep and troubled waters, my dear," he replied, but he would not be more explicit. He had no doubt in his mind that the murder of Walter Hine had been deliberately agreed upon by Garratt Skinner and the unknown man in London. But just as Sylvia had spared him during his months of absence, so now he was minded to spare Sylvia. Only, in order that he might spare her, in order that he might prevent shame and distress greater than she had known, he must needs go on with his questioning. He must discover, if by any means he could, the identity of the unknown man who was so concerned in the destiny of Walter Hine.

"Of your father's friends, was there one who was rich? Who came to the house? Who were his companions?"

"Very few people came to the house. There was no one amongst them who fits in"; and upon that she started. "I wonder--" she said, thoughtfully, and she turned to her lover. "After my father had gone away, I found a telegram in a drawer in one of the rooms. There was no envelope, there was just the telegram. So I opened it. It was addressed to my father. I remember the words, for I did not know whether there was not something which needed attention. It ran like this: 'What are you waiting for? Hurry up.'"

"Was it signed?" asked Chayne.

"Yes. 'Jarvice,'" replied Sylvia.

"Jarvice," Chayne repeated; and he spoke it yet again, as though in some vague way it was familiar to him. "What was the date of the telegram?"

"It had been sent a month before I found it. So I put it back into the drawer."

"'What are you waiting for? Hurry up. Jarvice,'" said Chayne, slowly, and then he remembered how and when he had come across the name of Jarvice before. His face grew very grave.

"We are in deep waters, my dear," he said.

There had been trouble in his regiment, some years before, in which the chief figures had been a subaltern and a money-lender. Jarvice was the name of the money-lender--an unusual name. Just such a man would be likely to be Garratt Skinner's confederate and backer. Chayne ran over the story in his mind again, by this new light. It certainly strengthened the argument that the Mr. Jarvice who sent the telegram was Mr. Jarvice, the money-lender. Thus did Chayne work it out in his thoughts:

"Jarvice, for some reason unknown, pays Walter Hine an allowance. Walter Hine gives it out that he receives it from his grandfather, whose heir he undoubtedly is, and being a vain person much exaggerates the amount. He falls into Garratt Skinner's hands, who, with the help of Barstow and others, proceeds to pluck him. Walter Hine loses more than he has and applies to Jarvice for more. Jarvice elicits the facts, and instead of disclosing who Garratt Skinner is, and the obvious swindle of which Hine is the victim, takes Garratt Skinner into his confidence. What happened at the interview between Mr. Jarvice and Garratt Skinner in London the subsequent facts make plain. At Jarvice's instigation the plot to swindle Walter Hine becomes a cold-blooded plan to murder him. That plan has been twice frustrated, once by me in Dorsetshire, and a second time by Sylvia."

So far the story worked out naturally, logically. But there remained two questions. For what reason did Mr. Jarvice make Walter Hine an allowance? And how would Walter Hine's death profit him? Chayne pondered over those two questions and then the truth flashed upon him. He remembered how the subaltern had been extracted from his difficulties. Money had been raised by a life insurance. Again Chayne ranged his facts in order.

"Walter Hine is the heir to great wealth. But he has no money now. Mr. Jarvice makes him an allowance, the money to be repaid with a handsome interest on the grandfather's death. But in order to insure Jarvice from loss, if Walter Hine should die first, Walter Hine's life is insured for a large sum. Thus Mr. Jarvice makes his position tenable should his conduct be called in question. Having insured Walter Hine's life, he arranges with Garratt Skinner to murder him. The attempt failed the first time, the slower method is then adopted by Garratt Skinner, and as a result comes the impatient telegram: 'What are you waiting for? Hurry up!'"

The case was thus so far clear. But anxiety remained. Was the plan abandoned altogether, now that Sylvia had stood bravely up and warned her father that she would not keep silent? So certainly Sylvia thought. But then she did not know all that Chayne knew. It seemed that she had not understood the incident of the lighted window. Nor was Chayne surprised. For she was unaware of what was in Chayne's eyes the keystone of the whole argument. She did not know that her father had worked as a convict in the Portland quarries.

"So they are abroad together, your father and Walter Hine," said Chayne, slowly.

"Yes!" replied Sylvia, with a smile. "Guess where they are now!" and she turned to him with a tender look upon her face which he did not understand.

"I can't guess."

"At Chamonix!"

She saw her lover flinch, his face grow white, his eyes stare in horror. And she wondered. For her the little town, overtopped by its tumbled glittering fields of snow and tall rock spires was a place apart. She cherished it in her memories, keeping clear and distinct the windings of its streets, where they narrowed, where they broadened into open spaces; yet all the while her thoughts transformed it, and made of its mere stones and bricks a tiny city magical with light and grace. For while she stayed in it her happiness had dawned and she saw it always roseate with that dawn. It seemed to her that plots and thoughts of harm could there hardly outlive one starlit night, one sunlit day. Had she mapped out her father's itinerary, thither and nowhere else would she have sent him.

"You are afraid?" she asked. "Hilary, why?"

Chayne did not answer her question. He was minded to spare her, even as she had spared him. He talked of other things until the restaurant grew empty and the waiters began to turn out the lights as a hint to these two determined loiterers. Then in the darkness, for now there was but one light left, and that at a little distance from their table, Chayne leaned forward and turning to Sylvia, as they sat side by side:

"You have been happy to-night?"

"Very," she answered, and there was a thrill of joyousness in her clear, low voice, as though her heart sang within her. Her eyes rested on his with pride. "No man could quite understand," she said.

"Well then, why should we wait longer, Sylvia?" he said. "We have waited long enough, my dear. We have after all no one but ourselves to please. I should like our marriage to take place as soon as possible."

Sylvia answered him without affectation.

"I, too," she whispered.

"To-morrow then! I'll get a special license to-morrow morning, and make the arrangements. We can go away together at once."

Sylvia smiled, and the smile deepened into a laugh.

"Where shall we go, Hilary?" she cried. "To some perfect place."

"To Chamonix," he answered. "That was where we first met. There could be no better place. We can just go and tell your father what we have done and then go up into the hills."

It was well done. He spoke without wakening Sylvia's suspicions. She had never understood the episode of the lighted window; she did not know that her father was Gabriel Strood, of whose exploits in the Alps she had read; she believed that all danger to Walter Hine was past. Chayne on the other hand knew that hardly at any time could Hine have stood in greater peril. To Chamonix he must go; and to Chamonix he must take Sylvia too. For by the time when he could reach Chamonix, he might already be too late. There might be publicity, inquiries, and for Garratt Skinner ruin, and worse than ruin. Would Sylvia let her lover share the dishonor of her name? He knew very surely she would not. Therefore he would have the marriage.

"By the way," he said, as he draped her cloak about her shoulders. "You have that telegram from Jarvice?"

"Yes."

"That's good," he said. "It might be useful."

CHAPTER XXII
REVAILLOUD REVISITED

Never that familiar journey across France seemed to Chayne so slow. Would he be in time? Would he arrive too late? The throb of the wheels beat out the questions in a perpetual rhythm and gave him no answer. The words of Jarvice's telegram were ever present in his mind, and grew more sinister, the more he thought upon them. "What are you waiting for? Hurry up!" Once, when the train stopped over long as it seemed to him he muttered the words aloud and then glanced in alarm at his wife, lest perchance she had overheard them. But she had not. She was remembering her former journey along this very road. Then it had been night; now it was day. Then she had been used to seek respite from her life in the shelter of her dreams. Now the dreams were of no use, since what was real made them by comparison so pale and thin. The blood ran strong and joyous in her veins to-day; and looking at her, Chayne sent up his prayers that they might not arrive in Chamonix too late. To him as to her Walter Hine was a mere puppet, a thing without importance--so long as he lived. But he must live. Dead, he threatened ruin and dishonor, and since from the beginning Sylvia and he had shared--for so she would have it--had shared in the effort to save this life, it would be well for them, he thought that they should not fail.

The long hot day drew to an end, and at last from the platform at the end of the electric train they saw the snow-fields lift toward the soaring peaks, and the peaks purple with the after glow stand solitary and beautiful against the evening sky.

"At last!" said Sylvia, with a catch in her breath, and the clasp of her hand tightened upon her husband's arm. But Chayne was remembering certain words once spoken to him in a garden of Dorsetshire, by a man who lay idly in a hammock and stared up between the leaves. "On the most sunny day, the mountains hold in their recesses mystery and death."

"You know where your father is staying?" Chayne asked.

"He wrote from the Hotel de l'Arve," Sylvia replied.

"We will stay at Couttet's and walk over to see him this evening," said Chayne, and after dinner they strolled across the little town. But at the Hotel de l'Arve they found neither Garratt Skinner nor his friend, Walter Hine.

"Only the day before yesterday," said the proprietor, "they started for the mountains. Always they make expeditions."

Chayne drew no satisfaction from that statement. Garratt Skinner and his friend would make many expeditions from which both men would return in safety. Garratt Skinner was no blunderer. And when at the last he returned alone with some flawless story of an accident in which his friend had lost his life, no one would believe but that here was another mishap, and another name to be added to the Alpine death-roll.

"To what mountain have they gone?" Chayne asked.

"To no mountain to-day. They cross the Col du Geant, monsieur, to Courmayeur. But after that I do not know."

"Oh, into Italy," said Chayne, in relief. So far there was no danger. The Col du Geant, that great pass between France and Italy across the range of Mont Blanc, was almost a highway. There would be too many parties abroad amongst its ice seracs on these days of summer for any deed which needed solitude and secrecy.

"When do you expect them back?"

"In five days, monsieur; not before." And at this reply Chayne's fears were all renewed. For clearly the expedition was not to end with the passage of the Col du Geant. There was to be a sequel, perhaps some hazardous ascent, some expedition at all events which Garratt Skinner had not thought fit to name.

"They took guides, I suppose," he said.

"One guide, monsieur, and a porter. Monsieur need not fear. For Monsieur Skinner is of an excellence prodigious."

"My father!" exclaimed Sylvia, in surprise. "I never knew."

"What guide?" asked Chayne.

"Pierre Delouvain"; and so once again Chayne's fears were allayed. He turned to Sylvia.

"A good name, sweetheart. I never climbed with him, but I know him by report. A prudent man, as prudent as he is skilful. He would run no risks."

The name gave him indeed greater comfort than even his words expressed. Delouvain's mere presence would prevent the commission of any crime. His great strength would not be needed to hinder it. For he would be there, to bear witness afterward. Chayne was freed from the dread which during the last two days had oppressed him. Perhaps after all Sylvia was right and the plot was definitely abandoned. Chayne knew very well that Garratt Skinner's passion for the Alps was a deep and real one. Perhaps it was that alone which had brought him back to Chamonix. Perhaps one day in the train, traveling northward from Italy, he had looked from the window and seen the slopes of Monte Rosa white in the sun--white with the look of white velvet--and all the last twenty years had fallen from him like a cloak, and he had been drawn back as with chains to the high playground of his youth. Chayne could very well understand that possibility, and eased of his fears he walked away with Sylvia back to the open square in the middle of the town. Darkness had come, and both stopped with one accord and looked upward to the massive barrier of hills. The rock peaks stood sharply up against the clear, dark sky, the snow-slopes glimmered faintly like a pale mist, and incredibly far, incredibly high, underneath a bright and dancing star, shone a dim and rounded whiteness, the snow-cap of Mont Blanc.

"A year ago," said Sylvia, drawing a breath and bethinking her of the black shadows which during those twelve months had lain across her path.

"Yes, a year ago we were here," said Chayne. The little square was thronged, the hotels and houses were bright with lights, and from here and from there music floated out upon the air, the light and lilting melodies of the day. "Sylvia, you see the cafe down the street there by the bridge?"

"Yes."

"A year ago, on just such a night as this, I sat with my guide, Michel Revailloud. I was going to cross the Col Dolent on the morrow. He had made his last ascent.

We were not very cheerful. And he gave me as a parting present the one scrap of philosophy his life had taught him. He said: 'Take care that when the time comes for you to get old that you have some one to share your memories. Take care that when you go home in the end, there shall be some one waiting in the room and the lamp lit against your coming.'"

Sylvia pressed against her side the hand which he had slipped through her arm.

"But he did more than give advice," Chayne continued, "for as he went away to his home in the little village of Les Praz-Conduits, just across the fields, he passed Couttet's Hotel and saw you under the lamp talking to a guide he knew. You were making your arrangements to ascend the Charmoz. But he dissuaded you."

"Yes."

"He convinced you that your first mountain should be the Aiguille d'Argentiere. He gave you no doubt many reasons, but not the real one which he had in his thoughts."

Sylvia looked at Chayne in surprise.

"He sent you to the Aiguille d'Argentiere, because he knew that so you and I would meet at the Pavilion de Lognan."

"But he had never spoken to me until that night," exclaimed Sylvia.

"Yet he had noticed you. When I went up to fetch down my friend Lattery, you were standing on the hotel step. You said to me, 'I am sorry.' Michel heard you speak, and that evening talked of you. He had the thought that you and I were matched."

Sylvia looked back to the night before her first ascent. She pictured to herself the old guide coming down the narrow street and out of the darkness into the light of the lamp above the doorway. She recalled how he had stopped at the sight of her, how cunningly he had spoken. He had desired that her last step on to her first summit should bring to her eyes and soul a revelation which no length of after years could dim. That was the argument, and it was just the argument which would prevail with her.

"So it was his doing," she cried, with a laugh, and at once grew serious, dwelling, as lovers will, upon the small accident which had brought them together, and might so easily never have occurred. An unknown guide speaks to her in a doorway, and lo! for her the world is changed, dark years come to an end, the pathway broadens to a road; she walks not alone. Whatever the future may hold--she walks not alone. Suppose there had been no lamp above the doorway! Suppose there had been a lamp and she not there! Suppose the guide had passed five minutes sooner or five minutes later!

"Oh, Hilary!" she cried, and put the thought from her.

"I was thinking," he said, "that if you were not tired we might walk across the fields to Michel's house. He would, I think, be very happy if we did."

A few minutes later they knocked upon Michel's door. Michel Revailloud opened it himself and stood for a moment peering at the dim figures in the darkness of the road.

"It is I, Michel," said Chayne, and at the sound of his voice Michel Revailloud drew him with a cry of welcome into the house.

"So you have come back to Chamonix, monsieur! That is good"; and he looked his "monsieur" over from head to foot and shook him warmly by the hand. "Ah, you have come back!"

"And not alone, Michel," said Chayne.

Revailloud turned to the door and saw Sylvia standing there. She was on the threshold and the light reached to her. Sylvia moved into the low-roofed room. It was a big, long room, bare, and with a raftered ceiling, and since one oil lamp lighted it, it was full of shadows. To Chayne it had a lonely and a dreary look. He thought of his own house in Sussex and of the evening he had passed there, thinking it just as lonely. He felt perhaps at this moment, more than at any, the value of the great prize which he had won. He took her hand in his, and, turning to Michel, said simply:

"We are married, Michel. We reached Chamonix only this evening. You are the first of our friends to know of our marriage."

Michel's face lighted up. He looked from one to the other of his visitors and nodded his head once or twice. Then he blew his nose vigorously. "But I let you stand!" he cried, in a voice that shook a little, and he bustled about pushing chairs forward, and of a sudden stopped. He came forward to Sylvia very gravely and held out his hand. She put her hand into his great palm.

"Madame, I will not pretend to you that I am not greatly moved. This is a great happiness to me," he said with simplicity. He made no effort to hide either the tears which filled his eyes or the unsteadiness of his voice. "I am very glad for the sake of Monsieur Chayne. But I know him well. We have been good friends for many a year, madame."

"I know, Michel," she said.

"And I can say therefore with confidence I am very glad for your sake too. I am also very glad for mine. A minute ago I was sitting here alone--now you are both here and together. Madame, it was a kind thought which brought you both here to me at once."

"To whom else should we come?" said Sylvia with a smile, "since it was you, Michel, who would not let me ascend the Aiguille des Charmoz when I wanted to."

Michel was taken aback for a moment; then his wrinkled and weatherbeaten face grew yet more wrinkled and he broke into a low and very pleasant laugh.

"Since my diplomacy has been so successful, madame, I will not deny it. From the first moment when I heard you with your small and pretty voice say on the steps of the hotel 'I am sorry' to my patron in his great distress, and when I saw your face, too thoughtful for one so young, I thought it would be a fine thing if you and he could come together. In youth to be lonely--what is it? You slip on your hat and your cloak and you go out. But when you are old, and your habits are settled, and you do not want to go out at nights to search for company, then it is as well to have a companion. And it is well to choose your companion in your youth, madame, so that you may have many recollections to talk over together when the good of life is chiefly recollection."

He made his visitors sit down, fetched out a bottle of wine and offered them the hospitalities of his house, easily and naturally, like the true gentleman he was. It seemed to Chayne that he looked a little older, that he was a little more heavy in his gait, a little more troubled with his eyes than he had been last year. But at all events to-night he had the spirit, the good-humor of his youth. He talked of old exploits upon peaks then unclimbed, he brought out his guide's book, in which his messieurs had written down their names and the dates of the climbs, and the photographs which they had sent to him.

"There are many photographs of men grown famous, madame," he said, proud-

ly, "with whom I had the good fortune to climb when they and I and the Alps
were all young together. But it is not only the famous who are interesting. Look,
madame! Here is your husband's friend, Monsieur Lattery--a good climber but not
always very sure on ice."

"You always will say that, Michel," protested Chayne. "I never knew a man so
obstinate."

Michel Revailloud smiled and said to Sylvia:

"I knew he would spring out on me. Never say a word against Monsieur Lattery if you would keep friends with Monsieur Chayne. See, I give you good advice
in return for your kindness in visiting an old man. Nevertheless," and he dropped
his voice in a pretence of secrecy and nodded emphatically: "It is true. Monsieur
Lattery was not always sure on ice. And here, madame, is the portrait of one whose
name is no doubt known to you in London--Professor Kenyon."

Sylvia, who was turning over the leaves of the guide's little book, looked up at
the photograph.

"It was taken many years ago," she said.

"Twenty or twenty-five years ago," said Michel, with a shrug of the shoulders,
"when he and I and the Alps were young."

Chayne began quickly to look through the photographs outspread upon the
table. If Kenyon's portrait was amongst Revailloud's small treasures, there might
be another which he had no wish for his wife to see, the portrait of the man who
climbed with Kenyon, who was Kenyon's "John Lattery." There might well be the
group before the Monte Rosa Hotel in Zermatt which he himself had seen in Kenyon's rooms. Fortunately however, or so it seemed to him, Sylvia was engrossed in
Michel's little book.

CHAPTER XXIII
MICHEL REVAILLOUD'S FUEHRBUCH

The book indeed was of far more interest to her than the portrait of any mountaineer. It had a romance, a glamour of its own. It was just a little note-book with
blue-lined pages and an old dark-red soiled leather cover which could fit into the

breast pocket and never be noticed there. But it went back to the early days of mountaineering when even the passes were not all discovered and many of them were still uncrossed, when mythical peaks were still gravely allotted their positions and approximate heights in the maps; and when the easy expedition of the young lady of to-day was the difficult achievement of the explorer. It was to the early part of the book to which she turned. Here she found first ascents of which she had read with her heart in her mouth, ascents since made famous, simply recorded in the handwriting of the men who had accomplished them--the dates, the hours of starting and returning, a word or two perhaps about the condition of the snow, a warm tribute to Michel Revailloud and the signatures. The same names recurred year after year, and often the same hand recorded year after year attempts on one particular pinnacle, until at the last, perhaps after fifteen or sixteen failures, weather and snow and the determination of the climbers conspired together, and the top was reached.

"Those were the grand days," cried Sylvia. "Michel, you must be proud of this book."

"I value it very much, madame," he said, smiling at her enthusiasm. Michel was a human person; and to have a young girl with a lovely face looking at him out of her great eyes in admiration, and speaking almost in a voice of awe, was flattery of a soothing kind. "Yes, many have offered to buy it from me at a great price--Americans and others. But I would not part with it. It is me. And when I am inclined to grumble, as old people will, and to complain that my bones ache too sorely, I have only to turn over the pages of that book to understand that I have no excuse to grumble. For I have the proof there that my life has been very good to live. No, I would not part with that little book."

Sylvia turned over the pages slowly, naming now this mountain, now that, and putting a question from time to time as to some point in a climb which she remembered to have read and concerning which the narrative had not been clear. And then a cry of surprise burst from her lips.

Chayne had just assured himself that there was no portrait of Gabriel Strood amongst those spread out upon the table.

"What is it, madame?" asked Michel.

Sylvia did not answer, but stared in bewilderment at the open page. Chayne saw the book which she was reading and knew that his care lest she should come across her father's portrait was of no avail. He crossed round behind her chair and looked over her shoulder. There on the page in her father's handwriting was the signature: "Gabriel Strood."

Sylvia raised her face to Hilary's, and before she could put her question he answered it quietly with a nod of the head.

"Yes, that is so," he said.

"You knew?"

"I have known for a long time," he replied.

Sylvia was lost in wonder. Yet there was no doubt in her mind. Gabriel Strood, of whom she had made a hero, whose exploits she knew almost by heart, had suffered from a physical disability which might well have kept the most eager mountaineer to the level. It was because of his mastery over his disability that she had set him so high in her esteem. Well, there had been a day when her father had tramped across the downs to Dorchester and had come back lame and in spite of his lameness had left his companions behind. Other trifles recurred to her memory. She had found him reading "The Alps in 1864," and yes--he had tried to hide from her the title of the book. On their first meeting he had understood at once when she had spoken to him of the emotion which her first mountain peak had waked in her. And before that--yes, her guide had cried aloud to her, "You remind me of Gabriel Strood." She owed it to him that she had turned to the Alps as to her heritage, and that she had brought to them an instinctive knowledge. Her first feeling was one of sheer pride in her father. Then the doubts began to thicken. He called himself Garratt Skinner.

"Why? But why?" she cried, impulsively, and Chayne, still leaning on her chair, pressed her arm with his hand and warned her to be silent.

"I will tell you afterward," he said, quietly, and then he suddenly drew himself upright. The movement was abrupt like the movement of a man thoroughly startled--more startled even than she had been by the unexpected sight of her father's handwriting. She looked up into his face. He was staring at the open page of Michel's book. She turned back to it herself and saw nothing which should so trouble him. Over Gabriel Strood's signature there were just these words written in his hand and nothing more:

"Mont Blanc by the Brenva route. July, 1868."

Yet it was just that sentence which had so startled Hilary. Gabriel Strood **had** then climbed Mont Blanc from the Italian side--up from the glacier to the top of the great rock-buttress, then along the world-famous ice-arete, thin as a knife edge, and to right and left precipitous as a wall, and on the far side above the ice-ridge up the hanging glaciers and the ice-cliffs to the summit of the Corridor. From the Italian side of the range of Mont Blanc! And the day before yesterday Gabriel Strood had crossed with Walter Hine to Italy, bound upon some expedition which would take five days, five days at the least.

It was to the Brenva ascent of Mont Blanc that Garratt Skinner was leading Walter Hine! The thought flashed upon Chayne swift as an inspiration and as convincing. Chayne was sure. The Brenva route! It was to this climb Garratt Skinner's thoughts had perpetually recurred during that one summer afternoon in the garden in Dorsetshire, when he had forgotten his secrecy and spoken even with his enemy of the one passion they had in common. Chayne worked out the dates and they fitted in with his belief. Two days ago Garratt Skinner started to cross the Col du Geant. He would sleep very likely in the hut on the Col, and go down the next morning to Courmayeur and make his arrangements for the Brenva climb. On the third day, to-day, he would set out with Walter Hine and sleep at the gite on the rocks in the bay to the right of the great ice-fall of the Brenva glacier. To-morrow he would ascend the buttress, traverse the ice-ridge with Walter Hine--perhaps-- yes, only perhaps--and at that thought Chayne's heart stood still. And even if he did, there were the hanging ice-cliffs above, and yet another day would pass before any alarm at his absence would be felt. Surely, it would be the Brenva route!

Garratt Skinner himself would run great risk upon this hazardous expedition-- that was true. But Chayne knew enough of the man to be assured that he would not hesitate on that account. The very audacity of the exploit marked it out as Gabriel Strood's. Moreover, there would be no other party on the Brenva ridge to spy upon his actions. There was just one fact so far as Chayne could judge to discredit his inspiration--the inconvenient presence of a guide.

"Do you know a guide Delouvain, Michel?"

"Indeed, yes! A good name, monsieur, and borne by a man worthy of it."

"So I thought," said Chayne. "Pierre Delouvain," and Michel laughed scornfully and waved the name away.

"Pierre! No, indeed!" he cried. "Monsieur, never engage Pierre Delouvain for your guide. I speak solemnly. Joseph--yes, and whenever you can secure him. I thought you spoke of him. But Pierre, he is a cousin who lives upon Joseph's name, a worthless fellow, a drunkard. Monsieur, never trust yourself or any one whom you hold dear with Pierre Delouvain!"

Chayne's last doubt was dispelled. Garratt Skinner had laid his plans for the Brenva route. Somewhere on that long and difficult climb the accident was to take place. The very choice of a guide was in itself a confirmation of Chayne's fears. It was a piece of subtlety altogether in keeping with Garratt Skinner. He had taken a bad and untrustworthy guide on one of the most difficult expeditions in the range of Mont Blanc. Why, he would be asked? And the answer was ready. He had confused Pierre Delouvain with Joseph, his cousin, as no doubt many another man had done before. Did not Pierre live on that very confusion? The answer was not capable of refutation.

Chayne was in despair. Garratt Skinner had started two days before from Chamonix, was already, now, at this moment, asleep, with his unconscious victim at his side, high up on the rocks of the upper Brenva glacier. There was no way to hinder him--no way unless God helped. He asked abruptly of Michel:

"Have you climbed this season, Michel?"

Michel laughed grimly.

"Indeed, yes, to the Montanvert, monsieur. And beyond--yes, beyond, to the Jardin."

Chayne broke in upon his bitter humor.

"I want the best guide in Chamonix. I want him at once. I must start by daylight."

Michel glanced up in surprise. But what he saw in Chayne's face stopped all remonstrance.

"For what ascent, monsieur?" he asked.

"The Brenva route."

"Madame will not go!"

"No, I go alone. I must go quickly. There is very much at stake. I beg you to help me."

In answer Michel took his hat down from a peg, and while he did so Chayne turned quickly to his wife. She had risen from her chair, but she had not interrupted him, she had asked no questions, she had uttered no prayer. She stood now, waiting upon him with a quiet and beautiful confidence which deeply stirred his heart.

"Thank you, sweetheart!" he said, quietly. "You can trust. I thank you," and he added, gravely: "Whatever happens--you and I--there is no altering that."

Michel opened the door.

"I will walk with you into Chamonix, and I will bring the best guides I can find to your hotel."

They passed out, and crossed the fields quickly to Chamonix.

"Do you go to your hotel, monsieur," said Revailloud, "and leave the choice to me. I must go about it quietly. If you were to come with me, we should have to choose the first two guides upon the rota and that would not do for the Brenva climb."

He left them at the door of the hotel and went off upon his errand. Sylvia turned at once to Hilary; her face was very pale, her voice shook.

"You will tell me everything now. Something terrible has happened. No doubt you feared it. You came to Chamonix because you feared it, and now you know that it has happened."

"Yes," said Chayne. "I hid it from you even as you spared me your bad news all this last year."

"Tell me now, please. If it is to be 'you and I,' as you said just now, you will tell me."

Chayne led the way into the garden, and drawing a couple of chairs apart from the other visitors told her all that he knew and she did not. He explained the episode of the lighted window, solved for her the riddle of her father's friendship for Walter Hine, and showed her the reason for this expedition to the summit of Mont Blanc.

She uttered one low cry of horror. "Murder!" she whispered.

"To think that we are two days behind, that even now they are sleeping on the rocks, *he* and Walter Hine, sleeping quite peacefully and quietly. Oh, it's horrible!" he cried, beating his hands upon his forehead in despair, and then he broke off. He saw that Sylvia was sitting with her hands covering her face, while every now and then a shudder shook her and set her trembling.

"I am so sorry, Sylvia," he cried. "Oh, my dear, I had so hoped we should be in time. I would have spared you this knowledge if I could. Who knows? We may be still in time," and as he spoke Michel entered the garden with one other man and came toward him.

"Henri Simond!" said Michel, presenting his companion. "You will know that name. Simond has just come down from the Grepon, monsieur. He will start with you at daylight."

Chayne looked at Simond. He was of no more than the middle height, but broad of shoulder, deep of chest, and long of arm. His strength was well known in Chamonix--as well known as his audacity.

"I am very glad that you can come, Simond," said Chayne. "You are the very man;" and then he turned to Michel. "But we should have another guide. I need two men."

"Yes," said Michel. "Three men are needed for that climb," and Chayne left him to believe that it was merely for the climb that he needed another guide. "But there is Andre Droz already at Courmayeur," he continued. "His patron was to leave him there to-day. A telegram can be sent to him to-morrow bidding him wait. If he has started, we shall meet him to-morrow on the Col du Geant. And Droz, monsieur, is the man for you. He is quick, as quick as you and Simond. The three of you together will go well. As for to-morrow, you will need no one else. But if you do, monsieur, I will go with you."

"There is no need, Michel," replied Chayne, gratefully, and thereupon Sylvia plucked him by the sleeve.

"I must go with you to-morrow, Hilary," she pleaded, wistfully. "Oh, you won't leave me here. Let me come with you as far as possible. Let me cross to Italy. I will go quick. If I get tired, you shall not know."

"It will be a long day, Sylvia."

"It cannot be so long as the day I should pass waiting here."

She wrung her hands as she spoke. The light from a lamp fixed in the hotel wall fell upon her upturned face. It was white, her lips trembled, and in her eyes Chayne saw again the look of terror which he had hoped was gone forever. "Oh, please," she whispered.

"Yes," he replied, and he turned again to Simond. "At two o'clock then. My wife will go, so bring a mule. We can leave it at the Montanvert."

The guides tramped from the garden. Chayne led his wife toward the hotel, slipping his arm through hers.

"You must get some sleep, Sylvia."

"Oh, Hilary," she cried. "I shall bring shame on you. We should never have married," and her voice broke in a sob.

"Hush!" he replied. "Never say that, my dear, never think it! Sleep! You will want your strength to-morrow."

But Sylvia slept little, and before the time she was ready with her ice-ax in her hand. At two o'clock they came out from the hotel in the twilight of the morning. There were two men there.

"Ah! you have come to see us off, Michel," said Chayne.

"No, monsieur, I bring my mule," said Revailloud, with a smile, and he helped Sylvia to mount it. "To lead mules to the Montanvert--is not that my business? Simond has a rope," he added, as he saw Chayne sling a coil across his shoulder.

"We may need an extra one," said Chayne, and the party moved off upon its long march. At the Montanvert hotel, on the edge of the Mer de Glace, Sylvia descended from her mule, and at once the party went down on to the ice.

"Au revoir!" shouted Michel from above, and he stood and watched them, until they passed out of his sight. Sylvia turned and waved her hand to him. But he made no answering sign. For his eyes were no longer good.

"He is very kind," said Sylvia. "He understood that there was some trouble, and while he led the mule he sought to comfort me," and then between a laugh and a sob she added: "You will never guess how. He offered to give me his little book with all the signatures--the little book which means so much to him."

It was the one thing which he had to offer her, as Sylvia understood, and always thereafter she remembered him with a particular tenderness. He had been a good friend to her, asking nothing and giving what he had. She saw him often in the times which were to come, but when she thought of him, she pictured him as on that early morning standing on the bluff of cliff by the Montanvert with the reins of his mule thrown across his arm, and straining his old eyes to hold his friends in view.

Later during that day amongst the seracs of the Col du Geant, Simond uttered a shout, and a party of guides returning to Chamonix changed their course toward him. Droz was amongst the number, and consenting at once to the expedition which was proposed to him, he tied himself on to the rope.

"Do you know the Brenva ascent?" Chayne asked of him.

"Yes, monsieur. I have crossed Mont Blanc once that way. I shall be very glad to go again. We shall be the first to cross for two years. If only the weather holds."

"Do you doubt that?" asked Chayne, anxiously. The morning had broken clear, the day was sunny and cloudless.

"I think there may be wind to-morrow," he replied, raising his face and judging by signs unappreciable to other than the trained eyes of a guide. "But we will try, eh, monsieur?" he cried, recovering his spirits. "We will try. We will be the first on the Brenva ridge for two years."

But there Chayne knew him to be wrong. There was another party somewhere on the great ridge at this moment. "Had *it* happened?" he asked himself. "How was it to happen?" What kind of an accident was it to be which could take place with a guide however worthless, and which would leave no suspicion resting on Garratt Skinner? There would be no cutting of the rope. Of that he felt sure. That method might do very well for a melodrama, but actually--no! Garratt Skinner would have a better plan than that. And indeed he had, a better plan and a simpler one, a plan which not merely would give to any uttered suspicion the complexion of malignancy, but must even bring Mr. Garratt Skinner honor and great praise. But no idea of the plan occurred either to Sylvia or to Chayne as all through that long hot day they toiled up the ice-fall of the Col du Geant and over the passes. It was evening before they came to the pastures, night before they reached Courmayeur.

There Chayne found full confirmation of his fears. In spite of effort to dissuade them, Garratt Skinner, Walter Hine and Pierre Delouvain had started yesterday for the Brenva climb. They had taken porters with them as far as the sleeping-place upon the glacier rocks. The porters had returned. Chayne sent for them.

"Yes," they said. "At half past two this morning, the climbing party descended from the rocks on to the ice-fall of the glacier. They should be at the hut at the Grands Mulets now, on the other side of the mountain, if not already in Chamonix. Perhaps monsieur would wish for porters to-morrow."

"No," said Chayne. "We mean to try the passage in one day"; and he turned to his guides. "I wish to start at midnight. It is important. We shall reach the glacier by five. Will you be ready?"

And at midnight accordingly he set out by the light of a lantern. Sylvia stood outside the hotel and watched the flame diminish to a star, dance for a little while, and then go out. For her, as for all women, the bad hour had struck when there was nothing to do but to sit and watch and wait. Perhaps her husband, after all, was wrong, she said to herself, and repeated the phrase, hoping that repetition would carry conviction to her heart.

But early on that morning Chayne had sure evidence that he was right. For as he, Simond and Andre Droz were marching in single file through the thin forest behind the chalets of La Brenva, a shepherd lad came running down toward them. He was so excited that he could hardly tell the story with which he was hurrying to Courmayeur. Only an hour before he had seen, high up on the Brenva ridge, a man waving a signal of distress. Both Simond and Droz discredited the story. The distance was too great; the sharpest eyes could not have seen so far. But Chayne believed, and his heart sank within him. The puppet and Garratt Skinner--what did they matter? But he turned his eyes down toward Courmayeur. It was Sylvia upon whom the blow would fall.

"The story cannot be true," cried Simond.

But Chayne bethought him of another day long ago, when a lad had burst into the hotel at Zermatt and told with no more acceptance for his story of an avalanche which he had seen fall from the very summit of the Matterhorn. Chayne looked at his watch. It was just four o'clock.

"There has been an accident," he said. "We must hurry."

CHAPTER XXIV
THE BRENVA RIDGE

The peasant was right. He *had* seen a man waving a signal of distress on the slopes of Mont Blanc above the great buttress. And this is how the signal came to be waved.

An hour before Chayne and Sylvia set out from Chamonix to cross the Col du Geant, and while it was yet quite dark, a spark glowed suddenly on an island of rocks set in the great white waste of the Brenva glacier. The spark was a fire lit by Pierre Delouvain. For Garratt Skinner's party had camped upon those rocks. The morning was cold, and one by one the porters, Garratt Skinner, and Walter Hine, gathered about the blaze. Overhead the stars glittered in a clear, dark sky. It was very still; no sound was heard at all but the movement in the camp; even on the glacier a thousand feet below, where all night long the avalanches had thundered, in the frost of the early morning there was silence.

Garratt Skinner looked upward.

"We shall have a good day," he said; and then he looked quickly toward Walter Hine. "How did you sleep, Wallie?"

"Very little. The avalanches kept me awake. Besides, I slipped and fell a hundred times at the corner of the path," he said, with a shiver. "A hundred times I felt emptiness beneath my feet."

He referred to a mishap of the day before. On the way to the gite after the chalets and the wood are left behind, a little path leads along the rocks of the Mont de la Brenva high above the glacier. There are one or two awkward corners to pass where rough footsteps have been hewn in the rock. At one of these corners Walter Hine had slipped. His side struck the step; he would have dropped to the glacier, but Garratt Skinner had suddenly reached out a hand and saved him.

Garratt Skinner's face changed.

"You are not afraid," he said.

"You think we can do it?" asked Hine, nervously, and Garratt Skinner laughed.

"Ask Pierre Delouvain!" he said, and himself put the question. Pierre laughed in his turn.

"Bah! I snap my fingers at the Brenva climb," said he. "We shall be in Chamonix to-night"; and Garratt Skinner translated the words to Walter Hine.

Breakfast was prepared and eaten. Walter Hine was silent through the meal. He had not the courage to say that he was afraid; and Garratt Skinner played upon his vanity.

"We shall be in Chamonix to-night. It will be a fine feather in your cap, Wallie.

One of the historic climbs!"

Walter Hine drew a deep breath. If only the day were over, and the party safe on the rough path through the woods on the other side of the mountain! But he held his tongue. Moreover, he had great faith in his idol and master, Garratt Skinner.

"You saved my life yesterday," he said; and upon Garratt Skinner's face there came a curious smile. He looked steadily into the blaze of the fire and spoke almost as though he made an apology to himself.

"I saw a man falling. I saw that I could save him. I did not think. My hand had already caught him."

He looked up with a start. In the east the day was breaking, pale and desolate; the lower glacier glimmered into view beneath them; the gigantic amphitheater of hills which girt them in on three sides loomed out of the mists from aerial heights and took solidity and shape, westward the black and rugged Peuteret ridge, eastward the cliffs of Mont Maudit, and northward sweeping around the head of the glacier, the great ice-wall of Mont Blanc with its ruined terraces and inaccessible cliffs.

"Time, Wallie," said Garratt Skinner, and he rose to his feet and called to Pierre Delouvain. "There are only three of us. We shall have to go quickly. We do not want to carry more food than we shall need. The rest we can send back with our blankets by the porters."

Pierre Delouvain justified at once the ill words which had been spoken of him by Michel Revailloud. He thought only of the burden which through this long day he would have to carry on his back.

"Yes, that is right," he said. "We will take what we need for the day. To-night we shall be in Chamonix."

And thus the party set off with no provision against that most probable of all mishaps--the chance that sunset might find them still upon the mountain side. Pierre Delouvain, being lazy and a worthless fellow, as Revailloud had said, agreed. But the suggestion had been made by Garratt Skinner. And Garratt Skinner was Gabriel Strood, who knew--none better--the folly of such light traveling.

The rope was put on; Pierre Delouvain led the way, Walter Hine as the weakest of the party was placed in the middle, Garratt Skinner came last; the three men mounted by a snow-slope and a gully to the top of the rocks which supported the upper Brenva glacier.

"That's our road, Wallie," said Garratt Skinner. He pointed to a great buttress of rock overlain here and there with fields of snow, which jutted out from the ice-wall of the mountain, descended steeply, bent to the west in a curve, and then pushed far out into the glacier as some great promontory pushes out into the sea. "Do you see a hump above the buttress, on the crest of the ridge and a little to the right? And to the right of the hump, a depression in the ridge? That's what they call the Corridor. Once we are there our troubles are over."

But between the party and the buttress stretched the great ice-fall of the upper Brenva glacier. Crevassed, broken, a wilderness of towering seracs, it had the look of a sea in a gale whose breakers had been frozen in the very act of over toppling.

"Come," said Pierre.

"Keep the rope stretched tight, Wallie," said Garratt Skinner; and they descended into the furrows of that wild and frozen sea. The day's work had begun in earnest; and almost at once they began to lose time.

Now it was a perilous strip of ice between unfathomable blue depths along which they must pass, as bridge-builders along their girders, yet without the bridge-builders' knowledge that at the end of the passage there was a further way. Now it was some crevasse into which they must descend, cutting their steps down a steep rib of ice; now it was a wall up which the leader must be hoisted on the shoulders of his companions, and even so as likely as not, his fingers could not reach the top, but hand holds and foot holds must be hewn with the ax till a ladder was formed. Now it was some crevasse gaping across their path; they must search this way and that for a firm snow-bridge by which to overpass it. It was difficult, as Pierre Delouvain discovered, to find a path through that tangled labyrinth without some knowledge of the glacier. For, only at rare times, when he stood high on a serac, could he see his way for more than a few yards ahead. Pierre aimed straight for the foot of the buttress, working thus due north. And he was wrong. Garratt Skinner knew it, but said not a word. He stood upon insecure ledges and supported Delouvain upon his shoulders, and pushed him up with his ice-ax into positions which only involved the party in further difficulties. He took his life in his hands and risked it, knowing the better way. Yet all the while the light broadened, the great violet shadows crept down the slopes and huddled at the bases of the peaks. Then the peaks took fire, and suddenly along the dull white slopes of ice in front of them the fingers of the morning flashed in gold. Over the eastern rocks the sun had leaped into the sky. For a little while longer they advanced deeper into the entanglement, and when they were about half way across they came to a stop. They were on a tongue of ice which narrowed to a point; the point abutted against a perpendicular ice-wall thirty feet high. Nowhere was there any break in that wall, and at each side of the tongue the ice gaped in chasms.

"We must go back," said Pierre. "I have forgotten the way."

He had never known it. Seduced by a treble fee, he had assumed an experience which he did not possess. Garratt Skinner looked at his watch, and turning about led the party back for a little while. Then he turned to his right and said:

"I think it might go in this direction," and lo! making steadily across some difficult ground, no longer in a straight line northward to Mont Blanc, but westward toward the cliffs of the Peuteret ridge under Garratt Skinner's lead, they saw a broad causeway of ice open before them. The causeway led them to steep slopes of snow, up which it was just possible to kick steps, and then working back again to the east they reached the foot of the great buttress on its western side just where it forms a right angle with the face of the mountain. Garratt Skinner once more looked at his watch. It had been half-past two when they had put on the rope, it was now close upon half-past six. They had taken four hours to traverse the ice-fall, and they should have taken only two and a half. Garratt Skinner, however, expressed no anxiety. On the contrary, one might have thought that he wished to lose time.

"There's one of the difficulties disposed of," he said, cheerily. "You did very well, Wallie--very well. It was not altogether nice, was it? But you won't have to go back."

Walter Hine had indeed crossed the glacier without complaint. There had been times when he had shivered, times when his heart within him had swelled with a longing to cry out, "Let us go back!" But he had not dared. He had been steadied across the narrow bridge with the rope, hauled up the ice-walls and let down again on the other side. But he had come through. He took some pride in the exploit as he gazed back from the top of the snow-slope across the tumult of ice to the rocks on which he had slipped. He had come through safely, and he was encouraged to go on.

"We won't stop here, I think," said Garratt Skinner. They had already halted upon the glacier for a second breakfast. The sun was getting hot upon the slopes above, and small showers of snow and crusts of ice were beginning to shoot down the gullies of the buttress at the base of which they stood. "We will have a third breakfast when we are out of range." He called to Delouvain who was examining the face of the rock-buttress up which they must ascend to its crest and said: "It looks as if we should do well to work out to the right I think."

The rocks were difficult, but their difficulty was not fully appreciated by Walter Hine. Nor did he understand the danger. There were gullies in which new snow lay in a thin crust over hard ice. He noticed that in those gullies the steps were cut deep into the ice below, that Garratt Skinner bade him not loiter, and that Pierre Delouvain in front made himself fast and drew in the rope with a particular care when it came to his turn to move. But he did not know that all that surface snow might peel off in a moment, and swish down the cliffs, sweeping the party from their feet. There were rounded rocks and slabs with no hold for hand or foot but roughness, roughness in the surface, and here and there a wrinkle. But the guide went first, as often as not pushed up by Garratt Skinner, and Walter Hine, like many another inefficient man before him, came up, like a bundle, on the rope afterward. Thus they climbed for three hours more. Walter Hine, nursed by gradually lengthening expeditions, was not as yet tired. Moreover the exhilaration of the air, and excitement, helped to keep fatigue aloof. They rested just below the crest of the ridge and took another meal.

"Eat often and little. That's the golden rule," said Garratt Skinner. "No brandy, Wallie. Keep that in your flask!"

Pierre Delouvain, however, followed a practice not unknown amongst Chamonix guides.

"Absinthe is good on the mountains," said he.

When they rose, the order of going was changed. Pierre Delouvain, who had led all the morning, now went last, and Garratt Skinner led. He led quickly and with great judgment or knowledge--Pierre Delouvain at the end of the rope wondered whether it was judgment or knowledge--and suddenly Walter Hine found himself standing on the crest with Garratt Skinner, and looking down the other side upon a glacier far below, which flows from the Mur de la Cote on the summit ridge of Mont Blanc into the Brenva glacier.

"That's famous," cried Garratt Skinner, looking once more at his watch. He did not say that they had lost yet another hour upon the face of the buttress. It was now half past nine in the morning. "We are twelve thousand feet up, Wallie," and he swung to his left, and led the party up the ridge of the buttress.

As they went along this ridge, Wallie Hine's courage rose. It was narrow but not steep, nor was it ice. It was either rock or snow in which steps could be kicked. He stepped out with a greater confidence. If this were all, the Brenva climb was a fraud, he exclaimed to himself in the vanity of his heart. Ahead of them a tall black tower stood up, hiding what lay beyond, and up toward this tower Garratt Skinner led quickly. He no longer spoke to his companions, he went forward, assured and inspiring assurance; he reached the tower, passed it and began to cut steps. His ax rang as it fell. It was ice into which he was cutting.

This was the first warning which Walter Hine received. But he paid no heed to it. He was intent upon setting his feet in the steps; he found the rope awkward to handle and keep tight, his attention was absorbed in observing his proper distance. Moreover, in front of him the stalwart figure of Garratt Skinner blocked his vision. He went forward. The snow on which he walked became hard ice, and instead of sloping upward ran ahead almost in a horizontal line. Suddenly, however, it narrowed; Hine became conscious of appalling depths on either side of him; it narrowed with extraordinary rapidity; half a dozen paces behind him he had been walking on a broad smooth path; now he walked on the width of the top of a garden wall. His knees began to shake; he halted; he reached out vainly into emptiness for some support on which his shaking hands might clutch. And then in front of him he saw Garratt Skinner sit down and bestride the wall. Over Garratt Skinner's head, he now saw the path by which he needs must go. He was on the famous ice-ridge; and nothing so formidable, so terrifying, had even entered into his dreams during his sleep upon the rocks where he had bivouacked. It thinned to a mere sharp edge, a line without breadth of cold blue ice, and it stretched away through the air for a great distance until it melted suddenly into the face of the mountain. On the left hand an almost vertical slope of ice dropped to depths which Hine did not dare to fathom with his eyes; on the right there was no slope at all; a wall of crumbling snow descended from the edge straight as a weighted line. On neither side could the point of the ax be driven in to preserve the balance. Walter Hine uttered a whimpering cry:

"I shall fall! I shall fall!"

Garratt Skinner, astride of the ridge, looked over his shoulder.

"Sit down," he cried, sharply. But Walter Hine dared not. He stood, all his courage gone, tottering on the narrow top of the wall, afraid to stoop, lest his knees should fail him altogether and his feet slip from beneath him. To bend down until his hands could rest upon the ice, and meanwhile to keep his feet--no, he could not do it. He stood trembling, his face distorted with fear, and his body swaying a little from side to side. Garratt Skinner called sharply to Pierre Delouvain.

"Quick, Pierre."

There was no time for Garratt Skinner to return; but he gathered himself together on the ridge, ready for a spring. Had Walter Hine toppled over, and swung down the length of the rope, as at any moment he might have done, Garratt Skinner was prepared. He would have jumped down the opposite side of the ice-arete, though how either he or Walter Hine could have regained the ridge he could not tell. Would any one of the party live to return to Courmayeur and tell the tale? But Garratt Skinner knew the risk he took, had counted it up long before ever he brought Walter Hine to Chamonix, and thought it worth while. He did not falter now. All through the morning, indeed, he had been taking risks, risks of which Walter Hine did not dream; with so firm and yet so delicate a step he had moved from crack to crack, from ice-step up to ice-step; with so obedient a response of his muscles, he had drawn himself up over the rounded rocks from ledge to ledge. He shouted again to Pierre Delouvain, and at the same moment began carefully to work backward along the ice-arete. Pierre, however, hurried; Walter Hine heard the guide's voice behind him, felt himself steadied by his hands. He stooped slowly down, knelt upon the wall, then bestrode it.

"Now, forward," cried Skinner, and he pulled in the rope. "Forward. We cannot go back!"

Hine clung to the ridge; behind him Pierre Delouvain sat down and held him about the waist. Slowly they worked themselves forward, while Garratt Skinner gathered in the rope in front. The wall narrowed as they advanced, became the merest edge which cut their hands as they clasped it. Hine closed his eyes, his head whirled, he was giddy, he felt sick. He stopped gripping the slope on both sides with his knees, clutching the sharp edge with the palms of his hands.

"I can't go on! I can't," he cried, and he reeled like a novice on the back of a horse.

Garratt Skinner worked back to him.

"Put your arms about my waist, Wallie! Keep your eyes shut! You shan't fall."

Walter Hine clung to him convulsively, Pierre Delouvain steadied Hine from behind, and thus they went slowly forward for a long while. Garratt Skinner gripped the edge with the palms of his hands--so narrow was the ridge--the fingers of one hand pointed down one slope, the fingers of the other down the opposite wall. Their legs dangled.

At last Walter Hine felt Garratt Skinner loosening his clasped fingers from about his waist. Garratt Skinner stood up, uncoiled the rope, chipped a step or two in the ice and went boldly forward. For a yard or two further Walter Hine straddled on, and then Garratt Skinner cried to him:

"Look up, Wallie. It's all over."

Hine looked and saw Garratt Skinner standing upon a level space of snow in the side of the mountain. A moment later he himself was lying in the sun upon the level space. The famous ice-arete was behind them. Walter Hine looked back along it and shuddered. The thin edge of ice curving slightly downward, stretched away to the black rock-tower, in the bright sunlight a thing most beautiful, but most menacing and terrible. He seemed cut off by it from the world. They had a meal upon that level space, and while Hine rested, Pierre Delouvain cast off the rope and went ahead. He came back in a little while with a serious face.

"Will it go?" asked Garratt Skinner.

"It must," said Delouvain. "For we can never go back"; and suddenly alarmed lest the way should be barred in front as well as behind, Walter Hine turned and looked above him. His nerves were already shaken; at the sight of what lay ahead of him, he uttered a cry of despair.

"It's no use," he cried. "We can never get up," and he flung himself upon the snow and buried his face in his arms. Garratt Skinner stood over him.

"We must," he said. "Come! Look!"

Walter Hine looked up and saw his companion dangling the face of his watch before his eyes.

"We are late. It is now twelve o'clock. We should have left this spot two hours ago and more," he said, very gravely; and Pierre Delouvain exclaimed excitedly:

"Certainly, monsieur, we must go on. It will not do to loiter now," and stooping down, he dragged rather than helped Walter Hine to his feet. The quiet gravity of Garratt Skinner and the excitement of Delouvain frightened Walter Hine equally. Some sense of his own insufficiency broke in at last upon him. His vanity peeled off from him, just at the moment when it would most have been of use. He had a glimpse of what he was--a poor, weak, inefficient thing.

Above them the slopes stretched upward to a great line of towering ice-cliffs. Through and up those ice-cliffs a way had to be found. And at any moment, loosened by the sun, huge blocks and pinnacles might break from them and come thundering down. As it was, upon their right hand where the snow-fields fell steeply in a huge ice gully, between a line of rocks and the cliffs of Mont Maudit, the avalanches plunged and reverberated down to the Brenva glacier. Pierre Delouvain took the lead again, and keeping by the line of rocks the party ascended the steep snow-slopes straight toward the wall of cliffs. But in a while the snow thinned, and the ax was brought into play again. Through the thin crust of snow, steps had to be cut into the ice beneath, and since there were still many hundreds of feet to be ascended, the steps were cut wide apart. With the sun burning upon his face, and his feet freezing in the ice-steps, Walter Hine stood and moved, and stood again all through that afternoon. Fatigue gained upon him, fear did not let him go. "If only I get off this mountain," he said to himself with heartfelt longing, "never again!" When near to the cliffs Pierre Delouvain stopped. In front of him the wall was plainly inaccessible. Far away to the left there was a depression up which possibly a way might be forced.

"I think, monsieur, that must be the way," said Pierre.

"But you should *know*" said Garratt Skinner.

"It is some time since I was here. I have forgotten;" and Pierre began to traverse the ice-slope to the left. Garratt Skinner followed without a word. But he knew that when he had ascended Mont Blanc by the Brenva route twenty-three years before, he had kept to the right along the rocks to a point where that ice-wall was crevassed, and through that crevasse had found his path. They passed quickly beneath an overhanging rib of ice which jutted out from the wall, and reached the angle then formed at four o'clock in the afternoon.

"Our last difficulty, Wallie," said Garratt Skinner, as he cut a large step in which Hine might stand. "Once up that wall, our troubles are over."

Walter Hine looked at the wall. It was not smooth ice, it was true; blocks had broken loose from it, and had left it bulging out here, there, and in places fissured. But it stood at an angle of 65 degrees. It seemed impossible that any one should ascend it. He looked down the slope up which they had climbed--it seemed equally impossible that any one should return. Moreover, the sun was already in the West, and the ice promontory under which they stood shut its warmth from them. Walter Hine was in the shadow, and he shivered with cold as much as with fear. For half an hour Pierre Delouvain tried desperately to work his way up that ice wall, and failed.

"It is too late," he said. "We shall not get up to-night."

Garratt Skinner nodded his head.

"No, nor get down," he added, gravely. "I am sorry, Wallie. We must go back and find a place where we can pass the night."

Walter Hine was in despair. He was tired, he was desperately cold, his gloves were frozen, his fingers and his feet benumbed.

"Oh, let's stop here!" he cried.

"We can't," said Garratt Skinner, and he turned as he spoke and led the way down quickly. There was need for hurry. Every now and then he stopped to cut an intervening step, where those already cut were too far apart, and at times to give Hine a hand while Delouvain let him down with the help of the rope from behind.

Slowly they descended, and while they descended the sun disappeared, the mists gathered about the precipices below, the thunder of the avalanches was heard at rare intervals, the ice-cliffs above them glimmered faintly and still more faintly. The dusk came. They descended in a ghostly twilight. At times the mists would part, and below them infinite miles away they saw the ice-fields of the Brenva glacier. The light was failing altogether when Garratt Skinner turned to his left and began to traverse the slopes to a small patch of rocks.

"Here!" he said, as he reached them. "We must sit here until the morning comes."

CHAPTER XXV
A NIGHT ON AN ICE-SLOPE

At the base of the rocks there was a narrow ledge on which, huddled together, the three men could sit side by side. Garratt Skinner began to clear the snow from the ledge with his ice-ax; but Walter Hine sank down at once and Pierre Delouvain, who might have shown a better spirit, promptly followed his example.

"What is the use?" he whispered. "We shall all die to-night.... I have a wife and family.... Let us eat what there is to eat and then die," and drowsily repeating his words, he fell asleep. Garratt Skinner, however, roused him, and drowsily he helped to clear the ledge. Then Walter Hine was placed in the middle that he might get what warmth and shelter was to be had, the rope was hitched over a spike of rock behind, so that if any one fell asleep he might not fall off, and Delouvain and Skinner took their places. By this time darkness had come. They sat upon the narrow ledge with their backs to the rock and the steep snow-slopes falling away at their feet. Far down a light or two glimmered in the chalets of La Brenva.

Garratt Skinner emptied the *Ruecksack* on his knees.

"Let us see what food we have," he said. "We made a mistake in not bringing more. But Pierre was so certain that we should reach Chamonix to-night."

"We shall die to-night," said Pierre.

"Nonsense," said Garratt Skinner. "We are not the first party which has been caught by the night."

Their stock of food was certainly low. It consisted of a little bread, a tin of sardines, a small pot of jam, some cold bacon, a bag of acid-drops, a couple of cakes of chocolate, and a few biscuits.

"We must keep some for the morning," he said. "Don't fall asleep, Wallie! You had better take off your boots and muffle your feet in the *Ruecksack*. It will keep them warmer and save you from frost-bite. You might as well squeeze the water out of your stockings too."

Garratt Skinner waked Hine from his drowsiness and insisted that his advice should be followed. It would be advisable that it should be known afterward in Courmayeur that he had taken every precaution to preserve his companion's life. He took off his own stockings and squeezed the water out, replaced them, and laced on his boots. For to him, too, the night would bring some risk. Then the three men ate their supper. A very little wine was left in the gourd which Garratt Skinner had carried on his back, and he filled it up with snow and thrust it inside his shirt that it might melt the sooner.

"You have your brandy flask, Wallie, but be sparing of it. Brandy will warm you for the moment, but it leaves you more sensitive to the cold than you were before. That's a known fact. And don't drink too much of this snow-water. It may make you burn inside. At least so I have been told," he added.

Hine drank and passed the bottle to Pierre, who took it with his reiterated moan: "What's the use? We shall all die to-night. Why should a poor guide with a wife and family be tempted to ascend mountains. I will tell you something, monsieur," he cried suddenly across Walter Hine. "I am not fond of the mountains. No, I am not fond of them!" and he leaned back and fell asleep.

"Better not follow his example, Wallie. Keep awake! Slap your limbs!"

Above the three men the stars came out very clear and bright; the tiny lights in the chalets far below disappeared one by one; the cold became intense. At times Garratt Skinner roused his companions, and holding each other by the arm, they rose simultaneously to their feet and stamped upon the ledge. But every movement hurt them, and after a while Walter Hine would not.

"Leave me alone," he said. "To move tortures me!"

Garratt Skinner had his pipe and some tobacco. He lit, shading the match with his coat; and then he looked at his watch.

"What time is it? Is it near morning?" asked Hine, in a voice which was very feeble.

"A little longer to wait," said Garratt Skinner, cheerfully.

The hands marked a quarter to ten.

And afterward they grew very silent, except for the noise which they made in shivering. Their teeth chattered with the chill, they shook in fits which lasted for minutes, Walter Hine moaned feebly. All about them the world was bound in frost; the cold stars glittered overhead; the mountains took their toll of pain that night. Yet there was one among those three perched high on a narrow ledge of rock amongst the desolate heights, who did not regret. Just for a night like this Garratt Skinner had hoped. Walter Hine, weak of frame and with little stamina, was exposed to the rigors of a long Alpine night, thirteen thousand feet above the level of the sea, with hardly any food, and no hope of rescue for yet another day and yet another night. There could be but one end to it. Not until to-morrow would any alarm at their disappearance be awakened either at Chamonix or at Courmayeur. It would need a second night before help reached them--so Garratt Skinner had planned it out. There could be but one end to it. Walter Hine would die. There was a risk that he himself might suffer the same fate--he was not blind to it. He had taken the risk knowingly, and with a certain indifference. It was the best plan, since, if he escaped alive, suspicion could not fall on him. Thus he argued, as he smoked his pipe with his back to the rock and waited for the morning.

At one o'clock Walter Hine began to ramble. He took Garratt Skinner and Pierre Delouvain for Captain Barstow and Archie Parminter, and complained that it was ridiculous to sit up playing poker on so cold a night; and while in his delirium he rambled and moaned, the morning began to break. But with the morning came a wind from the north, whirling the snow like smoke about the mountain-tops, and bitingly cold. Garratt Skinner with great difficulty stood up, slowly and with pain stretched himself to his full height, slapped his thighs, stamped with his feet, and then looked for a long while at his victim, without remorse, and without satisfaction. He stooped and sought to lift him. But Hine was too stiff and numbed with the cold to be able to move. In a little while Pierre Delouvain, who had fallen asleep, woke up. The day was upon them now, cold and lowering.

"We must wait for the sun," said Garratt Skinner. "Until that has risen and thawed us it will not be safe to move."

Pierre Delouvain looked about him, worked the stiffened muscles of his limbs and groaned.

"There will be little sun to-day," he said. "We shall all die here."

Garratt Skinner sat down again and waited. The sun rose over the rocks of Mont Maudit, but weak, and yellow as a guinea. Garratt Skinner then tied his coat to his ice-ax, and standing out upon a rock waved it this way and that.

"No one will see it," whimpered Pierre; and indeed Garratt Skinner would never have waved that signal had he not thought the same.

"Perhaps--one never knows," he said. "We must take all precautions, for the day looks bad."

The sunlight, indeed, only stayed upon the mountain-side long enough to tantalize them with vain hopes of warmth. Gray clouds swept up low over the crest of Mont Blanc and blotted it out. The wind moaned wildly along the slopes. The day frowned upon them sullen and cold with a sky full of snow.

"We will wait a little longer," said Garratt Skinner, "then we must move."

He looked at the sky. It seemed to him now very probable that he would lose the desperate game which he had been playing. He had staked his life upon it. Let the snow come and the mists, he would surely lose his stake. Nevertheless he set himself to the task of rousing Walter Hine.

"Leave me alone," moaned Walter Hine, and he struck feebly at his companions as they lifted him on to his feet.

"Stamp your feet, Wallie," said Garratt Skinner. "You will feel better in a few moments."

They held him up, but he repeated his cry. "Leave me alone!" and the moment they let him go he sank down again upon the ledge. He was overcome with drowsiness, the slightest movement tortured him.

Garratt Skinner looked up at the leaden sky.

"We must wait till help comes," he said,

Delouvain shook his head.

"It will not come to-day. We shall all die here. It was wrong, monsieur, to try the Brenva ridge. Yes, we shall die here"; and he fell to blubbering like a child.

"Could you go down alone?" Garratt Skinner asked.

"There is the glacier to cross, monsieur."

"I know. That is the risk. But it is cold and there is no sun. The snow-bridges may hold."

Pierre Delouvain hesitated. Here it seemed to him was certain death. But if he climbed down the ice-arete, the snow-slopes, and the rocks below, if the snow-bridges held upon the glacier, there would be life for one of the three. Pierre Delouvain had little in common with that loyal race of Alpine guides who hold it as their most sacred tradition not to return home without their patrons.

"Yes, it is our one hope," he said; and untying himself with awkward fumbling fingers from the kinked rope, and coiling the spare rope about his shoulders, he went down the slope. During the night the steps had frozen and in many places it was necessary to recut them. He too was stiff with the long vigil. He moved slowly, with numbed and frozen limbs. But as his ax rose and fell, the blood began to burn in the tips of his fingers, to flow within his veins; he went more and more firmly. For a long way Garratt Skinner held him in sight. Then he turned back to Walter Hine upon the ledge, and sat beside him. Garratt Skinner's strength had stood him in good stead. He filled his pipe and lit it, and watched beside his victim. The day wore on slowly. At times Garratt Skinner rubbed Hine's limbs and stamped about the ledge to keep some warmth within himself. Walter Hine grew weaker and weaker. At times he was delirious; at times he came to his senses.

"You leave me," he whispered once. "You have been a good friend to me. You can do no more. Just leave me here, and save yourself."

Garratt Skinner made no answer. He just looked at Hine curiously--that was all. That was all. It was a curious thing to him that Hine should display an unexpected manliness--almost a heroism. It could not be pleasant even to contemplate being left alone upon these windy and sunless heights to die. But actually to wish it!

"How did you come by so much fortitude?" he asked; and to his astonishment, Walter Hine replied:

"I learnt it from you, old man."

"From me?"

"Yes."

Garratt Skinner gave him some of the brandy and listened to a portrait of himself, described in broken words, which he was at some pains to recognize. Walter Hine had been seeking to model himself upon an imaginary Garratt Skinner, and thus, strangely enough, had arrived at an actual heroism. Thus would Garratt Skinner have bidden his friends leave him, only in tones less tremulous, and very likely with a laugh, turning back, as it were, to snap his fingers as he stepped out of the world. Thus, therefore, Walter Hine sought to bear himself.

"Curious," said Garratt Skinner with interest, but with no stronger feeling at all. "Are you in pain, Wallie?"

"Dreadful pain."

"We must wait. Perhaps help will come!"

The day wore on, but what the time was Garratt Skinner could not tell. His watch and Hine's had both stopped with the cold, and the dull, clouded sky gave him no clue. The last of the food was eaten, the last drop of the brandy drunk. It was bitterly cold. If only the snow would hold off till morning! Garratt Skinner had only to wait. The night would come and during the night Walter Hine would die. And even while the thought was in his mind, he heard voices. To his amazement, to his alarm, he heard voices! Then he laughed. He was growing light-headed. Exhaustion, cold and hunger were telling their tale upon him. He was not so young as he had been twenty years before. But to make sure he rose to his knees and peered down the slope. He had been mistaken. The steep snow-slopes stretched downward, wild and empty. Here and there black rocks jutted from them; a long way down four black stones were spaced; there was no living thing in that solitude. He sank back relieved. No living thing except himself, and perhaps his companion. He looked at Hine closely, shook him, and Hine groaned. Yes, he still lived--for a little time he still would live. Garratt Skinner gathered in his numbed palm the last pipeful of tobacco in his pouch and, spilling the half of it--his hands so shook with cold, his fingers were so clumsy--he pressed it into his pipe and lit it. Perhaps before it was all smoked out--he thought. And then his hallucination returned to him. Again he heard voices, very faint, and distant, in a lull of the wind.

It was weakness, of course, but he started up again, this time to his feet, and as he stood up his head and shoulders showed clear against the white snow behind him. He heard a shout--yes, an undoubted shout. He stared down the slope and then he saw. The four black stones had moved, were nearer to him--they were four men ascending. Garratt Skinner turned swiftly toward Walter Hine, reached for his ice-ax, grasped it and raised it, Walter Hine looked at him with staring, stupid eyes, but raised no hand, made no movement. He, too, was conscious of an hallucination. It seemed to him that his friend stood over him with a convulsed and murderous face, in which rage strove with bitter disappointment, but that he held his ax by the end with the adz-head swung back above his head to give greater force to the blow, and that while he poised it there came a cry from the confines of the world, and that upon that cry his friend dropped the ax, and stooping down to him murmured:

"There's help quite close, Wallie!"

Certainly those words were spoken--that at all events was no hallucination. Walter Hine understood it clearly. For Garratt Skinner suddenly stripped off his coat, passed it round Hine's shoulders and then, baring his own breast, clasped Hine to it that he might impart to him some warmth from his own body.

Thus they were found by the rescue party; and the story of Garratt Skinner's great self-sacrifice was long remembered in Courmayeur.

Garratt Skinner watched the men mounting and wondered who they were. He recognized his own guide, Pierre Delouvain, but who were the others, how did they come there on a morning so forbidding? Who was the tall man who walked last but one? And as the party drew nearer, he saw and understood. But he did not change from his attitude. He waited until they were close. Then he and Hilary Chayne exchanged a look.

"You?" said Garratt Skinner.

"Yes--" Chayne paused. "Yes, Mr. Strood," he said.

And in those words all was said. Garratt Skinner knew that his plan was not merely foiled, but also understood. He stood up and looked about him, and even to Chayne's eyes there was a dignity in his quiet manner, his patience under defeat. For Garratt Skinner, rogue though he was, the mountains had their message. All through that long night, while he sat by the side of his victim, they had been whispering it. Whether bound in frost beneath the stars, or sparkling to the sun, or gray under a sky of clouds, or buried deep in flakes of whirling snow, they spoke to him always of the grandeur of their indifference. They might be traversed and scaled, but they were unconquered always because they were indifferent. The climber might lie in wait through the bad weather at the base of the peak, seize upon his chance and stand upon the summit with a cry of triumph and derision. The mountains were indifferent. As they endured success, so they inflicted defeat--with a sublime indifference, lifting their foreheads to the stars as though wrapt in some high communion. Something of their patience had entered into Garratt Skinner. He did not deny his name, he asked no question, he accepted failure and he looked anxiously to the sky.

"It will snow, I think."

They made some tea, mixed it with wine and gave it first of all to Walter Hine.

Then they all breakfasted, and set off on their homeward journey, letting Hine down with the rope from step to step.

Gradually Hine regained a little strength. His numbed limbs began to come painfully to life. He began to move slowly of his own accord, supported by his rescuers. They reached the ice-ridge. It had no terrors now for Walter Hine.

"He had better be tied close between Pierre and myself," said Garratt Skinner. "We came up that way."

"Between Simond and Droz," said Chayne, quietly.

"As you will," said Garratt Skinner with a shrug of the shoulders.

Along the ice-ridge the party moved slowly and safely, carrying Hine between them. As they passed behind the great rock tower at the lower end, the threatened snow began to fall in light flakes.

"Quickly," said Chayne. "We must reach the chalets to-night."

They raced along the snow-slopes on the crest of the buttress and turned to the right down the gullies and the ledges on the face of the rock. In desperate haste they descended lowering Walter Hine from man to man, they crawled down the slabs, dropped from shelf to shelf, wound themselves down the gullies of ice. Somehow without injury the snow-slopes at the foot of the rocks were reached. The snow still held off; only now and then a few flakes fell. But over the mountain the wind was rising, it swept down in fierce swift eddies, and drew back with a roar like the sea upon shingle.

"We must get off the glacier before night comes," cried Chayne, and led by Simond the rescue party went down into the ice-fall. They stopped at the first glacier pool and made Hine wash his hands and feet in the water, to save himself from frost-bite; and thereafter for a little time they rested. They went on again, but they were tired men, and before the rocks were reached upon which two nights before Garratt Skinner had bivouacked, darkness had come. Then Simond justified the praise of Michel Revailloud. With the help of a folding lantern which Chayne had carried in his pocket, he led the way through that bewildering labyrinth with unerring judgment. Great seracs loomed up through the darkness, magnified in size and distorted in shape. Simond went over and round them and under them, steadily, and the rescue party followed. Now he disappeared over the edge of a cliff into space, and in a few seconds his voice rang upward cheerily.

"Follow! It is safe."

And his ice-ax rang with no less cheeriness. He led them boldly to the brink of abysses which were merely channels in the ice, and amid towering pinnacles which seen, close at hand, were mere blocks shoulder high. And at last the guide at the tail of the rope heard from far away ahead Simond's voice raised in a triumphant shout.

"The rocks! The rocks!"

With one accord they flung themselves, tired and panting, on the sheltered level of the bivouac. Some sticks were found, a fire was lighted, tea was once more made. Walter Hine began to take heart; and as the flames blazed up, the six men gathered about it, crouching, kneeling, sitting, and the rocks resounded with their laughter.

"Only a little further, Wallie!" said Garratt Skinner, still true to his part.

They descended from the rocks, crossed a level field of ice and struck the rock path along the slope of the Mont de la Brenva.

"Keep on the rope," said Garratt Skinner. "Hine slipped at a corner as we came up"; and Chayne glanced quickly at him. There were one or two awkward corners above the lower glacier where rough footsteps had been hewn. On one of these Walter Hine had slipped, and Garratt Skinner had saved him--had undoubtedly saved him. At the very beginning of the climb, the object for which it was undertaken was almost fulfilled, and would have been fulfilled but that instinct overpowered Garratt Skinner, and since the accident was unexpected, before he had had time to think he had reached out his hand and saved the life which he intended to destroy.

Along that path Hine was carefully brought to the chalets of La Brenva. The peasants made him as comfortable as they could.

"He will recover," said Simond. "Oh yes, he will recover. Two of us will stay with him."

"No need for that," replied Garratt Skinner. "Thank you very much, but that is my duty since Hine is my friend."

"I think not," said Chayne, standing quietly in front of Garratt Skinner. "Walter Hine will be safe enough in Simond's hands. I want you to return with me to Courmayeur. My wife is there and anxious."

"Your wife?"

"Yes, Sylvia."

Garratt Skinner nodded his head.

"I see," he said, slowly. "Yes."

He looked round the hut. Simond was going to watch by Hine's side. He was defeated utterly, and recognized it. Then he looked at Chayne, and smiled grimly.

"On the whole, I am not sorry that you have married my daughter," he said. "I will come down to Courmayeur. It will be pleasant to sleep in a bed."

And together they walked down to Courmayeur, which they reached soon after midnight.

CHAPTER XXVI
RUNNING WATER

In two days' time Walter Hine was sufficiently recovered to be carried down to Courmayeur. He had been very near to death upon the Brenva ridge, certainly the second night upon which Garratt Skinner had counted would have ended his life; he was frostbitten; and for a long while the shock and the exposure left him weak. But he gained strength with each day, and Chayne had opportunities to admire the audacity and the subtle skill with which Garratt Skinner had sought his end. For Walter Hine was loud in his praises of his friend's self-sacrifice. Skinner had denied himself his own share of food, had bared his breast to the wind that he might give the warmth of his own body to keep his friend alive--these instances lost nothing in the telling. And they were true! Chayne could not deny to Garratt Skinner a certain criminal grandeur. He had placed Hine in no peril which he had not shared himself; he had taken him, a man fitted in neither experience nor health, on an expedition where inexperience or weakness on the part of one was likely to prove fatal to all. There was, moreover, one incident, not contemplated by Garratt Skinner in his plan, which made his position absolutely secure. He had actually saved Walter Hine's life on the rocky path of the Mont de la Brenva. There was no doubt of it. He had reached out his hand and saved him. Chayne made much of this incident to his wife.

"I was wrong you see, Sylvia," he argued. "For your father could have let him fall, and did not. I have been unjust to him, and to you, for you have been troubled."

But Sylvia shook her head.

"You were not wrong," she answered. "It is only because you are very kind that you want me to believe it. But I see the truth quite clearly"; and she smiled at him. "If you wanted me to believe, you should never have told me of the law, a year ago in the Chalet de Lognan. My father obeyed the law--that was all. You know it as well as I. He had no time to think; he acted upon the instinct of the moment; he could not do otherwise. Had there been time to think, would he have reached out his hand? We both know that he would not. But he obeyed the law. What he knew, that he did, obeying the law upon the moment. He could save, and knowing it he *did* save, even against his will."

Chayne did not argue the point. Sylvia saw the truth too clearly.

"Walter Hine is getting well," he said. "Your father is still at another hotel in Courmayeur. There's the future to be considered."

"Yes," she said, and she waited.

"I have asked your father to come over to-night after dinner," said Chayne.

And into their private sitting-room Garratt Skinner entered at eight o'clock that evening. It was the first time that Sylvia had seen him since she had learned the whole truth, and she found the occasion one of trial. But Garratt Skinner carried it off.

There was nothing of the penitent in his manner, but on the other hand he no longer affected the manner of a pained and loving parent. He greeted her from the door, and congratulated her quietly and simply upon her marriage. Then he turned to Chayne.

"You wished to speak to me? I am at your service."

"Yes," replied Chayne. "We--and I speak for Sylvia--we wish to suggest to you that your acquaintanceship with Walter Hine should end altogether--that it should already have ended."

"Really!" said Garratt Skinner, with an air of surprise. "Captain Chayne, the laws of England, revolutionary as they have no doubt become to old-fashioned people like myself, have not yet placed fathers under the guardianship of their sons-in-law. I cannot accept your suggestion."

"We insist upon its acceptance," said Chayne, quietly.

Garratt Skinner smiled.

"Insist perhaps! But how enforce it, my friend? That's another matter."

"I think we have the means to do that," said Chayne. "We can point out to Walter Hine, for instance, that your ascent from the Brenva Glacier was an attempt to murder him."

"An ugly word, Captain Chayne. You would find it difficult of proof."

"The story is fairly complete," returned Chayne. "There is first of all a telegram from Mr. Jarvice couched in curious language."

Garratt Skinner's face lost its smile of amusement.

"Indeed?" he said. He was plainly disconcerted.

"Yes." Chayne produced the telegram from his letter case, read it aloud with his eyes upon Garratt Skinner, and replaced it. "'What are you waiting for? Hurry up! Jarvice.' There is no need at all events to ask Mr. Jarvice what he was waiting for, is there? He wanted to lay his hands upon the money for which Hine's life was insured."

Garratt Skinner leaned back in his chair. His eyes never left Chayne's face, his face grew set and stern. He had a dangerous look, the look of a desperate man at bay.

"Then there is a certain incident to be considered which took place in the house near Weymouth. You must at times have been puzzled by it--perhaps a little alarmed too. Do you remember one evening when a whistle from the shadows on the road and a yokel's shout drove you out of Walter Hine's room, sent you creeping out of it as stealthily as you entered--nay, did more than that, for that whistle and that shout drove you out of Dorsetshire. Ah! I see you remember."

Garratt Skinner indeed had often enough been troubled by the recollection of that night. The shout, the whistle ringing out so suddenly and abruptly from the darkness and the silence had struck upon his imagination and alarmed him by their mystery. Who was the man who had seen? And what had he seen? Garratt Skinner had never felt quite safe since that evening. There was some one, a stranger, going about the world with the key to his secret, even if he had not guessed the secret.

"It was I who whistled. I who shouted."

"You!" cried Garratt Skinner. "You!"

"Yes. Sylvia was with me. You thought to do that night what you thought to do a few days ago above the Brenva ridge. Both times together we were able to hinder you. But once Sylvia hindered you alone. There is the affair of the cocaine."

Chayne looked toward his wife with a look of great pride for the bravery which she had shown. She was sitting aloof in the embrasure of the window with her face averted and a hand pressed over her eyes and forehead. Chayne looked back to Garratt Skinner, and there was more anger in his face than he had ever shown.

"I will never forgive you the distress you have caused to Sylvia," he said.

But Garratt Skinner's eyes were upon Sylvia, and in his face, too, there was a humorous look of pride. She had courage. He remembered how she had confronted him when Walter Hine lay sick. He said no word to her, however, and again he turned to Chayne, who went on:

"There is also your past career to add weight to the argument, Mr.--Strood."

Point by point Chayne set out in detail the case for the prosecution. Garratt Skinner listened without interruption, but he knew that he was beaten. The evidence against him was too strong. It might not be enough legally to secure his conviction at a public trial--though even upon that question there would be the gravest doubt--but it would be enough to carry certitude to every ear which listened and to every eye which read.

"The game is played out," Chayne continued. "We have Walter Hine, and we shall not let him slip back into your hands. How much of the story we shall tell him we are not yet sure--but all if it be necessary. And, if it be necessary, to others beside."

There was a definite threat in the last words. But Garratt Skinner had already made up his mind. Since the game was played out, since defeat had come, he took it without anger or excuse.

"Very well," he said. "Peace in the family circle is after all very desirable--eh, Sylvia? I agree with the deepest regret to part from my young friend, Walter Hine. I leave him in your hands." He was speaking with a humorous magnanimity. But his eyes wandered back to Sylvia, who sat some distance away in the embrasure of the window, with her face in her hands; and his voice changed.

"Sylvia," he said, gently, "come here."

Sylvia rose and walked over to the table.

The waiting, the knowledge which had come to her during the last few days, had told their tale. She had the look which Chayne too well remembered, the dark shadows beneath her eyes, the languor in her walk, the pallor in her cheeks, the distress and shame in her expression.

"Sit down," he said; and she obeyed him reluctantly, seating herself over against him. She gazed at the table-cloth with that mutinous look upon her face which took away from her her womanhood and gave to her the aspect of a pretty but resentful child. Garratt Skinner for the life of him could not but smile at her.

"Well, Sylvia, you have beaten me. You fought your fight well, and I bear you no malice," he said, lightly. "But," and his voice became serious again, "you sit in judgment on me."

Sylvia raised her eyes quickly.

"No!" she cried.

"I think so," he persisted. "I don't blame you. Only I should like you to bear this in mind; that you have in your own life a reason to go gently in your judgments of other people."

Chayne stepped forward, as though he would interfere, but Sylvia laid her hand upon his arm and checked him.

"I don't think you understand, Hilary," she said, quickly. She turned to her father and looked straight at him with an eager interest.

"I wonder whether we are both thinking of the same thing," she said, curiously.

"Perhaps," replied her father. "All your life you have dreamed of running water."

And Sylvia nodded her head.

"Yes, yes," she said, with a peculiar intentness.

"The dream is part of you, part of your life. For all you know, it may have modified your character."

"Yes," said Sylvia.

"It is a part of you of which you could not rid yourself if you tried. When you are asleep, this dream comes to you. It is as much a part of you as a limb."

And again Sylvia answered: "Yes."

"Well, you are not responsible for it," and Sylvia leaned forward.

"Ah!" she said. She had been wondering whether it was to this point that he was coming.

"You know now why you hear it, why it's part of you. You were born to the sound of running water in that old house in Dorsetshire. Before you were born, in the daytime and in the stillness of the night your mother heard it week after week. Perhaps even when she was asleep the sound rippled through her dreams. Thus you came by it. It was born in you."

"Yes," she answered, following his argument step by step very carefully, but without a sign of the perplexity which was evident in Hilary Chayne. Chayne stood a little aloof, looking from Sylvia's face to the face of her father, in doubt whither the talk was leading. Sylvia, on the other hand, recognized each sentence which her father spoke as the embodiment of a thought with which she was herself familiar.

"Well, then, here's a definite thing, an influence most likely, a characteristic most certainly, and not of your making! One out of how many influences, characteristics which are part of you but not of your making! But we can lay our finger on it. Well, it is a pleasant and a pretty quality--this dream of yours, Sylvia--yes, a very pleasant one to be born with. But suppose that instead of that dream you had been born with a vice, an instinct of crime, of sin, would you have been any the more responsible for it? If you are not responsible for the good thing, are you responsible for the bad? An awkward question, Sylvia--awkward enough to teach you to go warily in your judgments."

"Yes," said Sylvia. "I was amongst the fortunate. I don't deny it."

"But that's not all," and as Chayne moved restively, Garratt Skinner waved an indulgent hand.

"I don't expect you, Captain Chayne, to take an interest in these problems. For a military man, discipline and the penal code are the obvious unalterable solutions. But it is possible that I may never see my daughter again and--I am speaking to her"; and he went back to the old vexed question.

"It's not only that you are born with qualities, definite characteristics, definite cravings, for which you are no more responsible than the man in the moon, and which are part of you. But there's something else. How much of your character, how much of all your life to come is decided for you during the first ten or fifteen years of your life--decided for you, mind, not by you? Upon my soul, I think the whole of it. You don't agree? Well, it's an open question. I believe that at the age of fifteen the lines along which you will move are already drawn, your character formed, your conduct for the future a settled thing."

To that Sylvia gave no assent. But she did not disagree. She only looked at her father with a questioning and a troubled face. If it were so, she asked, why had she hated from the first the circle in which her mother and herself had moved. And the answer--or at all events *an* answer--came as she put the question to herself. She had lived amongst her dreams. She was in doubt.

"Well, hear something of my boyhood, Sylvia!" cried her father, and for the first time his voice became embittered. "I was brought up by a respectable father. Yes, respectable," he said, with a sneer. "Everything about us was respectable. We lived in a respectable house in a respectable neighborhood, and twice every Sunday we went to church and listened to a respectable clergyman. But!--Well, here's a chapter out of the inside. I would go to bed and read in bed by a candle. Not a very heinous offence, but contrary to the rule of the house. Sooner or later I would hear a faint scuffling sound in the passage. That was my father stealing secretly along to listen at my door and see what I was doing. I covered the light of the candle with my hand, or perhaps blew it out--but not so quickly but that he would see the streak of light beneath the door. Then the play would begin. 'You are not reading in bed, are you?' he would say. 'Certainly not,' I would reply. 'You are sure?' he would insist. 'Of course, father,' I would answer. Then back he would go, but only for a little way, and I would hear him come stealthily scuffling back again. Perhaps the candle would be lit again already, or at all events uncovered. Would he say anything? Oh, no! He had found out I was lying. He felt that he had scored a point, and he would save it up. So we would meet the next morning at breakfast, he knowing that I was a liar, I knowing that he knew that I was a liar, and both pretending that we were all in all to each other. A small thing, Sylvia. But crowd your life with such small things? Spying and deceit and a game of catch-as-catch-can played by the father and son! My letters were read--I used to know, for roundabout questions would be put leading up to the elucidation of a sentence which to any one but myself would be obscure! Do you think any child could grow up straight, if his boyhood passed in that atmosphere of trickery? I don't know. Only I think that before I was fifteen my way of life was a sure and settled thing. It was certain that I should develop upon the lines on which I was trained."

Garratt Skinner rose from his seat.

"There, I have done," he said. He looked at his daughter for a little while, his eyes dwelling upon her beauty with a certain pleasure, and even a certain wistfulness; he looked at her now much as she had been wont to look at him in the early days of the house in Dorsetshire. It was very plain that they were father and daughter.

"You are too good for your military man, my dear," he said, with a smile. "Too pretty and too good. Don't you let him forget it!" And suddenly he cried out with a burst of passion. "I wish to God you had never come near me!" And Sylvia, hearing the cry, remembered that on the Sunday evening when she had first come to the house in Hobart Place, her father had shown a particular hesitation, had felt some of that remorse of which she heard the full expression now, in welcoming her to his house and adapting her to his ends. She raised her downcast eyes and with outstretched hands took a step forward. "Father!" she said. But her father was already gone. She heard his step upon the stairs.

Chayne, however, followed her father from the room and caught him up as he was leaving the hotel.

"I want to say," he began with some difficulty, "that, if you are pressed at all for money--"

Garratt Skinner stopped him. He pulled some sovereigns out of one pocket and some banknotes out of another.

"You see, I have enough to go on with. In fact--" and he looked northward toward the mountains. Dimly they could be seen under the sickle of a new moon. "In fact, I propose to-morrow to take your friend Simond and cross on the high-level to Zermatt."

"But afterward?" asked Chayne.

Garratt Skinner laughed and laughed like a boy. There was a rich anticipation of enjoyment in the sound.

"Afterward? I shall have a great time. I shall squeeze Mr. Jarvice. It's what they call in America a cinch."

And with a cheery good-night Garratt Skinner betook himself down the road.

The Codes Of Hammurabi And Moses
W. W. Davies

QTY

The discovery of the Hammurabi Code is one of the greatest achievements of archaeology, and is of paramount interest, not only to the student of the Bible, but also to all those interested in ancient history...

Religion   **ISBN:** *1-59462-338-4*   **Pages:132**

MSRP $12.95

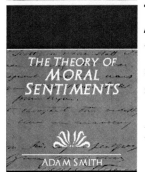

The Theory of Moral Sentiments
Adam Smith

QTY

This work from 1749. contains original theories of conscience amd moral judgment and it is the foundation for systemof morals.

Philosophy   **ISBN:** *1-59462-777-0*   **Pages:536**

MSRP $19.95

Jessica's First Prayer
Hesba Stretton

QTY

In a screened and secluded corner of one of the many railway-bridges which span the streets of London there could be seen a few years ago, from five o'clock every morning until half past eight, a tidily set-out coffee-stall, consisting of a trestle and board, upon which stood two large tin cans, with a small fire of charcoal burning under each so as to keep the coffee boiling during the early hours of the morning when the work-people were thronging into the city on their way to their daily toil...

Childrens   **ISBN:** *1-59462-373-2*   **Pages:84**

MSRP $9.95

My Life and Work
Henry Ford

QTY

Henry Ford revolutionized the world with his implementation of mass production for the Model T automobile. Gain valuable business insight into his life and work with his own auto-biography... "We have only started on our development of our country we have not as yet, with all our talk of wonderful progress, done more than scratch the surface. The progress has been wonderful enough but..."

Biographies/   **ISBN:** *1-59462-198-5*   **Pages:300**

MSRP $21.95

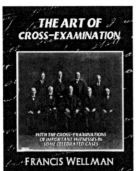

The Art of Cross-Examination
Francis Wellman

QTY

I presume it is the experience of every author, after his first book is published upon an important subject, to be almost overwhelmed with a wealth of ideas and illustrations which could readily have been included in his book, and which to his own mind, at least, seem to make a second edition inevitable. Such certainly was the case with me; and when the first edition had reached its sixth impression in five months, I rejoiced to learn that it seemed to my publishers that the book had met with a sufficiently favorable reception to justify a second and considerably enlarged edition. ..

Pages:412

Reference   **ISBN:** *1-59462-647-2*   *MSRP $19.95*

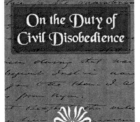

On the Duty of Civil Disobedience
Henry David Thoreau

QTY

Thoreau wrote his famous essay, On the Duty of Civil Disobedience, as a protest against an unjust but popular war and the immoral but popular institution of slave-owning. He did more than write—he declined to pay his taxes, and was hauled off to gaol in consequence. Who can say how much this refusal of his hastened the end of the war and of slavery ?

Law   **ISBN:** *1-59462-747-9*   **Pages:48**

MSRP $7.45

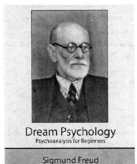

Dream Psychology Psychoanalysis for Beginners
Sigmund Freud

QTY

Sigmund Freud, born Sigismund Schlomo Freud (May 6, 1856 - September 23, 1939), was a Jewish-Austrian neurologist and psychiatrist who co-founded the psychoanalytic school of psychology. Freud is best known for his theories of the unconscious mind, especially involving the mechanism of repression; his redefinition of sexual desire as mobile and directed towards a wide variety of objects; and his therapeutic techniques, especially his understanding of transference in the therapeutic relationship and the presumed value of dreams as sources of insight into unconscious desires.

Pages:196

Psychology   **ISBN:** *1-59462-905-6*   *MSRP $15.45*

The Miracle of Right Thought
Orison Swett Marden

QTY

Believe with all of your heart that you will do what you were made to do. When the mind has once formed the habit of holding cheerful, happy, prosperous pictures, it will not be easy to form the opposite habit. It does not matter how improbable or how far away this realization may see, or how dark the prospects may be, if we visualize them as best we can, as vividly as possible, hold tenaciously to them and vigorously struggle to attain them, they will gradually become actualized, realized in the life. But a desire, a longing without endeavor, a yearning abandoned or held indifferently will vanish without realization.

Pages:360

Self Help   **ISBN:** *1-59462-644-8*   *MSRP $25.45*

QTY

The Rosicrucian Cosmo-Conception Mystic Christianity *by Max Heindel*   ISBN: *1-59462-188-8* $38.95
The Rosicrucian Cosmo-conception is not dogmatic, neither does it appeal to any other authority than the reason of the student. It is: not controversial, but is: sent forth in the, hope that it may help to clear...   *New Age/Religion Pages 646*

Abandonment To Divine Providence *by Jean-Pierre de Caussade*   ISBN: *1-59462-228-0* $25.95
"The Rev. Jean Pierre de Caussade was one of the most remarkable spiritual writers of the Society of Jesus in France in the 18th Century. His death took place at Toulouse in 1751. His works have gone through many editions and have been republished...   *Inspirational/Religion Pages 400*

Mental Chemistry *by Charles Haanel*   ISBN: *1-59462-192-6* $23.95
Mental Chemistry allows the change of material conditions by combining and appropriately utilizing the power of the mind. Much like applied chemistry creates something new and unique out of careful combinations of chemicals the mastery of mental chemistry...   *New Age/Business Pages 354*

The Letters of Robert Browning and Elizabeth Barret Barrett 1845-1846 vol II   ISBN: *1-59462-193-4* $35.95
by Robert Browning and Elizabeth Barrett   *Biographies Pages 596*

Gleanings In Genesis (volume I) *by Arthur W. Pink*   ISBN: *1-59462-130-6* $27.45
Appropriately has Genesis been termed "the seed plot of the Bible" for in it we have, in germ form, almost all of the great doctrines which are afterwards fully developed in the books of Scripture which follow...   *Religion/Inspirational Pages 420*

The Master Key *by L. W. de Laurence*   ISBN: *1-59462-001-6* $30.95
In no branch of human knowledge has there been a more lively increase of the spirit of research during the past few years than in the study of Psychology, Concentration and Mental Discipline. The requests for authentic lessons in Thought Control, Mental Discipline and...   *New Age Pages 422*

The Lesser Key Of Solomon Goetia *by L. W. de Laurence*   ISBN: *1-59462-092-X* $9.95
This translation of the first book of the "Lernegton" which is now for the first time made accessible to students of Talismanic Magic was done, after careful collation and edition, from numerous Ancient Manuscripts in Hebrew, Latin, and French...   *New Age Occult Pages 92*

Rubaiyat Of Omar Khayyam *by Edward Fitzgerald*   ISBN:*1-59462-332-5* $13.95
Edward Fitzgerald, whom the world has already learned, in spite of his own efforts to remain within the shadow of anonymity, to look upon as one of the rarest poets of the century, was born at Bredfield, in Suffolk, on the 31st of March, 1809. He was the third son of John Purcell...   *Music Pages 172*

Ancient Law *by Henry Maine*   ISBN: *1-59462-128-4* $29.95
The chief object of the following pages is to indicate some of the earliest ideas of mankind, as they are reflected in Ancient Law, and to point out the relation of those ideas to modern thought.   *Religion/History Pages 452*

Far-Away Stories *by William J. Locke*   ISBN: *1-59462-129-2* $19.45
"Good wine needs no bush, but a collection of mixed vintages does. And this book is just such a collection. Some of the stories I do not want to remain buried for ever in the museum files of dead magazine-numbers an author's not unpardonable vanity..."   *Fiction Pages 272*

Life of David Crockett *by David Crockett*   ISBN: *1-59462-250-7* $27.45
"Colonel David Crockett was one of the most remarkable men of the times in which he lived. Born in humble life, but gifted with a strong will, an indomitable courage, and unremitting perseverance...   *Biographies New Age Pages 424*

Lip-Reading *by Edward Nitchie*   ISBN: *1-59462-206-X* $25.95
Edward B. Nitchie, founder of the New York School for the Hard of Hearing, now the Nitchie School of Lip-Reading, Inc, wrote "LIP-READING Principles and Practice". The development and perfecting of this meritorious work on lip-reading was an undertaking...   *How-to Pages 400*

A Handbook of Suggestive Therapeutics, Applied Hypnotism, Psychic Science   ISBN: *1-59462-214-0* $24.95
by Henry Munro   *Health/New Age/Health Self-help Pages 376*

A Doll's House: and Two Other Plays *by Henrik Ibsen*   ISBN: *1-59462-112-8* $19.95
Henrik Ibsen created this classic when in revolutionary 1848 Rome. Introducing some striking concepts in playwriting for the realist genre, this play has been studied the world over.   *Fiction/Classics/Plays 308*

The Light of Asia *by sir Edwin Arnold*   ISBN: *1-59462-204-3* $13.95
In this poetic masterpiece, Edwin Arnold describes the life and teachings of Buddha. The man who was to become known as Buddha to the world was born as Prince Gautama of India but he rejected the worldly riches and abandoned the reigns of power when...   *Religion/History/Biographies Pages 170*

The Complete Works of Guy de Maupassant *by Guy de Maupassant*   ISBN: *1-59462-157-8* $16.95
"For days and days, nights and nights, I had dreamed of that first kiss which was to consecrate our engagement, and I knew not on what spot I should put my lips..."   *Fiction/Classics Pages 240*

The Art of Cross-Examination *by Francis L. Wellman*   ISBN: *1-59462-309-5* $26.95
Written by a renowned trial lawyer, Wellman imparts his experience and uses case studies to explain how to use psychology to extract desired information through questioning.   *How-to Science/Reference Pages 408*

Answered or Unanswered? *by Louisa Vaughan*   ISBN: *1-59462-248-5* $10.95
Miracles of Faith in China   *Religion Pages 112*

The Edinburgh Lectures on Mental Science (1909) *by Thomas*   ISBN: *1-59462-008-3* $11.95
This book contains the substance of a course of lectures recently given by the writer in the Queen Street Hall, Edinburgh. Its purpose is to indicate the Natural Principles governing the relation between Mental Action and Material Conditions...   *New Age/Psychology Pages 148*

Ayesha *by H. Rider Haggard*   ISBN: *1-59462-301-5* $24.95
Verily and indeed it is the unexpected that happens! Probably if there was one person upon the earth from whom the Editor of this, and of a certain previous history, did not expect to hear again...   *Classics Pages 380*

Ayala's Angel *by Anthony Trollope*   ISBN: *1-59462-352-X* $29.95
The two girls were both pretty, but Lucy who was twenty-one who supposed to be simple and comparatively unattractive, whereas Ayala was credited, as her Bombwhat romantic name might show, with poetic charm and a taste for romance. Ayala when her father died was nineteen...   *Fiction Pages 484*

The American Commonwealth *by James Bryce*   ISBN: *1-59462-286-8* $34.45
An interpretation of American democratic political theory. It examines political mechanics and society from the perspective of Scotsman James Bryce   *Politics Pages 572*

Stories of the Pilgrims *by Margaret P. Pumphrey*   ISBN: *1-59462-116-0* $17.95
This book explores pilgrims religious oppression in England as well as their escape to Holland and eventual crossing to America on the Mayflower, and their early days in New England...   *History Pages 268*

QTY

The Fasting Cure *by Sinclair Upton*   ISBN: *1-59462-222-1* **$13.95**
In the Cosmopolitan Magazine for May, 1910, and in the Contemporary Review (London) for April, 1910, I published an article dealing with my experiences in fasting. I have written a great many magazine articles, but never one which attracted so much attention... New Age/Self Help/Health Pages 164

Hebrew Astrology *by Sepharial*   ISBN: *1-59462-308-2* **$13.45**
In these days of advanced thinking it is a matter of common observation that we have left many of the old landmarks behind and that we are now pressing forward to greater heights and to a wider horizon than that which represented the mind-content of our progenitors...   Astrology Pages 144

Thought Vibration or The Law of Attraction in the Thought World   ISBN: *1-59462-127-6* **$12.95**
by William Walker Atkinson   *Psychology/Religion Pages 144*

Optimism *by Helen Keller*   ISBN: *1-59462-108-X* **$15.95**
Helen Keller was blind, deaf, and mute since 19 months old, yet famously learned how to overcome these handicaps, communicate with the world, and spread her lectures promoting optimism. An inspiring read for everyone...   Biographies/Inspirational Pages 84

Sara Crewe *by Frances Burnett*   ISBN: *1-59462-360-0* **$9.45**
In the first place, Miss Minchin lived in London. Her home was a large, dull, tall one, in a large, dull square, where all the houses were alike, and all the sparrows were alike, and where all the door-knockers made the same heavy sound...   Childrens/Classic Pages 88

The Autobiography of Benjamin Franklin *by Benjamin Franklin*   ISBN: *1-59462-135-7* **$24.95**
The Autobiography of Benjamin Franklin has probably been more extensively read than any other American historical work, and no other book of its kind has had such ups and downs of fortune. Franklin lived for many years in England, where he was agent...   Biographies/History Pages 332

Name	
Email	
Telephone	
Address	
City, State ZIP	

☐ **Credit Card**   ☐ **Check / Money Order**

Credit Card Number	
Expiration Date	
Signature	

Please Mail to: Book Jungle
PO Box 2226
Champaign, IL 61825
or Fax to: 630-214-0564

ORDERING INFORMATION
web: *www.bookjungle.com*
email: *sales@bookjungle.com*
fax: *630-214-0564*
mail: *Book Jungle PO Box 2226 Champaign, IL 61825*
or PayPal *to sales@bookjungle.com*

Please contact us for bulk discounts

DIRECT-ORDER TERMS

**20% Discount if You Order
Two or More Books**
Free Domestic Shipping!
Accepted: Master Card, Visa,
Discover, American Express

Breinigsville, PA USA
28 February 2010
233322BV00004B/4/P